A Spy Among Them

Tempie W. Wade

A Spy Among Them
By Tempie W. Wade

Printed in the United States of America.

First Edition Print - ISBN: 978-1-7363975-3-4

Digital Edition - ISBN: 978-1-7363975-2-7

For more information, please visit
www.TempieWade.com

A Spy Among Them

By Tempie W. Wade

A Novel

"The Prince of Darkness is a gentleman."

—William Shakespeare

"All is fair in love and war when a devilishly handsome rogue holds the key to what you desire most."

—Tempie W. Wade

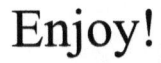

Enjoy!

CHAPTER ONE

1766

James City County, Virginia

Ten-year-old Emma Eldridge slumped forward, propping her elbow on the desk, staring longingly through the window while her father studied the sheet of spelling words she had just finished penning. She swung her feet back and forth, the thump of her feet hitting the base of the chair the only sound to be heard in the room.

Roger Eldridge used the palm of his left hand to conceal the amused expression on his face as he peered over the rim of his spectacles at his rather impatient daughter.

"Well?" she asked.

Forcing a solemn face for her benefit, he shifted his eyes to the page he was holding in his right hand and cleared his throat. "Your 't's need a bit more of a flourish and your 'a's need to be more rounded; however, overall, I would have to say your handwriting has much improved. As to your spelling," the corners of his lips twitched up in approval, "as always— impeccable." He laid the page down and rested his forearms on the table to look his daughter in the eye. "I am very pleased with the progress you have made on your lessons, young lady, and you have made me very proud."

Her face lit up with excitement and she grinned. "Does that mean I can go now?"

"*May* you go now?" he corrected.

"May I go now?" she parroted.

"Yes, my sweet girl, you may go!"

Emma sprang from her chair, wrapped her arms around his neck, and kissed his cheek. "Thank you, Papa! I will be home in plenty of time to help Mama with supper, I promise!"

The elated little girl bolted by her mother and out of the house before anyone could say another word.

Martha Eldridge came into the drawing-room, wiping her hands on a towel, catching a glimpse of her daughter hurrying down the hill through the nearby window. "I take it her lessons are finished for the day?"

"She lost all interest about an hour ago," her husband replied with a chuckle, straightening his stack of books. "I held her back as long as I could."

Martha went over to him and placed her hands lovingly on his shoulders. "She has been working hard lately, and I think she has earned it. Children need to have time to be children."

"And adults need time to be adults," he countered with a

wink. Wrapping his arms around her waist, he caught her off guard and pulled her onto his lap.

The unexpected action caused her to let out a 'whoop' before she broke into a bout of laughter. "Roger Eldridge, you are incorrigible!" She swatted at him with the towel in her hand. Then, she touched his face tenderly and kissed him. "I suppose that is why I fell in love with you!"

"Do you ever regret giving it all up for me?" He tightened his hold and rocked her on his knee.

"Not even for one moment. All the money in the world could not buy what we have. I am blissfully happy in our cozy little home, with my adoring husband, and our beautiful, happy, healthy daughter. I wouldn't trade it for anything in this world or the next!"

"I am beyond glad to hear that," he said, pulled her to his chest, and ravaged her with kisses.

Emma untied the ribbon from her hair and tossed it away as she ran, her bouncy, brown curls now unconfined and free to fly in the gentle breeze. She had been looking forward to this all day—her two best friends were already at the edge of the woods at their meeting spot.

"Finally!" called eleven-year-old Charlie Taylor when he caught sight of her. "We have been waiting forever!"

"We have not!" scolded his fourteen-year-old sister, Francis, wrinkling her nose at him. "Pay him no mind!

We just got here ourselves."

"Papa made me finish my lessons first," Emma explained, "but I am here now."

Charlie and Francis were the Eldridge's closest neighbors. Emma's father had been hired as a private tutor for their children and the farm they lived on was conveniently adjacent to the Taylor's estate. The three friends escaped to meet halfway between their homes to play every chance they could break free.

Being an unusually warm day, the trio decided to follow a narrow game trail that led to a babbling brook deep in the woods.

Upon reaching the bank, each quickly shed their stockings and shoes. Charlie rolled up the legs of his breeches while the girls pulled the hems of their dresses up to their knees and tied them in knots.

Emma was the first to jump in.

"Mother would have a fit if she saw me like this!" Francis's face was lit with a cheeky grin and she double-checked to make sure her skirts weren't going to get wet as she spoke. Stepping into the refreshing water, she deepened her voice and offered her best imitation of the woman who kept her in line. "Proper young ladies must look their best, no matter what! Your gown must be clean, your hair styled in the latest fashion, and there should always be a smile upon your face."

Emma lifted her chin in the air and joined the fun. "Because you never know when a suitable young man may come along and want to make you his wife!" Placing one hand on her hip, and holding the other out, she strutted around in the water. "And don't forget to always lift your little pinky in the air when you sip your tea. No proper gentleman will pay you any mind if you do not."

Emma and Francis collapsed against each other laughing.

"She just wants to get you married off so she can get rid of you," teased Charlie and jumped feet first into the stream, splattering water all over the two girls.

"Who wants to get married anyway?" asked Emma, stopping to pick up a shell. She closed her eyes and grinned, taking the time to enjoy the feel of the cool mud squishing between her toes.

"Girls are meant to take husbands and have babies! What else would they do?" asked Charlie.

Emma shrugged and nonchalantly picked up a stick lying on the bank. Raising it in the air, she waved it around. "Maybe I will be a soldier," she brought it down and stabbed at a fish swimming between them, "or a fisherman," grinning, she tossed it aside and dramatically bowed, "or an actress perhaps. Who says the only thing I am allowed to do is get married and have babies?"

"Society, unfortunately!" Francis groaned and carefully sat down on a large rock in the middle of the stream as to not get her dress dirty. "Father says it is our duty as women!"

Emma made a face and stuck out her tongue. "That sounds terribly boring, and those babies cry all the time. Who needs that kind of grief in their life? Besides, my Papa says all I have to be when I grow up is 'happy'! He doesn't care about anything else!"

Francis dipped her hand in the water and flicked it on Emma, making them both giggle. "Just another reason I like Mr. Eldridge a great deal! You are a lucky girl to have him as your father."

Emma was covered in mud by the time she arrived back home. Trying to sneak in and get cleaned up before her mother saw how filthy she had gotten, she was taken by surprise when she almost ran smack dab into a group of men on horseback between the house and the barn. Emma skirted around several trees, keeping a close eye on the men, and was able to get through the back door unnoticed—or so she thought until her mother met her in the kitchen and grabbed her by the arms.

"Slip up the back stairs and go straight to your room," she whispered anxiously.

Emma's mother had never spoken to her in that manner before. "Mama, what's happening?"

In a low voice, she said, "Shh! Keep quiet! Just go and stay out of sight. I will be up in a little while to explain everything."

Nodding, Emma did as she was told, washing up in the basin and changing her clothes before sitting in silence

6

on her bed, waiting nervously.

Martha came into her room about an hour later and softly closed the door.

"Mama?"

Martha went to her and pulled her to the far corner away from the door so they would not be heard. "The army soldiers need somewhere to stay for a couple of nights, and they will be quartering in our stables. I don't want them to know you are here, so you are to remain quiet in your room until they are gone."

"Why?" Emma asked, seeing the worry in her mother's eyes.

Pointing to the bed, Martha urged her to sit. "Because, while most British soldiers are kind and courteous, there are a few who are not, and some of those men would hurt little girls like you." Her mother brushed the hair back from her face. "You are the most precious gift your father and I have ever been given and we will do anything to ensure you are safe," she smiled, "so I need you to hide up here and do as you are told until they leave. Do you understand?"

"Yes, Mama!"

Martha kissed her forehead. "Good girl. I will bring you up some supper in a bit, but in the meantime," she reached over to the small table next to the bed and handed her a book, "you can practice your reading."

Emma wrinkled her nose and groaned. "Do I have to?"

"Yes!" Her mother laughed softly. "Someday, you will

appreciate the fact you are a girl who can read and write because not every girl is lucky enough to have a father who is a teacher. I promise it will come in handy when you are older."

Taking the book, Emma settled back on her bed and watched her mother leave the room.

Stopping at the door, her mother turned back. "I love you, sweetheart, and don't ever forget that!"

"I love you too, Mama," and Emma blew her a kiss.

Emma was lost in a dream. She was having a tea party with Francis, Charlie, and a fish in the middle of the creek. The table was set with the finest cups and saucers she had ever seen, and the fish, with impeccable manners and a crisp British accent, was instructing them on proper etiquette.

A commotion from the window overlooking the side yard pulled her from it. It was early morning.

Rubbing her eyes and yawning, she climbed out of bed and stumbled over to the window to see what was going on. She became fully awake when she saw one of the soldiers in a red coat had taken her mother by the arm. Emma pushed open the window just enough to hear what they were saying.

"Mrs. Eldridge, the invitation for your presence at my breakfast table was not a request."

"I am a married woman, Lieutenant Finch, and it would not be proper without my husband present! We may be required by the Crown to provide you with outside quarters, but my company is not included."

Martha turned to go, but the Lieutenant grabbed her around the waist and started dragging her towards the stable.

"I am afraid I must insist!" he growled through gritted teeth.

Martha kicked and screamed, reaching up and clawing at his face.

The Lieutenant attempted to clamp his hand over her mouth, but instead, she managed to crane her head and bite down sharply on the fleshy part of his palm. Enraged, he cursed and threw her forcefully to the ground. Martha landed hard and her body went still, her head having come to rest on a large rock that was lying nearby.

"Mama?" Emma tried to understand what was happening.

Her father came running from the house. He stopped short and his knees buckled when he saw her lifeless body on the ground — blood spilling from the back of her head, the rock now completely covered in red.

"Martha? Martha?" Looking to the Lieutenant in disbelief, "What have you done?" he demanded and collapsed beside her on his knees, resting his hand on her still-warm cheek. "What did you do to my wife?"

"She attacked me when I spurned her advances!" replied the indignant Lieutenant Finch. "I was simply defending myself!"

By that point, the rest of the soldiers under his command had appeared, hovering nearby, watching the scene unfold, but not one coming to the defense of the Eldridge man.

With tears in his eyes, Roger spat, "Martha would never! You're lying, and you will answer for this!"

"I have witnesses," he replied and waved his hand towards his men, all with their eyes cast downward, looking uncomfortable and ashamed. "You shouldn't have married a woman with a roving eye."

"I know what you did!" shouted Roger, anger filling the words, "And I will tell everyone what happened! You will hang for this!"

Lieutenant Finch pulled a handkerchief from his coat pocket and casually wiped the blood from his hand where Martha had bitten him. "Oh dear, this has turned into a most unfortunate situation. I am afraid I cannot have you besmirching my good name." He moved behind Roger, who was now cradling his wife's head and sobbing. Finch removed a knife from his belt, planted his feet, and sank it deep into the man's back, twisting the blade several times before pulling it back out.

Looking up in bewilderment, Roger's face went ghostly white, his body convulsing as the blood poured forth from his wound and his lips. He coughed several times and his eyes glazed over, the life force ebbing from his body. Looking back down at his wife, Roger Eldridge fell forward— and went to join his beloved in the next life.

Emma couldn't stop herself from crying out —and he heard it. When she saw Lieutenant Finch's head snap up, she quickly regained her wits and dropped to the floor out of sight before he turned to look towards the window for the source of the sound.

"Search the house for witnesses!" he ordered to the men, who dared not disobey him.

Emma scrambled underneath her bed and closed her eyes, tears spilling forth. She did her best to remain quiet, but one of her sobs managed to escape.

When she heard her door creak open, she covered her mouth and silently prayed she would somehow go unnoticed. She made an audible gasp and held her breath when a man's boots stopped at the foot of her bed. She relaxed a bit when the boots turned the other way as if the man were leaving— but instead, he bent down, and his face appeared in front of hers. Emma whimpered and remained still, staring into his eyes. She didn't know what to think when the man's hand came up— and he raised his finger to his lips in a 'shh' motion.

His face disappeared when he stood, walked to the window, and called down to his commander. "There is no one up here, just a bird that flew out of the window. That was the noise you heard."

As soon as the rest of the men had departed the house, he came back and stretched out on the floor. "Listen to me!" he whispered, "We will be leaving within the hour.

As soon as we are gone, run to your nearest neighbor and tell them your parents are dead. But Lieutenant Sherman Finch will kill you if he ever finds out you saw what happened, so you must be careful when choosing your words. Do you understand?"

Emma nodded and the man's face softened.

"I am sorry about your parents, little one. I truly am, and I don't want you to meet the same fate. Do not leave this room until you know for sure we are gone." He forced a half-smile, got up, and left the room.

Emma lay face down in a puddle of her tears for nearly three hours, too terrified to move. When she went nearly an hour without hearing anything, she rolled from underneath the bed and crept over to the window to make sure they were truly gone. A fresh stream of tears flooded her cheeks when she saw her parents still lying on the side yard, a sight that would now be etched into her memory until the day she joined them. Wiping the wetness from her face, she took one final look and ran from the house.

"Good Lord, who is banging on the door like that?" called Mrs. Taylor from the table where the family was having dinner.

A servant appeared, curtsied, and hurried to see. When she opened the door, exhausted and out of breath, Emma collapsed in a heap at her feet, her eyes red and swollen as she heaved.

"Emma?" Mrs. Taylor got up from the table and came into the hall. "What's wrong?"

"Soldiers came to the house. My parents— they are both dead!" she managed to get out.

Francis and Charlie went around their mother to her. The girl dropped to her knees, wrapped her arms around Emma, and pulled her face against her breast. "Shh! Charlie and I are here," she said and rubbed her back.

Charlie helped Emma to her feet, holding on to her to lead her into the drawing-room, and found her a chair.

Francis went into the dining room, brought back a cup of water, and forced her to drink it.

"What happened, dear?" asked Mrs. Taylor softly.

"A soldier killed them both," she replied between sniffles. "He would have killed me too, but he didn't know I was there."

"Oh, dear Lord!" Mr. Taylor touched his wife on the back and whispered in her ear. "I will take some of the men and ride out there to see what's happened."

That evening, a much different soldier came out to question Emma. She studied him and listened as he conversed with Mrs. Taylor. When the man spoke, he glanced over at her, nodded, and offered her a warm smile. This one appeared to have a kindness about him, unlike any other she had ever encountered. He didn't wear one of those powdered wigs she always thought looked so ridiculous —instead, he wore his blond hair

13

pulled neatly straight back and tied. The light smell of sandalwood moved with him when he came to sit down on the sofa beside her, taking the time to choose his words carefully, fidgeting with the hat in his hands.

"Hello Emma, my name is Gabe. It is a pleasure to meet you, although I wish it were under better circumstances," he shifted to face her better, "I want you to know how deeply sorry I am about your parents. This is something that never should have happened to anyone, and especially not to a lovely young girl such as you. I know it is difficult to think about and, I suspect, even worse to talk about," he said compassionately, "but I need to ask you a few questions about what happened this morning. We need to make sure we find out who is responsible for this, so it never happens again. Is that alright?"

She shrugged, tears still in her eyes.

A wretched look crossed his face when he saw one spill down her cheek. He pulled a handkerchief from his coat pocket and offered it to her.

She accepted it and held it tightly in her hands.

He took a moment to compose himself, visibly upset to have to question any child in this manner. "Did you recognize any of the men? From town perhaps?"

She stared down at his perfectly polished boots and shook her head.

"Did you hear anyone's names mentioned or called out?"

She shook her head again.

14

"Do you know how many there were?"

At that point, she didn't even bother to respond.

Gabe got down on one knee to be at her eye level. "Is there anything you can tell me about who did this? Anything at all?" he begged. "I want justice for you and your family, but I cannot get it without your help. Please!"

Emma swallowed hard. "There was only one man who did it, and he wore a red coat like yours," she said, barely audible, her eyes fixed on his sleeve.

Gabe followed her gaze, and it occurred to him she would never tell him anything— or see any other British soldier in a red coat in the same light again. Men she should have been able to look to for protection would, from now on, be seen only as men who took everything from her.

"Thank you for talking to me, Emma. I am going to do my best to find out who did this and make sure he answers for it."

She wiped her nose with his handkerchief and returned it.

Tucking it back in his coat pocket, Gabe gently caught another tear from her cheek with his finger, his own heart breaking for what this poor little girl had been through.

Gabe had the idea to send someone else in to speak to her without a uniform coat on, but each time she was asked, she always gave the same answers she gave him.

—but they were a lie.

15

Emma kept the truth to herself.

Lieutenant Sherman Finch was a name she would never forget for as long as she lived, at least not until she had made him pay for destroying her world.

Emma's parents only had one immediate family member in the Colonies—her mother's older sister, Lucile Wolfe. She had never met her aunt, who lived in New York, but learned she was about to because Aunt Lucile had just become her new guardian.

All the adults told her to expect a kindly, older woman who would know nothing about raising a child because she was something called a 'spinster'.

"I know it will be difficult, but you must do your best to not antagonize her," warned Mrs. Taylor when she sat her down to give her the news after the funerals. "Mistress Wolfe is older and will be set in her ways. She won't have the patience to put up with foolishness, and she will never love you like your mother, but she is the only family you have left. If she doesn't take you in, you will be sent to an orphanage and that is something you will want to avoid at all costs. They are horrible places for little girls. Do as you are told and stay out of her way."

"Yes ma'am," replied Emma sadly, desolation filling every part of her being. Not only had she lost both her parents but now she was being handed off to a complete stranger who she was just told already hated her.

"What's a spinster?" Emma asked Francis and Charlie when they were alone in Francis's bedroom that night after everyone else had gone to bed.

"It's an old woman who no one ever wanted to marry because she was so mean and ugly," replied Charlie. "She probably brings home stray cats off the street and feeds them. You might even have to share a bed with a few of them, maybe even a cream bowl," he teased, doing his best to get even a sliver of a smile out of her.

Francis swatted at him and he frowned back.

Charlie had never seen Emma like this, and he hated there was nothing he could do to make her feel better. The three were as close as could be and he felt what she felt, his own heart aching beyond measure.

Emma picked at the quilt, her watery eyes cast downward. "She is going to hate me!"

"She is going to love you," assured Francis and put her arm around her. "How could anyone not love you? Oh, Emma, Charlie and I are going to miss you terribly!" Francis burst into tears, which in turn caused Emma's own to erupt.

Charlie put his arms around both girls and gathered them to him comfortingly as the three spent their last night together as a group mourning what they were losing.

Lucile Wolfe was the complete opposite of what

everyone told Emma to expect—entering the Taylor home where Emma had been staying, like a destructive force of nature—blowing holes in misplaced stereotypical labels as big as the ocean and leaving a trail of chaos in her wake.

'Aunt Lucy' as she preferred to be called, was anyone but who Emma anticipated. Having been raised on the edge of a sleepy little town by reserved parents, Emma had never met anyone quite like this woman, and she found herself quite taken with her.

Aunt Lucy was a gorgeous, fuller figured woman with a voluptuous hourglass shape who arrived dressed in a fancy, dark-red gown that garnered a great deal of attention, especially from any man she happened to encounter. A black top hat holding back her blonde ringlet curls and a ruby necklace that rested in the 'V' of her breasts completed the ensemble.

Mr. Taylor, much to Mrs. Taylor's chagrin, immediately became the most attentive host in all of Virginia—Mrs. Taylor was quick to voice her opposition to the rather sudden change in his normal dreary, lackluster demeanor.

Emma, Francis, and Charlie all watched with curiosity from a hidden spot on the staircase.

"Please, Mistress Wolfe," he had said with a smile stretched so tight, you could see all his teeth, including the black holes in places of the missing ones in the back. Offering his arm, "allow me to escort you to our drawing room for refreshments. We are so honored to have you here in our humble abode, especially someone as kind and good-hearted as you, willing to take in a poor orphaned girl."

"Well, aren't you the sweetest thing?" she replied with a pat of his arm and a coy smirk. "What else would I do? That girl is family, after all."

Emma was called down about an hour later and left alone in the room with her new guardian. She was more nervous than she had ever been in her entire life.

"It is very nice to finally meet you," said Lucy sincerely with a smile on her face, "I am only sorry I have not had the pleasure sooner. I know you must have many questions, so feel free to ask me anything you like, but first let me say how sorry I am about your parents. Your mother was my best friend growing up and, though we didn't see each other as much as I would have liked, I never stopped loving her." Lucy reached out and touched her nose. "You look so much like her. It will be like having her around all over again. Now, what would you like to know?"

Emma chewed on her lip and looked down at her feet. "Do you have any cats?"

Lucy seemed a little taken aback before her lips curled into a grin. "I do not, but if you would like one, I am sure we can find the best cat in all of New York. He can sleep on your bed, eat from your dinner plate, or anything else you would like to have him do. You, my dear, will want for nothing while under my care, I give you my word."

A slow smile spread across Emma's face and she fell in love with her Aunt Lucy. They stayed up together all night talking and by morning, Emma felt better.

Lucy was ten years older than her sister. She had never been married because she simply had not met anyone she cared to marry. That, and the fact she didn't want any man to have that much control over her.

Emma was stunned to learn the Wolfe sisters had been the sole heirs to a massive fortune left behind when their parents had passed away. Martha had fallen in love with Roger at about the same time and chosen to live simply with him in Virginia. Lucy remained in the family's home in Pennsylvania and did as she wished since she had no husband to take her wealth or tell her what to do—a situation she had no intention of changing. And even though she was saddened and horrified to learn of her sister and her husband's deaths, she was thrilled beyond measure to have the honor of raising young Emma. She assured her she would have the finest tutors, only the latest in fashions, and anything else she wanted—and she would ensure she would also never have to marry unless it was something she truly wanted to do.

"You shall have whatever your heart desires!" vowed Lucy.

"Anything?" asked Emma, unsurely.

"Just say the word and if it is within my power, you will

have it!"

Hesitating, Emma looked down at her hands in her lap.

"Tell me," encouraged Lucy. "It can be our little secret if you like."

Emma swallowed hard. "I want the man who killed my parents to pay for what he did."

Lucy sucked in a deep breath and laid her hand over on Emma's. "Of course you do, and I would happily grant it given the opportunity, but it will be hard to do without knowing who committed the crime."

Emma closed her eyes and whispered, "I know his name. I lied."

"Oh, I see! And why would you do that?"

She opened her eyes, leaned closer to her aunt's face, and stated resolutely, "I want to be the one to make him pay."

Lucy nodded and squeezed her hand. "That would be your right, my dear, and as I said, if there is something you want within my power, you will have it. I give you my word."

Emma threw her arms around her aunt's neck and embraced her tightly.

At that moment, the two formed a bond that nothing would ever break.

After a long journey to New York with a few stops along the way, Emma stood in front of a grand mansion with a sprawling front porch and columns taller than she could see. It was the most magnificent thing she had ever laid eyes upon. Her face filled with wonder. "You live here?"

"*We* live here!" corrected Lucy, placing her hand on Emma's shoulder and following her gaze. "Welcome to your new home, 'Wolfe Manor'."

2
CHAPTER TWO

April 1779
Wolfe Manor, New York

Twenty-three-year-old Emma Eldridge placed her hat
and riding gloves on the table in the foyer. She had just
returned from her regular morning excursion on her
favorite horse, Mac—a fine, distinctive chestnut
thoroughbred with four black feet and a black mane.
Stopping to check her appearance in the gilded hallway
mirror, she took the time to tuck a strand of hair behind
her ear, before making her way into the dining room,
humming a lively tune.

"Good morning, Aunt Lucy," she said cheerfully and
kissed the older woman on the cheek.

"Good morning, my dear!" Laying her newspaper aside,
Lucy smiled at her niece. "Enjoy your morning ride?"

"Indeed, I did. It is a beautiful day—the sun is shining,

the birds are chirping, and all seems right with the world."

"You are in an exceptionally fine mood this morning," noted her aunt.

"Why wouldn't I be?" She took a seat as Midge, the housekeeper, placed a plate full of food in front of her. "My new gown has arrived, I am having a good hair day, and soon, we will have guests overflowing our home for the most anticipated event of the season. You know how much I adore a party, especially when we are the ones hosting it."

"You just like breaking the hearts of all those eligible bachelors who fall at your feet, hoping to be the Antony to your Cleopatra," teased Lucy. "Not that I can blame you. It's a thrilling game and one I rather enjoy playing myself."

Lucy Wolfe might be an unmarried woman near the age of fifty, but it didn't stop her from acting like a young, vital woman of the age of twenty. The ends of her lips curled up. "Or perhaps it's the 'other' game you are looking forward to, dear niece."

Emma winked and a sly smile appeared on her face. "So, tell me, who are we entertaining tonight, Auntie?" She spread her napkin across her lap and gave Lucy her full attention.

"The usual town residents, along with several high-ranking British officers and a few, who I understand, are in intelligence."

"Well, isn't that convenient?" asked Emma, her words dripping with sarcasm.

Lucile Wolfe and Emma Eldridge's allegiances were first and foremost to the Patriot cause, but not a single soul outside of their home knew it. The two prominent and desirable ladies of New York had become masters of the ultimate game, pretending to be loyal to the Crown, while throwing extravagant parties for British officers and using their charms to steal their secrets. As it turned out, the Wolfe family owned a second home in Virginia, which they had visited often when Lucy was a young girl, and a childhood friend of Lucy's also happened to be the leader of the American cause—General George Washington. Any useful information they gleaned from one of their much sought-after, invitation-only affairs was promptly relayed directly to the man himself. And while things had seemed hopeless, the few recent gains the Patriots had made were thanks mostly in part to the tireless efforts of the lovely 'femme fatales' of Wolfe Manor.

While she was garnering important details for the current cause, Emma was always on the lookout for any information she could learn concerning Lieutenant Sherman Finch, the man who murdered her parents—and one who seemed to have disappeared into thin air—thirteen years ago.

"What is the plan for the evening?" asked Emma.

"General Clinton will be here, so I will spend as much

time with him as possible."

"Wear the low-cut red gown," suggested Emma, picking up a piece of bread and taking a bite.

"Good idea! The amount of information I get from him does seem causally related to the amount of cleavage I expose." Lucy chuckled and drummed her fingers on the table. "Oh well, he is a widower, and I suppose it doesn't hurt to throw a dog a bone every now and then, especially given the number of particulars I tend to get out of him."

Emma nearly choked on her food at her aunt's impertinent remark, although she wasn't entirely surprised by it. Aunt Lucy was an outspoken, candid woman who rarely held back from telling the truth of the matter, no matter how inappropriate the timing might be. It was one of the things Emma loved most about her.

"It wouldn't hurt for you to show a little cleavage, as well," suggested Lucy. "I understand Captain Donald, who keeps the books for all the British ships coming in and out of port, will be one of the gentlemen accompanying General Clinton. George is always hungry for those kinds of facts and figures."

"The boring 'bean counter'? Seriously? Isn't he nearly forty?" Emma groaned and threw her napkin down on the table. "So much for looking forward to the night. Isn't there a handsome young intelligence officer with a strong shoulder and a firm derriere whose mind and pockets both need picking?"

"Unfortunately, not for this evening, my dear." Lucy reached across and patted her hand. "Don't worry, darling. Once we run these Redcoats out of the country, we will have the biggest party to celebrate you have ever seen, and you can have all the fun you like! I will settle for absolutely nothing less!"

Emma tied a set of double-stranded choker pearls around her neck and adjusted them. Standing in front of the long mirror, she smoothed the fabric of her gown down and turned to the side to make sure everything was tucked nicely in place. The dark blue satin ballgown she wore was cinched exceptionally tight for the occasion, emphasizing her small waist and placing her firm, round breasts on prominent display for the officers who would be attending—a small concession that always seemed to save her a great deal of time when eliciting sensitive information. Her hair was piled loosely on top of her head, secured with a beaded comb that matched the rest of the pearls she wore.

As she lightly dusted her face and chest, she stuck out her tongue and wondered why she was wasting perfectly good face powder on an army accountant of all people. Perhaps she could obtain the necessary information early on and then manage to enjoy the rest of the night. After placing a drop of expensive perfume behind each ear, she took one final look and headed into the hall.

Aunt Lucy was coming out of her room at the same

time, looking stunning, as always. "You look marvelous, my dear," she said and came to take Emma by the arm.

"Ready to welcome our guests?"

"Ready as I will ever be," she replied with a smile on her face.

The two ladies spent the next hour warmly receiving each person as they arrived. Invitations to any event at Wolfe Manor were highly coveted, and the hostesses were never ones to disappoint.

General Henry Clinton, the current Commander-in-Chief of the British army in the Colonies was one of the last to arrive. "Mistress Wolfe," he said, taking her hand and bending to kiss it. "Please forgive my late arrival. I am afraid I had some dull, last-minute business that held me."

"Oh, General Clinton, think nothing of it. We are honored to have you, as always."

Clinton's eyes couldn't help but drift to Lucy's rather amply exposed bosom. His gaze lingered a bit longer than socially acceptable until Lucy produced a folded fan from seemingly out of nowhere and tapped his chest a few times playfully with it to break his concentration.

"Henry, of course, you remember my niece, Emma."

The man cleared his throat, his cheeks now slightly flushed, and turned to take her hand. "How could I forget the lovely Miss Eldridge?" he said and greeted her. He took a step back and waved his hand as a man and woman came in behind him. "Please allow me to present Captain Jack Donald and his new wife of only two days…"

"FRANCIS?" exclaimed an astonished Emma, cutting him off.

The Captain's wife looked up. "Dear God! Emma?"

The two women rushed into each other's arms and embraced tightly.

Captain Donald clasped his hands behind his back and grinned. "I take it you two are acquainted?"

"Oh, Jack! Emma and I grew up together—I cannot believe I did not make the connection when you said we were coming to the home of Lucile Wolfe. It has been so long since we have been in contact, the association didn't even occur to me."

"It has been forever," said Emma, holding her at arm's length, "Look at you—and you are married now?"

"Only for two days—and look at *you*! Where is the little girl who traipsed through the mud from one end of the creek to the other and made swords from sticks to challenge any tree who dared cross our paths?"

"Finishing school sort of takes it out of a girl," Emma replied dryly and chuckled behind her hand.

"Well, that sounds like a rather intriguing childhood memory I would love to hear more about," said a man from behind them.

Everyone turned, and Emma was more than a little surprised to see a most handsome man smiling back at her.

"Ladies, allow me to introduce New York's newest resident, Major John André."

John stepped forward and bowed.

"John," continued General Clinton, "meet the mistress of Wolfe Manor, Lucile Wolfe and her lovely niece, Miss Emma Eldridge."

"It is indeed a pleasure," said John, taking both of Emma's hands in his and planting a long, lingering kiss on the back of each one. "I can already tell how much I am going to enjoy this fair city. Although I must admit, I also have the sudden urge to locate a muddy creek and take you on a stroll."

Emma was taken aback by his forwardness—and a bit amused. Her eyes drifted up to meet his, which were looking back intently at hers.

"Unfortunately for you, I haven't seen the first one since I left Virginia, so I am afraid you are out of luck, Major," she taunted.

"Ah, but you have no idea how determined I can be when there is something I wish to locate," he countered.

"You must be careful of this one, my dear," warned General Clinton good-naturedly, slapping the Major on the shoulder. "He will have you tied up in knots before you know what's happened."

"Of that, I have little doubt," she replied.

Emma had become exceptionally good over the years at reading people when she first met them, and she knew

Major John André's type a little too well. This man had grown accustomed to having women swoon over something as simple as the words that spilled from his lips, and she was certain he had found a way to use that to his advantage.

John laughed softly and turned to Lucy. "I hope you don't mind that General Clinton brought me along. I am aware my presence was quite unexpected, and I do not wish to be an undue burden."

"Nonsense," replied Lucy, her eyes sweeping over him indecently as she waved her fan back and forth in a frenzy. "We can always make room for one more." She gestured for her guests to continue inside. "Please, help yourself to the refreshments while I have a private word with my niece."

"Oh Emma, I want to catch up," protested Francis, still holding on to her arm.

"And we will," Emma assured. "Just as soon as my aunt and I make certain the food and drinks for the party are well-stocked."

After they went inside, Lucy pulled Emma off alone, craning her neck to get a better look at Major John André.

"Who is he?" whispered Emma.

"I have no idea, but I wouldn't mind finding out. He is quite a man!" Lucy shook her head, now back to reality as if just waking from a daydream. "Who is this Francis?

31

Wait! Is she the Taylor girl?"

Emma nodded. "We wrote back and forth for the first few months after I moved here, but we lost contact shortly thereafter."

"Now is as a good a time as any to get reacquainted and, given the fact she is now married to 'the bean counter', it should make it much easier to get information out of him and, lucky you, you don't have to come on to him to do it. Stay with the newlyweds as much as you can tonight and try to get what we need, but I don't need to tell you how to do that, do I?"

Emma chuckled. "Well, how could I not when I learned from the best on how to get exactly what I want from a man?" She stepped closer and fiddled with her aunt's gown to expose a little more of Lucy's cleavage. "The poor General is a widower after all, and he deserves a… 'bone'," she teased mockingly with a wink. "Your words, not mine!"

Lucy laughed, swatting at her behind with the fan as Emma bopped off to blend into the crowd, blowing a kiss over her shoulder for only her aunt to see.

Emma smiled to herself. Lucy had taught her everything she knew, and she could not be more grateful to the woman who took in a little girl she had never laid eyes on—and at a time in her life when she needed someone the most. The best tutors had been brought in to continue her education, teaching her not only English but several other languages, as well, not to mention how to be a proper lady of standing.

The clothes she had been given were made from the finest silk fabrics that could be brought in from all over the world, and Emma had been readily accepted into New York's high society as if she were born into it.

But it was Aunt Lucy herself who had taught her the most valuable lessons she had ever learned in her life about humility and humanity—showing her how people, not of their means, were treated by the British army. She had witnessed businesses and churches burned to the ground, entire families with children put out of their homes onto the streets to starve, and even been present at the hangings of men whose only crimes were giving food and shelter to wounded soldiers from the other army—not that Emma needed a lesson on the evils of British soldiers.

The sight of the murders of her parents still invaded her dreams each night, reminding her to hold fast to her vow to make the man who killed them pay. As relations between the Colonists and the British army had deteriorated, Aunt Lucy had impressed the importance of the Patriot cause, as well as making sure they maintained the appearance of being Loyalists for their own safety. In full agreement and wanting to do more to help their fellow countrymen, they had mutually decided to gather information when and where they could to pass along to General Washington—a man Emma had instantly liked the first time she met him. His impassioned words and hope for a better country had inspired her to want to do everything within her power to make his dream happen.

She and Aunt Lucy had stopped at his home, Mount Vernon, on their way to New York from Virginia. He and his wife, Martha, had been most kind and compassionate towards her when they learned of the death of her parents, especially given the circumstances.

Washington had been the one to come find her when she escaped the house to go sit by the river, not wanting her Aunt Lucy to see her tears when they overcame her. He didn't try to get her to talk about what happened as everyone else had—he had simply come out and sat down on the grass next to her without saying a word. Putting his arm around her, he had given her a shoulder to cry on, something she desperately needed. When she was all out of tears, he took a handkerchief from his pocket, wiped her face, and took her inside for cake—a surprising remedy for the grief she could not have anticipated.

After eating her fill, Emma had fallen asleep and when she woke up, she found herself ready to begin her new life. Ever since that day, each time they visited the delightful man, he always ensured cake was waiting for her, no matter what the occasion. When he came to their home, he would bring it along, even if it meant traveling days on horseback while carrying it. More often than not, it ended up being a little squished, but Emma didn't mind. She would happily devour it no matter what the condition just to see the man smile.

Emma looked around the room.

Francis and Jack, 'the bean counter', had located an empty sofa in the corner and were waving her over. Making her way to them, she noticed John André had managed to capture the attention of several women, including Colette Thompson, the snobbish daughter of a wealthy wine merchant. The young lady was looking to land a prominent husband—preferably a British officer— no doubt to secure her position depending on the outcome of the war. That was mainly given to the fact her grandfather was a well-respected member of the Continental army, a truth she didn't seem to like mentioned in polite company, especially these days. Colette looked rather pleased with herself, having backed the Major into a corner, a position John did not look to be the least bit uncomfortable in. In fact, he appeared to reciprocate the interest.

"I'm sure you two will be very happy together," she mumbled, crossing the room, smiling and stopping to speak to several guests before finally making it over to the newlyweds.

"Emma! Come! Sit!" Francis patted the seat next to her as Jack stood.

"Why don't I get you ladies something to drink?" he offered and kissed Francis on the cheek. "I will only be a few moments."

"Thank you, sweetheart," she touched his face and

35

smiled.

Emma sat down and embraced Francis once more. "I cannot believe you are here! I honestly thought I would never see you again."

"Neither did I!" Francis sighed and squeezed her hand tightly.

"So, tell me, how did you and Captain Donald over there end up married?"

"Oh, Emma, it was the craziest thing!" Francis beamed. "Charlie introduced us."

"Charlie? My God! How is he?"

"He is wonderful. The two are in the army together and when Jack had to come to Williamsburg on business, Charlie happened to be home for a brief visit and invited him to stay with us."

Emma looked down. "Charlie joined the army? Why in the world would he do that?"

"Indeed. He said he felt compelled by his conscience and he has done very well for himself. After father passed away—"

Holding up her hand, Emma interrupted. "Wait! Your father passed? When was that?"

"Two years ago, God rest his soul. His heart gave out when he was having a disagreement with one of the neighbors over this war business. It is horrible the way it has torn our little town apart. Father felt so strongly about supporting the Crown—and well, Charlie felt it was his duty to the family to join. I suppose it was a good thing

36

he did, because otherwise, I never would have met Jack and, since Mother passed last month, I would have been in that big house all alone."

"Oh, Francis! Your mother, as well? I am so sorry!"

"She never recovered from Father's death and spent most of her time confined to her room. She passed peacefully in her sleep." Francis glanced up to look over at her beloved. "I thank God Jack came into my life when he did. I know he is a bit older, but he is a good man who loves me and takes care of me."

Emma followed her gaze. "As long as you are happy, that is all that matters."

"Enough about me! Look at how beautiful you are!" Francis patted her leg. "Tell me about yourself. How have you been? How do you like it here?"

"Yes, well, New York is vastly different from Virginia, I can tell you that. There is a great deal more to do here and there is never a dull moment. I adore Aunt Lucy! She has been wonderful to me, and I have wanted for nothing under her care."

"I am glad to hear that. After all that happened, Charlie and I were worried to death about you, and when your letters stopped, we became even more concerned."

"That is my fault," explained Emma. "Aunt Lucy made sure to keep me busy once we got here to keep my mind off things and our correspondence slipped through the cracks. Please forgive me!"

"There is nothing to forgive. You were a child who

37

went through a horrible ordeal. No one could blame you for wanting to forget everything about Virginia and move on."

"That's the worst part," said Emma, her voice burdened, "I can never forget what happened there. It haunts me every day of my life."

The ladies looked up when Jack returned with two glasses of punch.

Plastering a smile on her face as she accepted the drink, Emma asked, "Tell me, Captain Donald, what is it you do for the army?"

"Please, call me Jack. After all, any childhood friend of my bride's is practically family."

"We were just speaking of what a shame it was that we lost touch," replied Emma. "We shall have to remedy that immediately."

"Yes!" agreed Francis with a smile. Proudly, Mrs. Donald was the one who answered Emma's question for her husband. "My dear Jack has the crucial task of keeping the records for all the army ships coming in and out of port here in New York."

"Of course, the most relevant vessel I checked in this week was the one that brought my dear sweet Francis to me to become my wife." The newlyweds gazed adoringly into each other's eyes. Emma sipped her glass and turned her head, feeling as if she were intruding on a private moment. She caught sight of John André with Colette's hand planted firmly on his chest, laughing, but John's

38

eyes were staring back at Emma, amusement alight in them. She quickly turned her attention back to the Donalds.

"Keeping up with all of those ships sounds like quite a task. I have always been rather curious as to how many were out there in the harbor. It seems like almost too many to count."

Before she could finish her glass, Emma had managed to find out the number of ships, the number of troops on those ships, the location of the armaments around the city, and what the men were having for supper for the next two weeks. She had gotten so skilled at retrieving information from men, in fact, she could do it in her sleep and they were never any the wiser.

The sound of giggling women reached her ear, causing her to turn to investigate the source. "Tell me about Major André."

The animated man stood with four enthralled women literally at his feet as he regaled them with some delightful story that had them hanging on his every word.

"Oh, Major André is a wonderful chap who arrived just a few days ago to settle into his new position."

"What position is that?" Emma asked and lifted her near-empty glass to her lips.

"General Clinton has just appointed him Head of Intelligence, a job I am certain he will excel at. From what I understand from the rumor mill coming out of Philadelphia, he has his own 'unique' way of gathering intelligence information." He smirked and nodded in the direction of the women.

Emma stopped mid-sip. "Major André? Well, isn't that intriguing?"

"Yes! According to General Clinton, his results are impressive, to say the least. It seems he learned a great deal from one of his retired predecessors on how to 'extract' pertinent information from the most unlikely of sources."

The four ladies clapped their hands and laughed as the Major concluded his story and bent to take a formal, dramatic bow.

Emma rose from her seat. "If you two will excuse me for a moment, I need to see that some of the refreshments are replenished. Please, enjoy yourselves."

She waded through the crowd to the doorway where she managed to get Lucy's attention while casting a wary eye in the Major's direction. Her aunt excused herself from General Clinton's company and met her in the kitchen, where they shooed the servants out of the room.

Emma picked through several bottles of wine on the table before settling on one. "Are you aware Major André is the new Head of Intelligence for the army?"

"So, I have been told," said Lucy and cautiously glanced towards the hall. "Perhaps, I should see what I can get out of him," she teased and held out her glass for a refill.

"Maybe more than you bargained for!" replied Emma

dryly and filled their glasses. "The word is, he uses some of the same tactics on women we do on men, although, I get the impression he doesn't stop at the bedroom door."

"Is that right?" Lucy's face lit up. "I can't say I would entirely hate being interrogated by the man. He is quite handsome and charming after all, and I have a feeling he might just make the exchange quite pleasurable."

"What about the General?" asked Emma, entertained by her aunt's enthusiasm.

Lucy straightened her back and adjusted her cleavage. "I am confident I can handle them both in one evening," she narrowed her eyes, "but I wouldn't want to deprive you of some enjoyment."

"Me?" Emma nearly choked on her wine. "What are you talking about?"

Lucy stepped closer and pulled the front of Emma's gown down in the 'V' between her breasts to showcase her assets a little more. "That man has had his eyes on you the entire night."

"While Colette Thompson has practically had her hands down the front of his breeches," Emma pointed out. "In case you haven't noticed, he has not rebuffed her in any way."

"Jealous? I am sure he wouldn't mind terribly if they were *your* hands instead," poked Lucy good-naturedly, making Emma scoff. "Besides, anyone who has been in this town for more than five minutes with half a mind can figure out that Colette Thompson is desperate for a husband and willing to do whatever it takes to rope one in. Most men find what is readily laid out in front of them difficult to resist at first, but easy to put down later."

Emma shook her head. "I don't know, Aunt Lucy. There is something about that man that makes me nervous."

"Good! Nerves are what keep you on your toes —and alive in this game."

Emma was just about to rejoin the party when she noticed Colette and John standing just inside the dining room on the other side of the doorway she entered. Making a quick retreat, she pressed her back against the wall and realized she could hear their conversation. Lifting her wine glass and smiling at guests as they passed, she remained in that spot, curious enough to eavesdrop.

"You must help me, my dear Colette. I am new here and terrible with names and faces and since you have resided here for so long, perhaps you could help me," he said in a low, sensual voice.

"I would be happy to tell you whatever you would like to know," she purred.

Emma stuck out her tongue as if she were gagging and, when a gentleman passed by, she lifted her hand and coughed to cover her somewhat childish behavior.

"The blond-haired young lady in the red gown who looks rather sad this evening," she heard him ask, "I was introduced to her earlier in town but cannot for the life of me recall her name. Do you by chance know it?"

"Oh yes, that is Beverly Conley. Her family are staunch Loyalists, but the poor girl is hopelessly in love with a young man under the command of Daniel Brodhead at Fort Pitt. Her parents are beside themselves she is so taken with a traitor and are trying to steer her into a more suitable match, but thus far, she has refused."

"Well, we cannot always choose who we fall in love with," he cooed. "She must feel very alone." Inclining his head, he continued, "And the lady by the refreshment table in the yellow gown? What is her story?"

"Oh, that is Molly Wright, a seamstress here in town. She lives with her elderly mother and has three brothers who joined up with Washington's army. She claims the family has not been in contact with any of them, but when the elder Mrs. Wright came by to order wine from my father, she let it slip she had received a letter from one of them only a few weeks ago."

Emma could hardly believe her ears. The Major was pulling information out of this foolish girl faster than water gushing over the falls after a hard afternoon thunderstorm—and the dimwitted ninny was none the wiser. She needed to find a way to shut Colette up, and fast, before she stupidly revealed her grandfather was one of Washington's top men. Cursing under her breath, she was just about to step around the corner and interrupt them when she heard John ask, "And what do you know

43

of our lovely hostesses for the evening?"

Her blood ran cold, and she froze.

"Lucile Wolfe is an extremely well-known and well-liked socialite here in New York. She inherited a great deal of wealth from her family, and they have been here for as far back as anyone can remember."

"And her niece, Miss Eldridge?" he inquired.

"Emma came here when she was only ten. Her parents were murdered in Virginia and her aunt was the only family she had left."

"Murdered?" his tone was troubled.

"Yes!" Collette's voice lowered. "The poor girl saw the whole thing happen. Of course, being an orphan and part of the noble and elite 'Wolfe' pedigree, everyone here immediately embraced her, especially knowing she will someday be the sole heir to the entire family fortune once her aunt is gone. Every single man in New York has tried to gain her affection, but so far, no one has managed to catch her attention."

Having heard more than enough, Emma decided it was time to put an end to John André's information-gathering session for the evening. She whirled around the corner, pretended to trip on the threshold, and landed on Colette, dumping her entire glass of red wine down the front of the young lady's white gown.

Colette let out a 'yelp'—one that dramatically morphed into a 'howl'—catching even the calm and collected Major André a bit off guard— if the discreet plugging of his ear with his index finger was any indication.

"Oh Colette, I am so sorry!" apologized Emma, casually glancing over her shoulder. "There must be a loose floorboard or something. You know how these old houses are."

Lucy, who was hovering nearby, seemed quite interested and curiously entertained by the scene playing out, doing her best to stifle her laughter. Locking eyes with her niece, she lifted her glass in a toast as if to say, 'well done'. Lucy composed herself before going over and putting her arm around Colette. "Come with me upstairs, my dear, and we will get you cleaned right up. Emma can see to our guests."

As they departed, the corners of Major André's lips twitched up and he stroked his chin, clearly amused. Nonchalantly slipping his hand around to the small of Emma's back, he guided her away from the center of attention. "Well, Miss Eldridge, it seems you are in need of a fresh drink."

"Well, would you look at that," she said, looking down at her glass, "It seems you are correct," and she let him escort her to the wine table.

"You really should have someone look at that floorboard," he smarted, refilling her glass. "That could be positively dangerous for an unsuspecting person who might happen along."

"I will get right on that," she half-chortled and glanced in that direction, only to see two officers thoroughly

45

inspecting the area where the 'accident' occurred. Turning back, she asked, "Are you enjoying the party, Major André?"

"Very much so," he replied and sipped from his glass, his eyes fixed on hers. "The entertainment thus far has been superb. I have also had the pleasure of meeting a great many interesting people."

"I am sure you have. You and Colette seem to have hit it off."

An impish grin crossed his lips. "She is a lovely young lady."

Emma shrugged. "Colette Thompson is also in the market for a husband, and I do believe she has set her sights upon you."

"Is that right?" he asked, never taking his attention off her.

A shiver darted down her spine, the Major's gaze making her a bit uncomfortable. Yes, there was something about this man that unnerved her in more ways than one.

"Indeed! I daresay she has already decided on the date, the time, and the menu. If I know her, she will be at the dressmaker first thing in the morning picking out fabrics."

He leaned close and whispered in her ear, "I am not exactly the marrying type."

She turned her head towards his. "If you are truly not the marrying kind, I suggest you save yourself some grief and cut your losses now. You are not the first handsome officer she has fixated upon."

"Well, Miss Eldridge, I must thank you for your candor, although I can't help but wonder if there is a note of something else in your words."

"Such as?"

The Major's eyes swept over her. "A tinge of jealousy perhaps?"

Emma blinked, stunned by the sheer audacity of the man's suggestion. "Jealousy? You think I am jealous of Colette Thompson?"

"You did just dump an entire glass of wine down the front of her gown to get me alone."

She scoffed. "Allow me to assure you— nothing could be further from the truth."

"My mistake," he muttered in a low, sensual voice, a sly smirk resting on his face.

A devilish smile crossed Emma's lips when she saw Willena Fitz sitting in a nearby chair, and it suddenly occurred to her how she could derail the Major's intelligence gathering for the entirety of the rest of the evening.

Taking John by the arm, she gently guided him in her direction. "You must forgive me, Major André! I have gotten so caught up in my hostess duties that I have become completely remiss in introducing you to some of our other guests. I would not want you to be under the mistaken assumption I was trying to keep you all to

47

myself, so please allow me to rectify that situation now."

Willena Fitz was the oldest current resident of New York at the age of 102. Hard of hearing, partially senile, and shaking from palsy, the tiny woman had buried four husbands, eight children, and outlived everyone except her great-grandson, Devon, who happily handed her off to anyone who expressed any interest in speaking to her whatsoever for the sake of his sanity. The poor man had deposited her into a chair and made a beeline out the back door to join some of the officers who had brought along their own supply of hard liquor for the occasion.

"John, I would like you to meet New York's most beloved resident, Mrs. Willena Fitz." Emma raised her voice and bent over. "Mrs. Fitz! I would like you to meet Major John André!" she shouted.

Willena lifted her head and leaned toward Emma. "Did you say something, dear?"

"Yes! This is Major John André!" she repeated louder.

John chuckled and chewed on his lip when he realized he was being toyed with. Determined to not let Emma get the better of him, he planted a wide smile on his face, reached for the old woman's hand, and planted a gentle kiss upon it. "It is a pleasure to be in the company of such a lovely young lady. Every man in the room is envious of me this evening because I am the one standing here with you."

"Well, aren't you a handsome fellow," the elderly woman said and leaned in for a closer look. Touching his face, she asked, "Have we met?"

"No ma'am, I am newly arrived here."

"What did you say? Speak up!" she yelled and firmly grasped his hand.

"I said—I am new here!" he said again in a firmer voice.

She used her free hand to spruce her hair. "Why yes, this is my new hairdo! Do you like it?"

Softly chuckling, he replied, "It's quite delightful—as are you!"

Willena patted his arm. "It is so nice of you to say. My third husband, Earl, never once noticed when I had my hair styled."

Emma turned her head to the side and snickered, catching sight of a playful expression on John's face aimed in her direction.

"Oh, I see my aunt trying to get my attention. If you will excuse me," she announced, before lightly tapping John on the shoulder and whispering in his ear, "Enjoy the rest of your evening, Major!"

John continued to smile at her impishly and proceeded to pull up a seat, still holding Willena's hand. "Don't worry about us! We will be just fine." Offering her a wink to let her know he knew exactly what she was up to, he proceeded to turn and give Willena his full, undivided attention.

"Has Colette gone home for the evening?" Emma asked Lucy when she rejoined her.

"Oh yes! That gown was completely ruined. Not that I didn't enjoy the show, but what was that all about anyway?"

"Colette was spewing information about some of our friends faster than the Major could keep up."

Lucy listened with keen interest as Emma explained what she had said about the others. "It seems the Head of Intelligence wasted no time finding the leakiest part of the sinking ship," she remarked.

"More like the rats trying to scurry off," Emma mumbled sarcastically.

Lucy grinned. "At any rate, I will make it a point to pay a visit to those ladies tomorrow and highly 'suggest' the Major is a well-known cad and one to steer clear of, for the sake of their virtues." Lucy nodded her head in the direction of the corner when she saw John entertaining Willena and laughed. "Your doing, I take it?"

"I thought she might keep him out of trouble for a while," replied Emma. "He is welcome to any and all information he can manage to get out of her." The two ladies toasted each other with their glasses.

At that very moment, John's mischief-filled eyes met hers—he shot her a wickedly handsome smile—and her heart skipped a beat.

The next morning, Emma bounded down the stairs in her riding outfit with a book in hand.

Lucy handed Emma a folded piece of paper where all the information she learned the night before had been written down in code in the form of a grocery list. When the ladies first started gathering information for Washington, they came up with a system known only to the three of them: Pounds of flour would represent the number of troops, one per thousand—bags of sugar would represent ships, one per hundred—and the locations of the most heavily placed armaments around the city would be listed in order of spirits from the most to the least—whisky for the north, rum for the south, beer for the east, and cider for the west. The list would be filled in with random items like any other, so were it ever found, no one would be any the wiser.

Emma rode Mac every morning to a nearby park, where she would spend time reading or writing in her journal while leaned against a particular old oak tree she was fond of—one that happened to have a slightly concealed opening where she could squirrel away the message without notice. At some time, later in the day, another person unknown to them, and vice versa, would retrieve the note and get it to Washington himself.

"I won't be long," she called out and left through the door.

She rode slowly that day, enjoying the nice weather. It was a crisp, clear morning and the town was slowly starting to come to life. She waved to and greeted those she knew.

After completing her mission, she decided to stop in at a nearby mercantile to pick up a wedding gift for Francis and Jack. While her silver serving dish for the Donalds was being wrapped, she wandered around the store and stopped to look at some newly arrived bolts of fabric. Glancing towards the front window, something— or rather someone— caught her eye.

It was Colette Thompson clinging tightly to the arm of none other than Major John André.

Eyes wide, her mouth agape, she let out an annoyed huff. When she realized they were headed inside the same store, she looked around and ducked down behind a table to hide. Hearing the small bell ring and the door open, she mouthed a curse word to herself when it occurred to her that she was now trapped.

"This is hands down the best place to get that tea you are so fond of," said Colette.

"It's good to know I can find a few familiar things here in the Colonies to make it feel more like home."

Emma shifted and stole a peak around the corner to see the Major with his hands folded behind his back, browsing the various tables. She reached for the display covering and pulled it up to see if there was anywhere to hide beneath the table closest to her, only to find there was just enough space for her to fit if she angled exactly right and curled her feet inward. She started to scooch into the spot when the Major exclaimed cheerfully, "Good morning, Miss Eldridge!"

Emma looked up to see John peering over the table and down at her with an amused look upon his face.

"Good morning, Major André!" she forced out.

"May I ask what you are doing on the floor?" He asked and walked around the table. "Did you drop something?" He pretended to look around.

"I was— um— looking for— more— fabric!" she lied.

"And is it normally on display under the table?" He extended his hand.

"No, it is not," she replied, reluctantly taking his proffered hand and standing up. "I was hoping there was more selection tucked away, but unfortunately, I was out of luck."

"Emma?" said Colette coolly. "What are you doing out so early this morning?"

"Actually, I was doing a little shopping—for you," she covered.

"For me? Why would you be shopping for me?"

Emma waved her hand over the table. "I felt so horrible about ruining your gown last evening, the least I thought I could do, was to replace the fabric so you could have a new gown made."

"Oh!" said Colette, surprised by the unexpected gesture. "Well, that is most kind of you."

Emma cut her eyes over to the Major and then back to Colette. "How fortunate you and Major André happened along when you did! You can pick out your favorite and save me the impossible task of deciding which would look more beautiful on you. There are simply too many choices and, as you well know, everything looks good on you." Pointing to a few bolts on the top, she asked, "Which one do you like best? Personally, I think this white silk would be absolutely stunning on you," Emma cast her eyes over to see John's reaction, "Wouldn't this make a beautiful formal gown, for something like a wedding or such?"

"Oh, you are right!" squealed Colette and took it from her hands.

Emma lifted her eyebrows and discretely shrugged in the Major's direction.

John dipped his head and ran his hand across some of the other choices as if contemplating a purchase.

"What do you think, John?" Colette stretched it out against her.

"Yes, Major. What do you think?" goaded Emma.

He raised his hand to his chin as if he were seriously pondering the question. "I think it is quite lovely indeed, although I prefer to see ladies wearing something a little more colorful, shades to match their tastes and personalities. White is so plain, innocent, and frankly — boring." He moved around the table and picked up a specific fabric. "Take this, for example. I think this would look splendid on Miss Eldridge. If I am not mistaken, green is definitely her color."

Emma narrowed her eyes and John gave her a roguish wink for only her to see.

"I have your gift wrapped for you," Mr. Miles, the shopkeeper, stepped out of the back and called out to Emma, interrupting the exchange.

"What sort of gift?" asked Colette absentmindedly, casually picking through the other choices.

"A wedding gift," she replied and winked back at the Major.

Colette turned to face John and smiled. "I simply adore weddings, don't you? Who is getting married?"

"My friend, Francis, married Captain Donald earlier this week and I just found out. Since I am having tea with her tomorrow afternoon, I felt I shouldn't show up empty-handed." Emma pointed at the fabric. "I have to run. Pick out whatever suits you, and as much of it as you like. Have it put on my bill, and again, my sincerest apologies, Colette, for ruining your fun last night."

"Oh, think nothing of it," she said and gathered her choices, excited for the free shopping spree.

"Major André!" Emma nodded and strode past him to the door.

"Miss Eldridge," he acknowledged with a sly grin before watching her leave.

Emma stormed into the house and slammed her package down on the table in the hall.

Lucy leaned out from the library with a book in hand. "Something wrong?"

Huffing, Emma traipsed around her and into the room.

Plopping down in a chair, she brushed her lips with her fingers. "John André and Colette were out together this morning after I clearly warned him last night she was only in the market for a husband, a position he plainly stated he was not interested in!"

"Oh!" Lucy pressed her lips together, snapping her book closed.

"What's that supposed to mean?" demanded Emma irately.

"Nothing! You just seem to be a little bothered by the fact the Major was in the company of another woman."

"It's not that—it's the fact it was Colette. You know how obtuse she can be. For Heaven's sakes, she was telling everyone's business like there was no tomorrow, including my own, which I do not appreciate at all!"

"Yours?" asked Lucy, suddenly concerned.

Emma picked at a spot on the chair. "She just met the man, and she was already telling him all about how I watched as my parents were murdered and had to come here because I had nowhere else to go. Not that it's any of her business," she added sullenly. "What does he see in her anyway?"

Lucy came over, put her arm around her, and rested against the chair. "Well, she is young—and beautiful—"

Emma wrinkled her nose contemptuously. "Are you trying to cheer me up? Because if you are, you are failing miserably."

Squeezing her niece tightly, Lucy continued, "—and the

56

granddaughter of one of Washington's most trusted men."

Leaning back, Emma looked up at her aunt, who was making a wry face. "What do you think the Head of Intelligence sees in that silly girl? Really Emma? Has this man gotten you so turned around you have forgotten how to think clearly?"

Understanding washed over Emma. She closed her eyes and rubbed her temples. "He has found out who she is, and he is using her for information."

"Ah, there's my smart girl! Welcome back!" Lucy patted her on the back. "The officers drink and play cards at one of the seedier taverns on Tuesday evenings with some of the men who work on the docks. From what I understand, Major André was the one plying them with alcohol at the last game, not long after he arrived."

"And exactly how did you find that out?" questioned Emma.

"Jacob happened to be there that night and recognized him when he came to the house for the party."

Jacob was the only stableman Emma trusted to care for her horse, Mac, and that wasn't all he was entrusted with. Unlike most other households, Lucile Wolfe kept no slaves—only highly-paid servants who were more than happy to remain loyal to their mistress out of appreciation for the excessive amount of coin she doled out to them for their services.

"If that's the case," pondered Emma aloud, "Colette is

going to end up giving him far more information than we can afford for him to have."

Lucy went over to her desk and sat down in her chair. "Well, I suppose you are just going to have to arrange for those two to have a falling out," she said with a gleam in her eye.

"Wouldn't it be easier to go ahead and cut Colette's tongue out?" retorted Emma sourly. "It will save us the trouble the next time she wants to get chatty!"

"Easier, yes, but where's the fun in that? I think the Major just needs a little distraction, and I think you are the perfect person to provide it."

3
CHAPTER THREE

"Tell me about Charlie."

Emma and Francis were enjoying their tea and cakes.

"I don't hear from him as often as I like and most of the time," replied Francis, "I don't even know where he is. I get the odd letter here and there, and occasionally, he just appears out of nowhere for a day or two to check in. I am not even sure exactly what he does for the army."

Emma added more sugar to her tea and stirred. "What do you mean 'you don't know what he does for them'? Have you never asked?"

"Of course, I have, but I always get the same response— 'whatever is needed'."

"That's a rather odd answer, don't you think?" Emma

tapped the spoon and laid it across the saucer.

Francis sighed. "Charlie is not the same person you once knew. Father's death took a great toll on him and something inside of him changed. It is as if he went from being a carefree boy to a burdened man overnight."

"It's no fun having to grow up that fast." Emma's tone was grim as her eyes drifted to the floor and the image of her parent's bodies flashed in her mind.

Seeing the light go out of her, Francis decided to change the subject. "Tell me, Emma, why have you not married? Don't tell me you haven't had at the very least, a dozen proposals."

Emma shook the dark image from her mind and smiled. "I suppose the right man hasn't come along. Fortunately, Aunt Lucy has not been one to press the matter, something I am extremely grateful for. I think she has rather enjoyed living the life of an unmarried lady without having a man to tell her what to do, and she wants me to have the luxury of doing the same." She winced as soon as the words left her lips. "Not that being married is a bad thing."

Francis chuckled softly and picked up her cup. "It's alright. While I will admit, our family's finances are not as vast as they once were, and that taking a husband with some family money in England turned out to be quite beneficial in the circumstance, I do love Jack. He has made me happier than I have ever been, and I am honored to be his wife."

Emma reached across and touched her hand. "I cannot tell you how glad I am to hear that."

"I only hope you find someone who makes you feel the same way." A sly grin crossed her lips. "Tell me, Emma, what do you think of Major André?"

Taking a sip of her tea, Emma pondered how best to answer. She thought a great many things about Major André, but it was probably best to not say them in polite company. Instead, all she said was, "He's seems nice enough. Why do you ask?"

"He stopped by to have a word with Jack yesterday afternoon about some army business, but of course Jack was working down by the dock, so we visited for a bit before he had to go."

Fully aware a man in John André's position would have known if Jack was home or not before he stopped by, she simply said, "Oh?"

Francis nodded. "After exchanging some pleasantries, our conversation topic turned to you. He seemed extremely interested in knowing more about you."

"I am sure he did," she said to herself. Then, aloud to Francis, "What specifically was he curious about?"

Francis set her teacup onto the saucer and tilted her head to one side. "Our childhood, of all things. He was asking about our families and how we knew each other growing up. If I didn't know any better, I would say he was a little sweet on you."

"I don't think 'sweet' is the word I would use," she

mumbled under her breath.

"What was that?" asked Francis.

"I just said 'not from what I have heard'," she covered. "He seems quite interested in Colette Thompson."

"I wouldn't be so sure about that," whispered Francis, leaning in, "I saw where his eyes were the other night, and they weren't on Miss Thompson."

Emma rested her head against the inside wall of the carriage on the way home. She had been in such a good mood, excited to have time alone with Francis, but the thought of Major André asking about her childhood behind her back had turned her mood sour. It was late afternoon by the time she got home, and she went straight to the library where the strongest alcohol was set out. Downing two glasses of whisky in rapid succession, she poured a third, kicked off her shoes, and sat down as she proceeded to finish that one off.

"Will you be wanting an early supper?" asked Midge when she came in the room.

"I am not hungry. Tell Aunt Lucy to eat without me."

"She is out for the evening, playing cards with some of the ladies. Are you sure you don't want some food to go with what you are drinking there?" asked Midge, suggesting more than asking.

"No, thank you. You can go for the evening."

Midge cast a wary eye towards her before leaving.

Emma continued to nurse her drink for the next hour, her anger towards John André for asking questions about her family growing by leaps and bounds. The thought occurred to her that perhaps she should tell him to mind his own business. The idea sounded better with each sip she took, and by the end of glass four, she was filled with a great deal of 'liquid courage'. Remembering Major André was billeted two streets over, she slipped on her shoes and stumbled out of the house. Bobbing and weaving from the effects of the alcohol, she made her way down the street. A quarter of an hour later, after some deliberation as to the actual location of the house, she stood on his stoop. Straightening her back and smoothing her gown, she swayed a bit before loudly banging on the door. A servant answered the call.

"I need—to see—John—Major—André," she slurred, reaching for the jamb to steady herself.

"Major André is not to be disturbed," said the servant and tried to close the door.

Emma planted her foot on the threshold and leaned forward. "I don't think you understand," she enunciated for emphasis, "I need to see him NOW!" and pushed past her, leaving the servant stunned.

Noticing the door to the left was to a parlour, she marched in and shouted, "Oh Major André," she half-sang, "I need a word with you!"

John appeared from the next room over, attached by two doorways, one on each side of a large fireplace. Napkin in hand and a perplexed expression on his face, he said, "Miss Eldridge?"

She stumbled and staggered over to where he was and repeatedly poked her index finger in the middle of his chest, her sense of propriety completely extinguished at this point. "Listen mister intelligence man, I have something to say to you!"

"Good Lord, how much have you had to drink?" he muttered when he caught a whiff of her breath and nervously glanced over his shoulder. Taking her by the arms, he whispered, "Now is not the time or the place for whatever you feel the need to get off your chest. Perhaps it is best you return home, and we can speak tomorrow when your thoughts are a bit clearer."

"I feel just fine, thank you very much!"

"Not as fine as you might think." He tried to gently guide her back in the direction from which she came.

Emma stubbornly planted her feet firmly and refused to budge. "Why were you asking about my childhood?" she demanded. "What happened to my family is none of your business or anyone else's for that matter. If you want to know something about me, why don't you ask me? Or maybe you are worried Colette will get jealous if you pay me a visit for something like that—and, no doubt, she will. She wants you all to herself. Tell me, Major John André, has she let you fuck her yet?"

John tightened his grip on her arms. "Please, for the love of God, stop talking!"

"Does that mean 'no'?" Emma cocked her head as if in thought. "Well, it shouldn't be too difficult, I mean that barn door was busted down a long time ago! I imagine after two glasses of wine and a little loosening of this," she fiddled with the cravat around his neck, "you will have her on her back in no time, especially if you are gazing at her with those beautiful eyes and that sweet smile of yours…" she trailed off before shaking her head as if waking from a trance and took a step back, "I mean, if she's your type and who you really want to be with."

A man appeared behind them and loudly cleared his throat.

Emma leaned to the side to see General Clinton standing there, his lips in a thin line, appearing rather unamused. "Is everything alright, Major André?" he asked.

"Yes General, my apologies. It seems Miss Eldridge is not feeling herself for some reason and was just about to return home to rest," he replied resolutely.

It was at that moment, Emma turned her head to look through the second doorway to see Major André was in the middle of having a supper party with several officers, their wives, and a few of the town's residents, including the Vicar from the church she attended.

She cursed under her breath and cringed. "Good evening, General Clinton!" she managed.

"Miss Eldridge," he acknowledged and stepped closer, catching the strong reek of whisky coming off her.

"Perhaps you should see her home to her aunt, Major André, since she is feeling rather 'unwell'."

Emma shook her head. "Oh no, that won't be necessary. I think I can make it on my own," she said, the gravity of the situation sobering her up rather quickly. Turning, she started towards the door but nearly fell when the heel of her shoe broke.

"Damn it!" she let slip before righting herself and limping towards the front hall.

John followed her outside and caught her by the arm once they were alone. "Oh, no you don't, Miss Eldridge! You are not getting off that easily! Just what the hell was that all about?"

"Nothing—I'm sorry—" she said and tried to pull free, but he refused to relinquish his firm grasp.

"You interrupted an extremely important gathering this evening to get something off your chest, and there is no need to stop now, so let's have it. What is it you wanted to say so badly to me?"

Emma looked down at the ground. "I didn't know you had company," she said quietly. "I just wanted to tell you—"

"Tell me what?" he demanded, his patience wearing thin.

She swallowed hard. "If you want to know about the death of my parents, ask me, not anyone else in this miserable fucking town. After all, I was the only witness that day to the murders, and I am the only one who knows what really happened. I remember it vividly because I see it happen all over again each night when I close my eyes." Tears threatened to burst like a dam, and he relaxed his grip, his face softening as she continued, lifting her chin, "Everyone wants to know, but are far too polite to ask me to my face, so instead, they gossip behind my back. They all have their own version of what happened, you know, but none of them ever get it right because it is far worse than their small, insignificant minds could ever possibly imagine."

Silent tears streaked down her face and she started to walk away, leaving him confused.

"Wait! I don't understand. I didn't ask anyone about the death of your parents," he called out.

Sniffling, Emma stopped and turned to face him. "But Francis Donald said you were asking about our childhood, and that was after I overheard Colette at the party the other night tell you I witnessed my parents' murders."

Sighing, John closed the distance between them and waved his hand towards a nearby bench, inviting her to sit with him.

"I wasn't trying to find out about your childhood specifically," he explained in a compassionate tone, "I was using you as a reason to inquire about the Taylor's background."

"Francis and Charlie?" Emma shook her head. "But why?"

He hesitated and glanced around to make sure they were alone before resting his arm on the back of the bench. "Her brother has been recommended for a special assignment under my command, and I need to be unequivocally certain of his devotion to our cause because of the delicate nature of what it entails. I had thought I was making a quiet inquiry, but apparently, I was not as surreptitious as I thought I was."

Emma covered her mouth. "Oh my God! What have I done?"

John gently brushed a tear from her cheek. "It seems I have as much culpability in this situation as you do," he said with a warm smile.

She dropped her face into her hands, embarrassed. "And I just made a complete ass of myself in front of all those people, including my own priest."

"I daresay he has heard worse in confession if it makes you feel any better." He chuckled softly.

"Major André, I know this means little after what I just did but allow me to offer my deepest apologies. I think it is past time I should be going." She tried to stand, toppling over on to him as her broken heel threw her off balance.

John caught her and steadied her, holding her in place for a long moment to gaze into her eyes. Finally, he spoke. "Let me see you home safely, Miss Eldridge."

"No, I think you need to see to your guests, and I very well may die of humiliation if I have to be around you much longer." She reached down and took her shoes in her hands before starting up the walkway.

"Miss Eldridge—Emma," he called out, causing her to stop. "I won't ever ask about the horrific thing that happened to your parents, but if you ever want to tell me, I will always be here and willing to listen."

Touched beyond measure by his words, she tried her best to control the tears, a nod the only acknowledgment she could muster before hurrying out of sight and completely falling apart.

The following morning, Emma lay in bed, groaning when the curtains were pulled back to let in the morning sun.

"Well, aren't we the talk of the town this morning?" announced a cheerful, almost giddy Lucy as she fluttered around the room.

"I made an absolute fool of myself last night," Emma confessed and pulled the covers over her head.

"So, I have heard!" Lucy sat down on the edge of the bed. "Did you really ask Major André if he had fucked Colette Thompson in front of Father Donley and then say that her barn door had been busted open long ago?"

Emma moaned and Lucy clapped her hands together in a boisterous fit of laughter. "Damn it! Of all the boring supper parties I must attend, why was I not invited to this one? I miss all the fun!"

"Oh Lucy, it was awful. I had so much whisky I didn't

notice an entire room full of people who were sitting right in front of me!"

"Oh, don't give it a second thought. This town has a rather large stick up its ass, and it needed a little excitement to stir things up."

"How can I show my face in town after my erratic behavior?"

"My dear, you are a young, wealthy socialite who has yet to take a husband. You could have walked into that room completely naked, with a rose between your teeth, and no one would have dared questioned you. In fact, they would have complimented you on your choice of attire and asked where you got the lovely flower. After last night, you will just be considered a spitfire who needs the right man to come along and tame you. All will be forgotten as soon as the next bit of juicy gossip comes along. Besides, Major André and General Clinton were kind enough to cover for you by saying, unbeknownst to them at the time, you had been nearly run over by a coach, falling and hitting your head as you were knocked out of the way. The whole town is now concerned about your well-being, and I have had visitors all morning stopping by to check in on you. Now that the matter has been addressed, do you mind telling me what it was really all about?" She handed Emma a cup of tea.

"Francis told me yesterday, the Major stopped by her home and was asking about our time as children in Virginia."

Lucy frowned. "Why would he do something like that?"

"I wrongly assumed it was about the murders, but he told me last night that Charlie, her brother, is up for a special assignment, and he was merely checking into his background."

"And you believe him?"

Emma shrugged. "He seemed sincere enough."

"What sort of special assignment?"

"I have no idea! He didn't elaborate and I was in no position to ask questions."

"We should probably find out what it is. If he is going to that kind of trouble to poke around, it must be important."

Emma sipped her tea and leaned back against the headboard. "How exactly are we going to do that?"

Lucy patted her leg. "I am sure we can come up with something that doesn't involve busting down your barn door, unless of course, it is something you want the Major to do. I am sure he would be happy to oblige!"

Setting her teacup on the side table, Emma shot a daggered glare at her aunt. "You know, most high-society spinster aunts who raise their nieces from a young age don't encourage such debauchery."

Lucy grinned. "Most high-society spinster aunts are boring and have never experienced the pleasure of having a man, who knows exactly what he is doing, take them to bed."

Emma decided to cower in her bedroom as visitors with food and notes of concern came and went all morning. She ventured downstairs just after sunset to spend some time with Lucy, who she found with her feet propped up on a footstool, gown askew and drinking a large glass of port.

"You look comfortable!"

Lucy wiggled her toes. "It has been an exhausting day of worrying about my niece's health. I have had no fewer than twenty people stop by and inquire as to your condition."

"What did you tell them?" asked Emma, plucking a few grapes from a tray on the table, before pouring herself a drink and sitting down.

"That you were sleeping it off—the bump on the head, that is," she replied with a sly grin. "I assured everyone you were being well cared for and would be up and about in no time."

"Can we delay my miraculous improvement until after the next church service? On second thought, perhaps we should just switch churches altogether—maybe even consider converting faiths."

Lucy flicked her hand. "We can always blame it on a fit of hysteria during your monthly courses. Nothing ends a conversation with a man faster than the mention of that."

"I don't know—asking a man if he has fucked another woman in front of a room full of people works pretty well too," added Emma dryly.

Lucy snorted. "I suppose it does!" Setting her glass aside, she sighed and said, "I think I am going to turn in for the evening. Good night, my dear," and she got up.

"Good night, Aunt Lucy!"

Needing to settle her mind, Emma went over and perused the books on the shelf. After choosing one, she curled up on the sofa in front of the fireplace, tucked her feet beneath her, and settled in. She had just finished the first three chapters when Midge stepped inside the room. "Pardon me, Miss Emma, but there is someone here to see you."

"This late? Who is it?"

"Major John André."

Emma's head dropped and she groaned. "Might as well get it out of the way," she mumbled and nodded for her to show him in.

John stepped inside the library with his hat in hand and a pleasant expression on his face.

"Come in, Major André."

"Good evening, Miss Eldridge. I hope you will forgive the lateness of the hour. I have been meaning to stop by all day and check in on you, but unfortunately, business has taken precedence."

"May I offer you something to drink?" she asked and motioned for him to sit.

He cast a wary eye at the glass in her hand and winced. "I hope that is not the same concoction you were drinking last evening."

"No, just a little bit of wine. I think I will lay off the hard stuff for a while."

"Probably a wise idea," he agreed and helped himself to a glass before taking a seat next to her. "How are you feeling today?"

Emma closed her eyes. "Embarrassed—humiliated—foolish—and a few more things I am sure I am leaving out." She opened her eyes and looked at him. "Major André, I cannot begin to apologize for my atrocious behavior. I have no idea what got into me. I also owe you a debt of gratitude for attempting to cover for me when I seemed to have taken leave of my senses. It was the very gentlemanly thing to do."

"It was the least I could do." He leaned back and crossed his legs. "I am afraid I bear some measure of responsibility for the situation, as well. I had no idea Mrs. Donald would mention a conversation I was convinced I had passed off as mere small talk. It was certainly not my intention to upset you by bringing up something so unpleasant from your past."

She stared into the flames of the fireplace. "I must admit, it has been on my mind a little more than usual as of late, and I may have let my emotions get the better of me."

"That is sometimes an easy thing to do." Noticing the book in her hand and deciding it was a good time to change the subject, he asked, "What are you reading?"

"Oh!" she held it up, "Gulliver's Travels by Jonathan Swift."

"A wonderful adventure indeed! Are you enjoying it?"

"It has been a nice escape from reality, especially today. Books have always been a comfort to me. I am fortunate to have an aunt who keeps our library well-stocked. Do you like to read?"

"I do! Shakespeare is my favorite. I have even been known to try my hand at composing a little poetry myself on occasion."

"You write?" she asked somewhat surprised.

He nodded and sipped his wine. "I write, I sketch, I paint, I make silhouettes, and I even play the flute when I have enough of the right encouragement. I have also taken the time to learn several languages. The arts are a large part of what makes life so interesting, and I find them essential for my peace of mind given the nature of my work."

"What are some of the other essentials that make life interesting?" The words slipping out before she considered what the answer might be.

"There are too many to name." He seemed to ponder his answer as he swirled the liquid in his glass around. He laughed softly before his face became serious and his voice dropped to a low, sultry, almost hypnotic tone. "The taste of a delicious, decadent food so rich it makes you want to take your time savoring each bite as if it were your last—the slow burn of a perfectly aged whisky as it splashes on the back of your throat while you sit by the warmth of a fire as the wind howls and the snow piles high outside your window—" he leaned in, mere inches separating them, "—the rapid beat of your heart as you take a beautiful woman in your arms and taste the sweetness of her lips for the very first time." John gently cupped her face and gazed into her eyes, the heat from his breath mingling with hers.

Her breathing had become ragged, shallow at the mere sound of his voice and with her heartbeat racing out of control, she closed her eyes, eagerly awaiting what came next—a desperate impulse had suddenly overcome her in the moment, and she yearned to feel his body pressed to hers. Prepared to surrender to whatever he desired, she was dismayed to only feel the brush of his cheek against hers and hear him whisper, "It is late, and I should be going."

"Huh?" she responded, completely confused.

He leaned back with his lips curled slyly. "I have an early morning, and I should not have called on you at such a late hour. I just wanted to see with my own eyes you were alright." He set his glass down and rose from his seat.

"Of course!" Emma quickly composed herself and stood. "I will see you out."

She walked him to the door.

"Good night, Miss Eldridge," he said with a devilish smile. "I hope you sleep well, and your dreams are filled

76

with all the things that make your life 'interesting'."

"Good evening, Major."

Emma groaned as she watched him walk away, her eyes still on him when he stopped to glance over his shoulder. She chided herself, closed the door, and sat down on the bottom step of the staircase. That man was nothing but trouble, yet she couldn't get her mind off him.

She tossed and turned the entire night, and what little sleep she did get was consumed with dreams of him covering her with his kisses and the feel of his touch in places she had never let any man experience before.

Exhausted, restless, and beyond frustrated, she got up and dressed just before dawn, careful not to wake her aunt, deciding to clear her head by taking a walk. Lost in her thoughts, when she looked around, she was surprised to find herself on the street where his house was.

"You have lost your mind," she muttered and wandered closer while debating whether she should pay him an early morning visit to repay his late-night one. As she stood there pondering the question on her mind, the movement of curtains in the upstairs window caught her attention. Curious to know if he were indeed already awake or if the servants were just opening the rooms for the day, she watched and waited. Emma's breath hitched and she felt her body go numb when the curtains parted—and the face of Colette Thompson appeared in the pane. "What in the world?" she said and moved to the

77

cover of a nearby tree for a better look. "What are you doing here?"

Her question was answered when John appeared next to her, wrapping his arms around her waist and planting a kiss on her shoulder. Colette turned and John took her into a tight embrace. Emma watched as he kissed her lips and slipped the robe she wore off, just before the two stepped out of sight.

"Oh, dear God!" Emma leaned against the tree and tried to catch her breath, feeling faint from the shock of what she had just seen. "He is fucking her."

She had been warned Major André used women to his advantage, yet, after spending some time with him, she had found herself doubting this kind, sincere man could do something as despicable as that. She had been one mere kiss from falling under his bewitching and seductive spell. At that moment, it dawned on her why he was so good at his job—he knew exactly how to make a woman feel like she was the only one in his world without uttering a word. While she assured herself her secrets and her true feelings regarding the war were safe no matter what, she realized a few short hours before, she had not been able to say the same about her virtue.

She also knew that women who fancied themselves in love would often lose all rational thinking and do stupid things for men they had feelings for. Aunt Lucy was right—John André was tying her up in knots and she had allowed it to make her vulnerable. It was a mistake she would not allow to happen again. No matter how much she desired the man physically, the cost of losing a high-stakes chess game with him was far too high, and the only way she would be able to win would be by removing herself from the board entirely.

Slowly, she made her way back home and slipped back into her room before anyone had any idea she was gone.

"Midge tells me Major André stopped in last evening," said Lucy as she spread butter on her bread. "What was that all about?"

"Nothing," replied Emma and shoved her food around with her fork. "He was just checking in on me."

Lucy sat her knife aside. "What's wrong, sweetheart?" She continued to press when Emma said nothing. "Tell me!"

Emma pushed her plate away. "I think it is best to steer clear of Major André. It is too big of a risk if he gets too close to either one of us, and I am not willing to take the chance."

"Did the two of you have a quarrel?"

Emma shook her head. "No. That man is not worth quarreling with." Rubbing the spot between her eyebrows, she added, "Colette has become a liability. Major André has taken her as a lover which means she is spilling everything she knows to him."

Lucy noticed the disheartened tone in her voice but chose not to address it. "Which also means she is telling him everything she learns about her grandfather's whereabouts and moves. He continues to write to her mother each week even though he knows where Colette and her father's loyalties lie. He needs to be warned to be careful of what information he sends. While something as simple as where they are may seem innocent enough, it is a tool the Major can use to his advantage." Lucy sighed. "This cannot be conveyed through our normal ways. Instead, it will require a more personal visit."

"I will go," offered Emma. "I could use a day away from town to clear my head. Write out the code for an in-person meeting and I will drop it in the tree. I will be ready to go in half an hour."

Lucy regarded her as she got up. "Is something else bothering you?"

"No," she replied and left the room.

Lucy picked up her bread and glanced towards the hall. "Oh, my dear Emma, you have made the mistake of falling for the enemy, haven't you? It's fine, well, and good to have your fun with them, in and out of bed, but you must learn to never develop true feelings for them. It will only cause you pain and heartache in the end." She took a bite of her food and slowly chewed, recalling her own unfortunate experience in that department.

Emma rode to the park, dismounted, and tied her horse before slowly making her way over to the tree. After settling in and placing the note, she opened her book and tried to concentrate on the words, but the only thing she could see was the image of Colette in Major André's arms. "You are a foolish girl with your head in the clouds to think a man like that might have been beginning to have feelings for you," she said to herself and slammed the book closed. After spending the next half an hour staring blankly into nothingness, she gathered herself and returned home.

"All taken care of?" asked Lucy.

"Yes," she replied and closed the door. "If picked up today, the meeting should be set for the day after tomorrow at the arranged place —and I will be there."

4

CHAPTER FOUR

Emma got an early start, planning to arrive at the
meeting place by mid-morning and return by early
afternoon. The pre-selected destination was an
abandoned cabin about an hour's ride outside of town in
a wooded area that was not well-traveled. She was
looking forward to the trip, even though the weather was
a bit overcast. Still feeling a little stung by the revelation
of the intimate relationship between Colette and the
Major, she thought a change of scenery might do her
some good. She arrived before General Washington and
tied her horse around back, out of sight. After making her
way inside, she pulled up a chair and waited. It wasn't
long before the back door creaked open, and a striking
young man dressed in farmer's clothing came inside.

Getting up from the chair and positioning it between them, she gripped it defensively and demanded, "Who are you?"

Startled and caught completely off guard, she chided herself for traveling with a knife for protection and then foolishly leaving it in her saddlebag on her horse thinking herself safe inside.

He held up one hand to indicate he meant no harm, holding something else in the other. "My name is Major Benjamin Tallmadge. General Washington sent me on his behalf because he was unable to break away. He sends his sincerest apologies and his warmest regards."

Emma started towards the front door. "I am afraid you have me confused with someone else. I was supposed to meet a young man I have been seeing here, and you are most certainly not him. Good day to you, sir."

As her hand touched the doorknob, he called out, "Wait! Please! General Washington said you would deny any and all knowledge of the meeting, you yourself, in fact, set up, so he asked me to bring something along to convince you that he did indeed send me in his place. He said you would understand what it meant."

Turning, Emma watched him lay something folded in cloth on the table. As he unwrapped it, she was surprised to see a piece of cake revealed.

"I take it you have a sweet tooth?" he inquired curiously.

Emma dropped her hand and shook her head, a slow

smile spreading across her face. "It's a rather long story," she said and came over to the table.

He pulled out the chair like a gentleman for her to sit. "I am afraid cake is hard to come by these days in an army encampment. I hope apple is alright—it was all I could scrounge up."

Emma took off her gloves and broke off a piece before popping it into her mouth. "The flavor doesn't matter. It's the thought that counts," she said and slid it over it in front of him to enjoy as well.

He sat down in the other chair and smiled. "I have to admit I am curious about the story that goes along with this. The General insisted I bring it along."

Emma rested her arm on the table. "I am afraid it is a sad and sordid tale."

"That is unfortunate, Miss...?" he questioned.

"Eldridge—but you may call me Emma."

He nodded. "Emma it is. I understand you have some information for the General."

"More of a stern warning for one of his close associates—a man by the name of Daniel Lawrence in his camp."

Tallmadge frowned. "Yes, I know who you mean. What's the problem?"

"He has a daughter in New York whom he has been writing to at every opportunity," she continued, "but her husband and daughter are loyal to the British. The new Head of Intelligence, Major John André, has taken his

84

granddaughter as a lover, and I am fairly sure he is using her to gain information for their cause."

"You are certain about this?"

"Oh, I am certain they are lovers," she grumbled.

He gave her a peculiar look. "I meant, are you certain he is getting information from her?" There was a guarded look on his face.

"Oh!" she said, slightly embarrassed that her obvious irritation with the Major had slipped out so easily. "Yes. It seems Major André's best source of information comes from exploitations of women he finds with connections to the Continental army. Given his interest in Miss Thompson, I can only assume he is receiving regular updates from her. I am sure Mr. Lawrence is not intentionally giving away information—probably only simple things like where he is at the time and where his men may be headed next—and to be honest, I would not be entirely surprised to learn his daughter is unaware of what is happening under her own nose. Miss Thompson is desperate to prove her worth to the English in hopes of bettering her station when this is all over with. Whatever the case, the Major is a smart, shrewd man who can ascertain a great deal from very little and those minor details are certainly giving him something of use if he is continuing the relationship."

Tallmadge sat back in his chair and pondered her words. Playing devil's advocate, he suggested, "Perhaps he has merely fallen in love with her and simply wants to be with her."

"He's not the type," she retorted dryly. "At any rate, any information they gain at this stage in the game, no matter how small, is entirely too much."

"Not necessarily." He drummed his fingers on the table.

"What do you mean?" she asked curiously.

"This might be an opportunity to feed the British some misguidance we could use to our advantage. I will discuss it with the General."

"Do what you wish with it," she said, "I am just the messenger, and we thought it was worth bringing to your attention."

"Indeed, it was. Do you have anything else?" he asked as he picked up a morsel of the cake and tasted it.

"No, I am afraid that is all for now. We will continue to send the troop numbers and movements within the city as we obtain them."

"Thank you, Emma. You have no idea how much we appreciate what you ladies are doing. The General also asked me to relay a message to you. He wanted to reiterate he does not want you or your aunt to put yourselves in any unnecessary danger. He is quite fond of both of you and wants to ensure you remain safe."

"Thank you for your concern, but we are taking the necessary precautions," she assured.

"At any rate, if you find yourself in some difficulty and need assistance, we have set up a way for you to signal us so someone can come to you. There is a small bakery on the north side of town called 'The Blackbird'. Go around to their back entrance where there is a slot in the door and when no one is looking, slide in a note that states you want them to deliver a spiced rum cake as a surprise to the last room at the top of the stairs at Underhill's Boarding House. Leave it unsigned and put no one else's name on it. That way, no incriminating information is exchanged, and all identities are protected."

"Spiced rum cake to the last room at the top of the stairs at Underhill's," she repeated. "Got it!"

Tallmadge smiled. "Do you mind if I ask why you are doing this?"

Emma shrugged. "Watching a British soldier murder your parents while his men stand by and do nothing as a child tends to leave a bad taste in your mouth," she replied matter-of-factly and stood. "You will relay the information?"

Not being the answer he was expecting, the soldier was taken aback. Quickly recovering, he rose from the chair and said, "I give you my word! Thank you, Emma."

He escorted her to her horse and helped her into the saddle. Leading Mac out to the trail, he made sure no one was around before sending her on her way with a wave.

Emma rode slowly towards home, so consumed by her thoughts she paid no mind to her surroundings or the darkening skies overhead. She was brought to attention, however, when the ground beneath her shook from the loud boom of rolling thunder. Mac whinnied and balked, causing her to look up at the sky. She had ridden into the edge of a thunderstorm without even realizing it. The cabin not being too far behind her and with an ominous-looking storm before her, she decided it was probably best to ride back the way she came and take cover until it passed.

Just as she turned Mac and spurred him in the side, she felt the hairs on the back of her arms stand up. The sudden flash of a lightning bolt and a deafening crack of thunder lit up everything around them as it struck a tree, splitting it in half, only about ten feet from where they were. The noise and commotion were too much for the poor frightened horse, who immediately reared up on his hind legs snorting and squealing, terrified.

Emma tried her best to hold on while hollering, "Whoa boy!" but her words went unheard. The sudden action and the powerful throw sent her flying off his back, landing her on her side before Mac galloped at full speed completely out of sight.

Laying still for a few moments, Emma was unable to move from the trauma of hitting the ground and the shock of the pain that racked her body. Another streak of lightning brought her around and she came to understand what a terrible predicament she was in.

Pushing up on her elbow to better survey her surroundings, she noticed off to the side of the trail two large pines had fallen side by side and caught on the next few trees over creating a small bit of cover low to the ground not far from where she was. When she tried to climb to her feet, an intense agony and a weakness shot from her foot to her knee causing her to fall again. With the next deafening roll of thunder came the torrential downpour. Emma used her arms to pull, and her non-injured leg to propel, herself until she finally reached the trees and managed to roll underneath, curling into the fetal position to fit under what little shelter it provided from the storm. The sky illuminated, the ground shook, and her eyes closed — she succumbed to the darkness.

By late that afternoon, Lucile Wolfe was a nervous wreck. She went over to the window and pulled back the curtains to search for any sign of Emma. She should have returned from her meeting hours ago and deep down inside, Lucy knew something was wrong. When a knock came at the door, she rushed to it and flung it open. She exhaled sharply when she saw it was Major André. "Oh, it's only you!" she said and turned away.

An amused look crossed his face. "I am terribly sorry to disappoint you, Mistress Wolfe." His smile faded and he stepped inside when he noticed her wringing her hands, seemingly upset. "Are you alright?" he asked worriedly. "Has something happened?"

Lucy regarded him for a long moment, hesitating before giving him an answer. "I am sorry, Major. I was hoping you were Emma."

He closed the door. "I don't understand. Is there some cause for concern?"

She walked back to the library with the Major close on her heels. "She went out for a ride this morning and I had expected her back a few hours ago, that's all."

"Perhaps she stopped off for a visit? To see Mrs. Donald or one of her other friends?"

"I am sure you are right," replied Lucy, unconvincingly. They each turned their attention to a commotion in the hall.

"Miss Lucy!" shouted Jacob and he hurried into the room.

"Jacob! What is it?"

He glanced warily at Major André before taking his hat off. "Miss Emma's horse came back but she wasn't with him. He is spooked something terrible, and he is soaked as if he has been through a storm. His saddlebags are still on him."

"Oh, dear God!" exclaimed Lucy.

"Where did she ride out to?" demanded John.

Lucy eyed him up and down. Something had happened, and while she wasn't sure what, she decided no matter what the situation, it might help to have friends on both sides. She went over to her desk and opened a drawer, pulling out a map. Pointing to a specific spot, she said, "She likes to ride out this way. It's a little off the beaten path, but there is an old trail that she fancies and usually sticks to it."

John nodded. "I will head out that way now and see if I can locate her. Perhaps, her horse just ran off when she stopped for a bit." He took a sheet of paper from her desk and wrote out a note. "Will you have this delivered to General Clinton for me?"

"Of course." She took it from him and grasped him by the arm. "Major André, my niece is everything to me. Please bring her back."

"On my word," he said and rushed from the house.

Emma had no idea how long she had been out when she finally came to. Cold and shivering, her clothes were completely soaked, and she lay in several inches of mud. The thunderstorm had abated, but the rain was still coming down hard. Her head hurt tremendously in one specific spot and when she touched it, she drew back blood on her hand. Trying to gauge the damage to her leg by attempting to stretch it out, she found it tender and unmovable. A soreness had settled into her ribs that pained her each time she took in a breath.

"Well, this is a fine mess," she said to herself.

Getting out from underneath the two fallen trees proved harder than she ever thought possible. Her body had stiffened from the cold, and she cried out in pain when she inched ever so slightly to the side until she had cleared them.

"Now what?" she asked, lying face down in the rain. With a series of careful, calculated moves, she made it to a sitting position and leaned against the frame of her makeshift shelter for support. Tilting back her head, she let the rain fall into her mouth to help quench her unbearable thirst.

She looked around to survey the situation. It was later than she thought, and it would be dark soon. A dismal feeling of apprehension settled into the pit of her stomach when she became aware she would be out here alone for the night, and very possibly, much longer. Pulling her riding coat tighter around her, she rested her forehead on her knees and allowed a few tears to spill just to keep herself from becoming overwhelmed.

"Okay," she said and tried to pull her thoughts together. "I have to make it through the night. Aunt Lucy will have someone out looking for me by tomorrow if she hasn't sent someone already."

The meeting place was a few miles back and she had no way of getting there. All the essentials she normally carried with her were in her saddlebag and that had disappeared with Mac. Searching her pockets, she found all she had on her were a few coins. With no way of starting a fire, it dawned on her it was going to be a long, cold night. Her hiding place afforded little protection, but it was better than nothing. Perhaps she could shore it up a bit by adding some leaves to the top and some pine needles for a bed. The only problem was she couldn't get up to gather anything.

"Well, you are just completely fucked, aren't you?"

That's when she thought she heard something off in the distance. Lifting her chin, she listened. "You are just hearing things," she mumbled after a moment of quiet— but then heard it once more, this time much closer.

"Hello!" she called out. "HELLO!" she said louder, but her voice had gone hoarse.

"EMMA! EMMA!"

"John?" Could it be? "JOHN!"

"EMMA! ARE YOU OUT HERE? CAN YOU HEAR ME?"

"I am over here!" She realized the rain was drowning out her voice. Noticing a large stick on the ground next to her, she picked it up and used what little strength she had left to strike a nearby tree trunk, making a loud 'thunk' noise. "JOHN!" Smacking it again, she screamed out his name, "JOHN!"

She dropped the stick and burst into tears when he appeared on the road.

"EMMA!" he shouted, relieved when he saw her. Pulling his horse to a stop, he slid off and rushed to her. "Dear God!" he said as he embraced her; she sobbed into his chest. Taking off his coat, he wrapped it around her and pulled it tight. "Can you stand?"

She shook her head. "Something is wrong with my leg and I can't move it."

"What happened?" He brushed back her hair to see where blood had formed.

"My horse got spooked when we rode into a storm and

93

he threw me off."

Nodding, he looked up at the sky, the droplets starting to pick up even more. "This rain has set in for the night and we will not make it back before nightfall. I noticed a barn a little ways back up the road. We can stay there until morning."

Gathering her up in his arms, he carefully lifted her, placing her on his horse before climbing in the saddle behind her and spurring the animal full speed towards shelter.

Emma had forgotten the place even existed, even though she had passed it many times. The barn was intact on one side and partially collapsed on the other—only one half open to the elements. After carrying her inside to the part most sheltered from the weather and carefully settling her in, Major Andre brought his horse over to the other side and tied him for the night. John gathered some of the drier wood that had fallen in on itself and returned with an armful, along with his saddlebags and a bedroll. Within a short amount of time, he had a fire going and was taking some things from his satchel. He took the top off a flask and pressed it in her hand. "Drink this!"

"How did you know?" Her teeth chattered as she took a long swig of the dark, amber liquid that blissfully burned as it went down.

"I stopped by your home for a visit and your aunt was worried when you had not returned from a ride." He poured some water from a canteen onto one of his handkerchiefs. "At the same time, your stableman came in to say your horse had returned without you. I immediately rode out to search for you." He used the cloth to clean the dirt, grime, and blood from her face.

She winced when he hit the spot that was bleeding earlier.

"I'm sorry. You have a nasty cut and a bad bruise there. It needs to be cleaned out."

"I am sure it's not the only place I have them," she said sarcastically before a chill hit her and she began to shiver.

"We need to get you out of those clothes before you catch your death!"

"I don't have anything else to wear," she pointed out.

"I have my bedroll and a blanket. You can use them." He grabbed the items and started laying them out close to the fire. When he was done, he looked at her and held out his hand. "It's not what you are used to, but it is warm and dry."

Emma lowered her gaze and took another long sip from the flask, a tinge of pink creeping across her cheeks.

John smiled. "Come now, Emma, surely giving up a little modesty beats dying of pneumonia out here." She narrowed her eyes at him, and he laughed softly. "I, of course, will turn my back while you undress."

"Honestly, I don't think I could if I wanted to," she said and tried to shift a bit, letting out a loud groan.

John's face filled with concern and he shifted closer to her. "Exactly how badly are you injured?"

"I am almost afraid to look," she snarked.

He carefully slipped his coat from around her and removed her riding jacket. He could already see the bruising on her shoulder through the thin white shift she wore underneath. "What places hurt the most?"

"My head, my ribs, and my leg."

Lifting her skirts to just above her knee, he removed her stocking and boot, frowning when he saw precisely how bad it looked. Pressing on her knee and leg, Emma jumped and cried out in pain when he touched a particular spot. He laid his palm flat over the area as she winced and looked to the ceiling. "I don't think anything is broken, but it is swollen and inflamed. You will not be able to walk on it for a while."

She nodded in agreement.

After gently removing her other stocking and boot, he positioned her skirts back in place and sighed. "Emma, there is no way possible you can undress yourself, and if you stay in those wet clothes, you most certainly will become ill. You are going to have to set your notions of propriety aside and allow me to help you."

"I am sure I can manage," she lied, knowing full well she could not.

He sat back and decided to call her bluff. "Very well, prove it."

Emma wrinkled her nose in defeat. "Alright, maybe I

cannot," she admitted begrudgingly. "But I am only going down to my shift!"

"Only if it's dry," he stated firmly. "I won't have you getting sick on my watch."

"You are very bossy," she remarked sourly.

"I won't look if it makes you feel any better," he teased and moved to help her. "I am fairly certain I can find my way around a woman's body with my eyes closed."

Emma rested her chin on his shoulder when he reached around to untie her skirts. "Oh, I know you know your way around a woman's body—Colette's anyway," she mumbled. Emma felt him stiffen at her sharp words.

"What do you mean by that?" he asked as he went about his work.

"I know you have taken her into your bed," she said quietly. "I saw the two of you together."

After a long moment of silence, he asked, "How long have you known?"

"Since the morning after your last visit with me. I couldn't sleep so I went for a walk early the next day and I saw her in your window just before you joined her."

Pulling back, he blew out a hard breath. "I am going to lift you out of your skirts and lay you down on the bedroll. Are you ready?"

She nodded.

He gently picked her up and carried her over to the pallet he laid out. After carefully laying her down, he spread the blanket over her. "I want to take a look at your ribs." He made sure she was covered except for the area he was checking. The right side looked much worse than the left and he determined it must have been the one she landed on. "Does it hurt when you breathe in?"

"Quite a bit."

"You may have broken a rib in the fall. The physician will be able to tell you tomorrow once we get you home." He pulled the blanket up to her chin, rested on one knee, and looked down into her eyes. "Yes, Colette was in my bed, but it is not for the reason you think. I have no feelings for her whatsoever in that regard."

"I don't understand. How can you lay with someone you have no feelings for?"

"You are very sweet and naïve, my dear Emma," he replied wearily, tucking one side of the blanket beneath her. "I am sometimes required to do unorthodox things in my line of work—pretending to have feelings for Miss Thompson is one of those."

"So, you are leading her to believe you have a future together?"

"Absolutely not! In fact, I have made it perfectly clear to her that our relationship will never go any further. That does not seem to deter her in the least. As you so rightly pointed out at my dinner party, Miss Thompson is not an innocent maid whose barn door had never been kicked in before."

"I still don't understand."

He rubbed his chin and continued, choosing his words

carefully. "My line of work requires me to often do things polite society would find unacceptable and I do them out of my sense of duty to the Crown. I am in the impossible situation of garnering information others cannot, and I will do what I must to ensure we win this war. I will see order restored to this place, no matter what the cost. Colette has useful information, and she has freely offered it in exchange for a few minor 'concessions' on my part."

"Isn't that taking advantage of women by luring them into your bed?"

"No!" he exclaimed, and a hurt look crossed his face. "Emma, let me make something clear to you—I have never lured a woman into my bed under false pretenses. I have never, nor will I ever, take a woman against her will. It has been quite the opposite. The women who find their way to my bed are there because it is exactly where they want to be, and if they willingly offer up information that helps our cause, I will not ignore it."

"It sounds like you have done this quite a bit. How many women have you been with?" she asked in a tone that said she was unsure she wanted to know the answer.

John sighed and touched her face with the back of his hand. "You ask the wrong question, my dear sweet Emma. The question you should be asking is — how many women have I truly had feelings for? I will not lie or pretend I do not enjoy certain aspects of my work, after all, I am a man, and the feel of a woman's touch is one of our Creator's most magnificent gifts. But as far as how many women have I truly desired because of the feelings I have for them, the answer is— only three."

"Three?" She snuggled into the bedroll, the warmth of the fire making her more comfortable.

He reached for the flask and made her take another long drink so it would numb her to the point she could get some rest. "The first woman I ever loved was one I met years ago when I was still young and idealistic. Her name was Honora and when she broke my heart, I joined the army to dull the considerable pain. They say you never forget your first love and truer words have never been spoken. The second was a woman I let slip through my fingers because I did not make my intentions clear enough in time and she ended up marrying another. They are blissfully happy together and I count them both as dear friends now. The third," he stopped when he noticed her eyes had closed and she had finally given in to her weariness. Reaching out to lightly stroke her forehead, he whispered, "may be a bit closer than I care to admit." Hesitating at first, he gave in and kissed her tenderly on the forehead. John downed a good portion of the flask himself before laying her clothes out to dry and positioning himself against the nearby wall to watch over her.

He had dozed off but was awakened shortly thereafter by the sounds of Emma struggling. John moved to her side to find her having a nightmare, fighting to push something—or someone—away. He touched her face and shook her lightly. "Emma, you are having a bad dream!"

Her eyes flew open wide, and tears stained her face. She swallowed hard as her eyes darted back and forth, her senses slowly coming back. "I'm sorry!"

"Why are you sorry?" He kept his tone gentle and sat down beside her. Reaching over, he tossed another piece of wood onto the fire.

"I wake everyone with my nightmares. I am fairly certain Aunt Lucy was ready to ship me back to Virginia after the first two weeks of sleepless nights when I first arrived in New York. She had no idea what she was signing up for when she brought me home."

"It happens often?" Stretching out on his side next to her, he propped on one elbow. Seeing the blanket had been pulled loose, he put it back around her so she would not be cold.

"Every night it happens," she wiped her face with her hand, staring up at the ceiling, refusing to look anywhere else as her story spilled forth.

"I came home from playing with Francis and Charlie that day and my mother rushed me upstairs. British soldiers had shown up and needed use of our stables for the night to camp. She told me to stay in my room the whole time they were there, hidden from them. The next morning, I woke up to the sounds of their Lieutenant trying to drag my mother off alone. When she fought

101

back, he shoved her to the ground causing her to hit her head and she died instantly. When my father rushed to her side, that same Lieutenant buried a knife in his back and twisted it as I watched."

John remained silent, but the expression on his face said he was clearly disturbed by the recounting of that day.

"He heard me cry out and sent some of his men inside to see what caused the noise. The only reason I am alive is because the one who found me took pity and pretended I didn't exist. He told me to remain hidden until they were gone and then to run to the nearest neighbor. I lay there facedown for hours praying it was just a nightmare, but it was one that I could not wake from. I finally worked up enough courage to run to the Taylor's home, but not before I had to see Mama and Papa still lying dead on the ground. They just left them laying there, like they meant absolutely nothing to anyone."

Slipping his hand over her midsection, he shifted closer.

She closed her eyes and went back to sleep as if she had never awakened.

John spent the rest of the night with his arm over her protectively, watching her slumber as if his mere presence might somehow stave off her demons, if only until daylight.

Emma became aware of the sun and the sound of multiple voices nearby. She opened her eyes to see John speaking with another officer. Seeing her awake, he sent the man off and came to her side. "Good morning!"

"Is it?" she moaned when she tried to move.

"Well, probably not for you," he said and knelt by her side.

"Who was that?"

"I sent General Clinton a note before I left yesterday to send out some men if we had not returned by morning. They arrived about an hour ago and I have sent some of them back to fetch a coach since I suspect you are in no shape to sit a horse for the trip back into town."

"You would be correct, sir."

"They also brought some food—if you are up to trying to eat something."

"Believe it or not, I am starving."

He smiled. "Well, that is an encouraging sign." He helped her to sit up and she rested against him, eating a piece of freshly baked bread and cheese.

"Emma, I hope you won't think too badly of me for the situation with Miss Thompson. I have decided I am going to end things completely with her."

"I thought you were getting useful information from your time together?" she said through gritted teeth.

"It has been nothing I cannot manage without," he assured.

Emma remembered what Tallmadge had said about using that outlet to their advantage and she felt torn. "I am not thrilled with the idea of you extracting information that way," she said carefully, "but, if you

103

need to continue, I would understand—for the good of the Crown."

He looked at her with a confused expression on his face. "You would be fine with—'that'? You seemed extremely bothered by 'that' last night. What changed your mind?"

"That was before you explained. After all, we must all do our part, right?" She forced the words out, nearly choking on the bile rising in the back of her throat at the thought of the two of them together. The truth was she wanted Colette to fall off the face of the Earth—and she desired to be the one in his bed—but she wanted Washington to win even more.

"Let's talk about something else, shall we?" he said rather nervously.

She decided to leave it at that. Chewing on her lip, she lowered her head and said in a low voice, "I am sorry I woke you last night."

"I'm not." He placed his finger under her chin and lifted it. "I feel honored you trusted me enough to share your story with me. My heart breaks for what happened to you that day. No child should ever have to go through something as horrendous as that. I now understand why you get so distressed whenever the subject is mentioned."

"Let's talk about something else," she parroted.

"Why don't you tell me why you were out here alone and how you got past the checkpoints?"

Thinking quickly, she replied, "I sometimes need to clear my head and I can't do it in town, so I bring Mac out to run. General Clinton was kind enough to write passage papers for my aunt to travel outside of New York — and I may have borrowed them."

"Emma!" he scolded. "You should not be out here alone. There are too many rebels that roam these woods, and you are lucky you didn't have the misfortune of running up on one of them." He pointed at her like a father lecturing his daughter. "And no more 'borrowing' papers or I will have General Clinton revoke them. If you want to come out and ride, you will be accompanied by an escort, or better yet, I will just bring you myself."

Deciding it was best not to press the issue, she nodded in agreement. "Whatever you say, Major."

"Good!" he smiled. "Let's get you home."

The carriage arrived not long after and, by mid-morning, John was carrying her inside where Lucy was anxiously waiting with General Clinton and the town physician, Dr. Reade.

"Oh, thank God!" Lucy and the others followed them up the stairs.

John laid her across her bed and the physician shooed them all out to examine her.

"What happened to her?" demanded Lucy as they waited in the hall.

"Emma rode her horse into a thunderstorm, and he bucked her off when he became frightened. I found her by the side of the road, soaked to the bone and freezing—

her knee is severely injured, and she was unable to walk to try and find shelter. Since the rain had set in for the night, we took refuge in an abandoned barn nearby until the men arrived this morning." He glanced towards the door. "She also hit her head and may have some broken ribs, not to mention a great deal of bruising."

"Well, thank goodness you found her." General Clinton clapped him on the shoulder. "You look like you could stand a hot bath and a warm bed yourself."

"Indeed," he said and smiled, "but I will wait until we hear what the doctor has to say."

Lucy gratefully took John by the hand. "I cannot thank you enough, Major André, for bringing her back to me. I am in your debt."

After a few minutes, Doctor Reade emerged.

"Well?"

"She will be fine after a few days in bed. There doesn't appear to be any broken bones, but she twisted her knee badly and there is one nasty cut on her head. She will have to stay off that leg until it heals. Otherwise, I think she will feel better after getting cleaned up, having a hot meal, and some much-needed sleep."

"Thank you, Dr. Reade. I will make sure she gets all of those things," said a relieved Lucy and showed him out.

While the others were distracted, John slipped into Emma's room where he found her resting against the headboard.

"I think I will live," she remarked, pulling a chunk of dried mud from her hair.

"I heard," he said and came to sit on the edge of the bed. Plucking a leaf from behind her ear, he laughed. "I think a bath may be in both our futures. How are you feeling?"

"Sore—exhausted—and extremely thankful you came to find me. Thank you!"

"It was my pleasure." Taking her hand, he pressed his lips to her palm. "I have to go but I was hoping you might give some consideration to having dinner with me once you are back on your feet—I mean, just the two of us, a nice bottle of wine, and a quiet place to get to know each other better?"

Emma linked her fingers in his. "I think I would like that."

John and General Clinton left together.

"Nice work," offered the General as they walked down the street. "Mistress Wolfe was a bundle of nerves when she came to my home to deliver the message you left with her." A sly grin spread across his face. "I spent most of the evening doing my best to soothe and comfort her restlessness."

"I am sure she was 'appreciative'," goaded John.

"I will say she is quite the woman," General Clinton replied. "Speaking of women, there is someone you need to meet with."

"Oh? Who might that be?"

"A young woman who presented herself to me yesterday with quite an intriguing story. She claims she fell in love with one of Washington's men stationed in New Jersey. He told her he loved her, wanted to carry her away from her less-than-ideal circumstances, and marry her, so she traveled to his camp to be with him. Apparently, once she arrived, she found out he had forgotten to mention he already had a wife and three small children."

"Well, that's inconvenient," smarted John.

"Quite! Anyway, when she discovered his betrayal, she became a little upset with him and decided to strike out, so to speak. They fought, she hit him in the head with a chamber pot and stole all of the army's papers that were in his tent at the time before fleeing for New York with several men on her trail."

"You know what they say about women scorned," John snickered, unable to resist.

"At any rate, she has offered what she has taken to us in exchange for our protection and a new start."

John clasped his hands together. "Wonderful! I will have a look at the papers immediately."

"Not so fast. It seems her conscience, if that is what you want to call it, has gotten the better of her, and she is having second thoughts."

"So, we give her back to the traitors, let them deal with her and we keep the information—a winning solution for everyone," suggested John.

General Clinton held up his finger. "Only, she was smart enough to hide the papers before she came to me, and we do not know where they are. I offered her protection and money, but that wasn't enough. I threatened to put her on one of the prison ships until she told us where they were, yet she remains defiant. Nothing seems to intimidate her."

"What exactly does she want in exchange?"

"It seems even she doesn't know. One moment she wants to run the man through with a sword and the next minute she wants him to keep his word of providing her a better home and life, even if it means becoming his mistress."

John stroked his chin, perplexed until a slow understanding washed over him. "Oh, dear Lord! She's a paid whore?"

The General nudged him with his elbow and chuckled. "Only until her acting career takes off."

John groaned. "Where is she now?"

"I placed her under house arrest until I could have a word with you." The General stopped and turned to face John, placing his hands on his shoulders. "We all know you have a unique way of getting information from the ladies, so I will need you to handle this delicate situation with that special charm and cleverness only John André can offer."

Wincing, John scratched his head. "Not that I am at all opposed to dealing with 'ladies of the night'—in fact, there are a few I am quite partial to—but, perhaps we could just offer more money? I mean, in fairness, we are the ones assuming all the risk here. We aren't even sure what we would be paying for."

"She claims her lover was a courier and had a full bag of correspondence on him at the time. The potential payoff is worth the risk." The older man sighed. "See what you can get out of her. Who knows, if she truly is an actress and you can get her to trust you, perhaps she will be useful to us on a long-term basis. This is an order, John. I want you to do whatever it takes to get what we need. Now, get some rest and get cleaned up. I will have her brought to your house for a late dinner."

John sighed and glanced back towards Wolfe Manor, trying to figure out how he was going to explain this to Emma. "Yes, sir."

As soon as everyone cleared out, Lucy went into Emma's room and closed the door.

"Are you alright?" she asked, full of concern.

"I will be fine," assured Emma, "thanks to John. If he hadn't come looking for me, things might have turned out very differently."

Lucy pulled a chair up to the side of the bed and sat down. "You seem to have had a change of heart regarding him."

"He's not so bad."

"So, what happened out there? Did you get a chance to meet with Washington?"

"Not Washington, but a man by the name of Tallmadge."

Lucy's eyes widened.

"Washington definitely sent him," Emma reassured her aunt when she saw the expression on Lucy's face. "He said Washington instructed him to bring cake so I would know he was sent by him."

Lucy relaxed a bit and smiled. "Ah!"

"Anyway," she continued, "I passed along the information and had started back when the storm came up out of nowhere and Mac threw me. Is he okay?"

"Your horse is fine. He was a bit spooked, but Jacob got him settled down."

"Good!"

"And the rest of the night?" pressed Lucy.

Emma shifted to get more comfortable. "The Major was a perfect gentleman. He also felt the need to tell me Colette was giving him information in exchange for—"

"For what?"

"It seems she was the one who desired him."

Lucy blinked several times as if in disbelief. "He said she was telling him what he wanted to know in exchange for sex?"

"That's what he said—but now that I say it aloud—" Emma wrinkled her nose, "it does sound a bit embellished, doesn't it?"

Lucy lifted her eyebrows.

"It made sense at the time," mumbled Emma. "Of course, I did hit my head pretty hard."

"Perhaps he was telling the truth. It may have been Colette's way of getting him to fall in love with her or, more likely, a chance to create a situation he would not be able to walk away from." Lucy held out her hands to indicate a swollen belly.

Emma pushed the hair back from her face and frowned. "He asked me to have dinner with him once I was feeling better."

"Did he? And what was your answer?"

Emma closed her eyes and rubbed the spot between them. "I said I would."

"Just to clarify, this would be the same man you were certain we needed to steer clear of just a couple of days ago?" Lucy bobbed her head up and down as Emma covered her face with her hands.

"I know and that is exactly how I felt two days ago, but after last night, he was so sweet and kind and honest about everything. What is it about that man that gets me so turned around?"

"I am sure Colette felt the same way when he started to show her some attention," countered Lucy. "The man is a master at manipulating women to get what he wants—it is his job after all." Lucy leaned forward and took her hand. "Answer me truthfully because I need to know. Are you having second thoughts about the work we do for

Washington's cause? If you are, I understand, but you need to tell me now."

Emma shook her head vigorously. "No! Never! My first loyalty is always to the betterment of this country, no matter what. I despise the British army! You know that!"

"The British army as an entity, just not the one man who will do anything to see them succeed at tearing this country apart." Lucy squeezed her hand. "I don't want to see you have your heart broken. Love and war are two different mistresses, demanding absolute, undivided attention, and at some point, you will have to make a choice of which is more important—the option to have both will simply not exist. The sooner you make that decision, the better for all concerned." Lucy stood and kissed Emma tenderly on the forehead, stopping to pull a twig out of her hair. "What do you say to a bath? Your hair looks like a bird has tried to make a nest in it."

Chuckling, Emma looked down at the grime on her arms. "I think a long, hot bath is just what the doctor ordered."

John sat in a chair by the window staring out, lost in thoughts of Emma. He looked up when Nelly called his name. "Major André, there is a Miss Sarah Tate here to see you."

"Yes, show her in."

Standing, John straightened his jacket and planted a smile on his face. "Miss Tate, it is a pleasure to meet you," he said and took her hand. The truth was he took no pleasure in this meeting. The woman was pleasant-looking enough—a brunette with a powdered face, a fake mole, and a low-cut gown. She smiled back at him. Her large eyes and small nose made her appear younger but the red stain on her lips added a few years. It was obvious she knew how to play with her appearance, more than likely to cater to the desires of her clientele.

"Major André," she purred.

He led her over to the sofa and offered her a seat before moving to the side buffet to pour two glasses of wine. He watched her from the corner of his eye, and she was looking him up and down as if she were sizing up a new horse.

Crossing the room, he handed her a glass. "I understand you are newly arrived," he said and sat down next to her.

"Yesterday," she replied and sipped her drink.

"What brings you here?"

"Major André, you know exactly what brings me here. I am sure General Clinton filled you in."

"A straight-forward woman—I can appreciate that." He set his wine aside and regarded her. "Let me guess, you were playing the emotionally wounded victim to the General to see how much he was willing to give up for what you supposedly have."

"I am an aspiring actress," she said with a wink. "And I can assure you, the information I have acquired is worth it."

Exasperated and short of patience, he asked, "What exactly is it you want Miss Tate? I am an extremely busy man, and I had an exceptionally long night. Let's not play games, shall we?"

She ran her tongue across her teeth, watching him. "I want what I have always wanted—a better station in life—one out of the whorehouse. I thought I could obtain it by marrying Silas, but the bastard was already taken, a fact he conveniently forgot to mention."

John held out his hands. "I am sure we can come to an agreement on payment which will give you a nice, new start."

"I want far more than that. The money will run out soon enough, but a rich husband endures."

John reached for his wine, downed it, and stood to refill it. "Well then, you are looking at the wrong man. I survive on a meager salary, and I do not come from money."

"But Major John André is a loved, well-respected man whom all of polite society has taken in as one of their own."

"Where did you hear that?" He leaned against the table and folded his arms curiously.

She held out her glass for a refill and he reluctantly obliged. "I was in Philadelphia before I relocated to New Jersey after an unfortunate incident. While I was there, all anyone could ever talk about was the charming, debonair Major André."

"Your point?"

"My point is you have standing, open invitations to the homes of the wealthiest people in New York, and I want to have that as well."

"And how do you propose to obtain that?"

"Well, if you and I present ourselves as a couple, I will be welcomed with open arms into the same circles you enjoy, and that will give me a chance to find a viable suitor. After all, any woman good enough for the great John André must be someone worth having."

John scoffed. "You cannot be serious."

"Oh, I am very serious. It has also come to my attention General Clinton has told you to do whatever you need to do to get what I have, so this is what we are going to do—I will move in here today, and tomorrow, you will begin to introduce me as your fiancé. As soon as I secure a husband, the information is all yours."

"Absolutely not!" he protested angrily.

"I thought you might need some encouragement, so I brought a little incentive." She reached down the front of her dress and pulled out a piece of paper that she held out for him.

Snatching it from her hand, he huffed and smoothed it out. He was astonished when he read the words. He had suspected there was a leak somewhere in New York. Washington's movements as of late suggested he had procured some inside knowledge of their layout in the city, and this certainly seemed to confirm that assumption.

"If I am not mistaken," she said, adjusting the front of her gown, "that is a list of places where messages are dropped for Washington's men to pick up. It seems one of them is right here—the trunk of a tree in a park not far from where we are now. That was the least interesting thing in the satchel. The others—well, let's just say—you will be a hero."

John regarded her and folded the page in half. After carefully considering the offer and with Clinton's words fresh on his mind, he blew out a long breath and conceded. "Very well. I will agree to your terms, all except one—you will not stay here. I will secure lodgings elsewhere for you—I will have peace and quiet in my own home."

"Fine!" she said obviously displeased and stood. "I suppose it would be looked down upon anyway." She walked past him, stopping to cup his cheek. "Oh, and we will have to sell the 'engagement'. You must tell no one of our deceit or the deal is off. I will expect you to play the part of the doting fiancé when we are in public, and if you perform well," glancing to just below his waist, "I may just reward you with a little something special." She quickly and unexpectedly kissed him, leaving the red stain on his lips, and left the house.

John stomped over to the buffet and poured a glass of whisky. After sucking it down, he caught a glimpse of his reflection in the mirror. Using his sleeve, he scrubbed until all the color was gone. The man staring back at him disgusted him—that man was going to have to hurt someone he had come to care a great deal for. In a fit of rage, he cursed, raked everything off the table onto the floor, and sprayed the room with shattered glass. When Nelly ran in to see what happened, he stalked by her into the hall, grabbed his hat, and slammed the front door on his way out.

"This is the epitome of madness!" he shouted as he paced the floor.

General Clinton laid the paper down and rested his forearms on the desk. "I know it is asking a great deal, John, but we need everything we can lay our hands on at this point, especially if you are correct about someone in this town funneling information to the enemy. You and I are both weary of this God-forsaken war and the sooner we can end it, the better."

"Her demands are outrageous!"

The General reached down and pulled open the bottom drawer of his desk, producing two glasses and a bottle. "Sit down!" he ordered, pouring and pushing one in his direction.

John obeyed and reached for the glass. "It's asking too much!" John spoke in a calmer, more solemn tone.

"Since when? You use women all the time for information and you have never had a problem with it before."

Resting the glass on his knee, he confessed, "It's different this time."

Clinton leaned back in his chair and took a sip as he gave John a good once over. "This wouldn't have anything to do with Miss Eldridge, would it?"

John's shoulders slumped, and he let out an exaggerated sigh.

Clinton straightened up, intrigued. "It does, doesn't it? Is there something going on between the two of you I am unaware of? Don't tell me you have bedded her already!"

"NO!" John replied emphatically. "I just had hoped we would be able to spend some time together, but this new development is going to make that impossible."

"Well, this is an interesting turn of events, and I must say, I am a bit surprised to see a woman has finally tickled John André's fancy enough to want to do things in the proper order," remarked Clinton. "And Miss Eldridge would be quite the catch. She is young, beautiful, extremely entertaining—and the heir to one of the biggest fortunes in the Colonies. Perhaps it is best to wait until this war business is finished anyway."

"I waited for this 'war business to be finished' to pursue another woman I fell in love with, and that delay cost me everything. She and her new husband are incredibly happy together. It seems my timing is always unfortunate."

"Well, if Miss Tate has any skill whatsoever as a whore, she will catch the fancy of one of these old geezers with

119

money before you know it and you will be off the hook—free to court Miss Eldridge as you like."

"I still have the matter of Miss Thompson."

"Get rid of her. What Miss Tate has for us far outweighs anything the Thompson girl ever provided—and while you are at it, check out this drop point at the park. See if anyone shows up."

"I had already planned to on both counts."

5

CHAPTER FIVE

Nearly a week after her accident, Emma was much improved. The only thing keeping her in bed was her knee, which was still swollen and painful to the touch, but on the mend.

Francis stopped by for a visit.

"I am so glad you are feeling better!" Francis unpacked a picnic basket filled with assorted pastries. "I thought since you were confined to your bed, we might gorge ourselves on sweets."

"Oh Francis, have I told you how much I love you?" asked a delighted and excited Emma.

Francis brought over a tea service set on a tray and placed it on the bed before settling next to Emma. "It's just like the tea parties we used to have at your house," said Francis as she poured. "Your mother made the best sweets. Even to this day, I have tasted none as good as hers."

"She did love to cook, and she was good at it, which is surprising given the extravagant way she and Aunt Lucy were raised. I don't even know how or where she learned."

"It's still amazing to me your mother never mentioned any of this to you. The love she had for your father must have been incredibly special and rare for her to give all of this up."

Emma nodded and took a bite of a small cake. "If only we had Charlie here, it would be just like old times. Remember how much he pretended to hate our tea parties—until he got to the eating part anyway?"

Francis touched her arm. "Oh, I remember. He would complain to our mother and father about being subjected to it just before sneaking off to enjoy the sweets he had stuffed in his pockets."

The two laughed and continued to reminisce.

"I am bored. Please tell me all about everything I am missing going on in town being confined to this bed," Emma pleaded.

"Well, I suppose the biggest news is that Major André broke things off with Miss Thompson," Emma smiled smugly and stuffed a pastry in her mouth as Francis continued, "and announced his engagement to a Miss Sarah Tate."

Emma sputtered, coughing while nearly choking on a combination of the food in her mouth and the words she had just heard, finally spewing a mouthful across the bed.

"Are you alright?" asked Francis, patting her on the back.

Once she'd finally gotten her throat cleared, she asked, "His what?"

Francis brushed the crumbs from the bed. "Oh yes! It seems it was all quite sudden. Miss Tate arrived in town on the same day as your accident and yesterday she accompanied him to a dinner party at the Miller's home where she was introduced as his fiancé."

"I—don't —understand!" stuttered Emma, dumbfounded with her stomach having suddenly twisted into knots. "He mentioned no fiancé to me the night he rescued me, and he certainly didn't mention one when he asked me to dinner."

"Oh my!" Francis's hand flew to her mouth. "I'm sorry, Emma. I didn't know he had asked to see you. I probably shouldn't have mentioned it."

"Oh no! Now, I want to know everything. Who is she anyway?"

Francis shrugged. "No one seems to know anything about her except her name."

"That explains why he hasn't been by to visit!" Emma looked up. "Francis, I'm sorry, I am suddenly exhausted. Do you mind if we continue this another day?"

"Of course!" Francis said and got up. "Your recovery is the most important thing. I will come back some other time when you are feeling better."

As Francis started out the door, Emma asked her to send Lucy in.

"THAT LYING BASTARD!" screamed Emma and hurled the teapot across the room.

"What on Earth is going on in here?" demanded Lucy, ducking just before a cup lobbed by and struck the wall, missing her by mere inches.

"That—fucking—miserable excuse—"

"EMMA!" shouted Lucy. "What is the matter?"

Emma seethed. "Major fucking John André is engaged!"

Lucy blinked hard, unsure if she had heard correctly. "What did you just say?"

"John André has a fiancé—some woman by the name of Sarah Tate who arrived in town the day of my accident."

Closing the door, Lucy came to sit on the edge of the bed. "Did he mention she would be arriving?"

"What do you think? He asked me to dinner the day we came back."

"Oh!" Lucy was taken aback. "What sort of game is he playing at?"

"I don't know, but I am going to find out." Emma shoved back the covers, swung her legs over the side, and cautiously stood, leaning on the bed to test her leg.

"Emma! Get back in this bed this instant!" scolded Lucy. "The doctor said—"

"I don't give a damn what the doctor said!" Emma shifted her weight to find it not nearly as painful as the news she had just received. Limping over to her

124

wardrobe, she flung it open and began looking through her gowns. "I want an explanation." Glancing over her shoulder, she asked, "When is the next planned dinner party where the main officers will be?"

Lucy thought for a moment. "The Richards, I believe, the day after tomorrow."

Emma examined the neckline of a bright satin evening dress. "We have an invitation?"

Lucy scoffed. "Of course, we do—no successful event occurs in this town without one of us in attendance, but I already turned down the invite because of your injury."

Spinning back to her aunt, Emma pulled in a long breath. "Send a note and tell them we will try to attend, but to please not make it known in case I am not up to it at the last minute."

"Alright? May I ask what you intend to do?" questioned Lucy with a curious expression on her face.

"I don't want the Major to see me coming so he has time to figure out some pathetic excuse for his behavior."

"Are you going to make a scene?" When Emma didn't reply, Lucy clapped her hands together. "Oh goody! Finally, some excitement in this boring little town! I will go write the note and send it over right now."

Emma called out to her aunt when she reached the door. "I am going to need something special to wear."

A slow smile spread across Lucy's face. "I think we can make that happen."

6

CHAPTER SIX

On Friday, Sarah fluffed her hair while looking in the mirror as John finished up some paperwork.

"Who should I have my eyes on this evening?" she asked.

"Anyone but me," he replied dryly and dipped his pen in the inkwell.

She turned and stuck out her tongue. "You are no fun—do you know that?"

"And you are a lying, manipulative whore," he retorted without looking up. "What's your point?"

She sashayed over to stand behind him and slipped her hand across his shoulder, down the front of his chest while pressing her breasts against him. "You know, you and I could have a great deal of fun if you would just loosen up a bit," she purred. "You seem very tense. Why don't you let me help you relax a bit?"

He made a wry face and concentrated on his letter. "You are getting your cheap perfume all over my freshly laundered shirt and I, for one, do not care to smell like a harlot."

She straightened up and turned to look out the window. "What has happened to the famous wooer of women I have heard so much talk about?"

"He is busy trying to win a war," he replied and shook the bottle of pounce over his page to help it dry. Looking over at her, he huffed. "You need to get on with the business of finding yourself a husband and giving me the information I have been promised. I am sure some of it is time-sensitive, if not already obsolete, since they are aware it was taken, and I am not willing to allow this charade to continue for much longer."

"What is your problem?" she grumbled, then stopped and spun around to face him. "Ah! There is a woman in your life and my presence is causing an issue with her, isn't it?"

"My personal life is none of your concern," he spat and stood up. "Get on with finding some poor, unsuspecting bastard to marry you so this matter between us can be concluded once and for all."

"Fashionably late," said Lucy in the carriage. "I like it. We will get to make a grand entrance, especially since no one is expecting us."

"More like a surprise attack," smarted Emma.

Lucy grinned. "My dear, you look stunning. Every man in that house is going to be standing in line to get a gander at you."

"I am only interested in one," her voice was full of venom.

Emma felt like a force to be reckoned with. She had forgone the accustomed attire for something a little more revealing, in the form of a form-fitted dark red gown, cut four inches lower than allowed by polite society and accented by the large diamond jewelry pieces dripping from her neck and ears. She wanted to make sure she was a sight John André would never forget.

Lucy had been right. Everyone turned to gape when they were announced, and every man in the place became extremely attentive to the 'ladies of Wolfe Manor'.

John's back was to the entrance when he heard the name, and he cursed under his breath. Planting a smile on his face, he turned, and the breath left his body when he caught sight of her. He was so taken aback by how devastatingly beautiful she looked, the glass nearly slipped from his hand.

"Who is that?" demanded Sarah.

"None of your concern," he whispered and moved away from her.

Emma spent the next thirty minutes surrounded by men who were suddenly interested in her well-being after the accident and were devoted to making sure she had whatever her heart desired. She was finally able to make her way past the hall and into the main body of the party to search the room.

"The one in blue, by the door going into the garden with her back turned," whispered Lucy from behind. "That is Sarah Tate!"

Emma's eyes locked on the woman's back like a target. "I see her," and she pushed through the crowd.

"John, you don't seem like your usual jovial self this evening," remarked the General, reaching for a drink.

"You wouldn't be either if you had to deal with that infernal woman," he said in a low voice so no one else would hear. "Can't you find a wealthy officer and order him to marry her?"

Clinton chuckled. "If it were only that easy!" His eyes swept the room. "I can certainly see why you are impatient. Miss Eldridge most assuredly lit up the room this evening."

"So, I noticed," mumbled John and turned up his glass.

"And it looks like she just found Miss Tate!"

Turning to see Emma taking Sarah by the arm, John's eyes widened, and he spat out his drink. "Oh, dear God in Heaven!" and he made haste crossing the room.

"I am Emma Eldridge of Wolfe Manor and you must be Major André's fiancé?" Emma said with a fake smile.

"I am indeed," the young woman replied. "My name is Sarah Tate." She cocked her head. "Wolfe Manor? Is that the lovely home at the end of Wolfe Street?"

"It is!" Taking her by the arm, Emma said, "I cannot tell you how delighted I am to meet you! John has told me absolutely nothing about you."

"Good evening, Emma," said John curtly when he reached them.

"Oh, hello Major André," Emma said with emphasis. "I have just met your lovely fiancé. I must say, I was more than a little surprised to hear the wonderful news."

"Should you be out of bed so soon after your ordeal?" he inquired.

"I am feeling much better, but you would have known that if you had not been so preoccupied with the arrival of your intended."

He nervously rubbed his forehead with his palm, wiping away a bead of perspiration that had formed.

"John, Miss Eldridge lives in that large, expensive place two streets over," said Sarah.

"Oh, the Major is well aware," remarked Emma. "He has visited our home on multiple occasions, and he knows his way around it very well."

John slid his hand around and rested it on the small of Emma's back. "Sarah, if you will excuse us, I need to have a word with Miss Eldridge alone."

"I don't think you and I have anything to talk about," she retorted through gritted teeth.

"Yes, we most certainly do!" John tightened his grip and practically lifted her off her feet, moving her through the door and into the garden. Looking around, he forced her around the corner of the house where they could be completely alone.

"Emma, I can explain—" he started.

"I am not sure you can!" she spat angrily. "How could you forget to mention you were engaged?"

"It's not what you think!"

She folded her arms. "Then, tell me, what is it?"

He blew out a hard breath and looked down. "I am not in a position to say at the moment, but I will tell you as soon as I am able. I just need you to be patient and a little understanding."

"You are un-fucking-believable!" and she shoved him away.

John grabbed her around the waist and pushed her against the wall, pressing his body firmly against hers.

Before she knew what was happening, a merciless assault was launched upon her lips—and it caused a sensation she desperately hoped would never end. The truth was, she wanted this man more than anything and she would be willing to sacrifice a great deal to have him. Melting against him, desire coursed throughout her entire being and she returned his fervor, much to his delight. When he pulled back to tenderly touch her face, she smiled, pressed her hands to his chest—and proceeded to knee him in the groin.

He doubled over in pain. "Damn it, Emma!" he growled and took two steps back.

Emma straightened her gown, patted her hair, and leaned down to whisper in his ear, "Once you have recovered, be sure to come inside. I want to propose a toast to you and your betrothed, and I think you will find the speech I have prepared quite enlightening." Emma spun away to leave but he grabbed her by the hand.

"Emma, I know you are upset, and you have every right to be, but you are making a terrible mistake. Please don't do this!"

"No! You are the one who made the mistake when you asked me to dinner knowing full well you already had a woman you intended to marry. I will not be made a fool of by John André or any other man."

As soon as she rounded the corner, her determination to not let him see her vulnerability faltered and she started to limp. She had impulsively assaulted him with her injured knee and now she was paying the painful price. After making her way inside, she located a secluded seat, sat down, and rubbed the aching joint.

"You aren't overdoing it, are you?" asked Lucy when she found her. "You really should still be at home, resting."

"It was fine until John André kissed me."

"The nerve of that man!" Lucy gave her a peculiar look and glanced down at her knee, confused. "Wait, exactly

132

where did the man's lips end up?" she asked curiously.

Emma followed her gaze and rolled her eyes. "I let him know exactly how I felt—hitting him right where it hurts a man the most."

"Oh!" Lucy chuckled. "I am guessing Miss Tate will be severely disappointed in the bedroom later this evening." Her aunt patted her on the shoulder. "Why don't we call it a night and get you, and that knee, home?"

"Not just yet!" said Emma, slowly standing. "I promised to offer a toast to the happy couple and that is what I intend to do."

"Alright!" conceded Lucy with a mischievous grin. "As long as I get to watch."

Emma made sure John was back inside before grabbing a glass and a spoon. She waited until she caught his attention, blew him a discreet kiss, and tapped the side of the glass loudly to get everyone's attention. "Pardon me! I have something to say." Waiting for the noise of the crowd to die down, she noticed John whisper to a young officer who stood just off to his side. Emma became curious when John then turned, blew her a kiss right back, and started moving in her direction.

"May I have everyone's attention please?" she said, wondering what he was up to and thinking it best to get the words out before he got close enough to stop her. "I ask that you lift your glasses in a toast this evening. It seems we have a new resident in our fair city, and I want you all to help me welcome—" she stopped when she felt two firm hands come around her waist and a warm breath on her neck. John was in front of her, and she wondered who dared to presume to be so familiar with her? Quickly spinning around, ready to chastise the man who had his hands where they shouldn't have been, her face went from anger to one of disbelief. "Charlie?"

"Hello, Emma," he whispered with a grin.

"CHARLIE!" she exclaimed excitedly and slung her arms around his neck.

"Yes!" interjected John, hijacking her announcement. She turned so she was directly face-to-face with him, his glass held high. "Welcome to the newly-arrived, Captain Charles Taylor. He and Miss Eldridge are childhood friends, and she could not wait any longer to introduce him to everyone. We hope you enjoy your time here!"

Emma growled when a smirk appeared on John's face and the crowd erupted in applause. She scrunched her nose at him in defeat.

Leaning close, he said, "I look forward to seeing you soon so we may sort all of this confusion out."

"Don't bother! I never want to see you again!" she snapped back as Charlie took her by the waist and spirited her away.

"What was that all about?" Sarah asked of John as they watched them walk away.

"'That' was your hourglass running out of time. You

have one week to find a suitable match. By then, I am washing my hands of this matter, one way or another."

Sarah looked again. "Oh, so the Eldridge woman is the one you are hung up on. I will gladly have a chat with her if you like."

He gripped her tightly by the arm and leaned in. "Stay the hell away from her or I will make you wish you had never stepped foot in New York." He downed his drink and left the party.

Charlie searched until he found a small empty room used as an office and pulled her inside. Once they were alone, he embraced her tightly. "Oh my God, Emma, it is so good to see you. Look at you, all grown up and beautiful."

"Me? Look at you! You finally grew into your ears and the rest of your body!" she teased. "What are you doing here Charlie?" she asked, delighted to see him.

"Business!"

She straightened his collar. "Francis didn't tell me you were coming."

"That's because she didn't know. I only arrived this afternoon and Major André insisted I come along this evening. I was going to stop by and see her tomorrow."

"Major André!" grumbled Emma disgustedly.

"What is going on between the two of you anyway?" he inquired. "Why did he order me to interrupt your toast and get you out of the room?"

"It's a long story!" She rubbed her leg and grimaced as a sharp pain hit her. "I need to sit down."

"What's wrong?" He took her arm, led her to a chair, and helped her to sit.

"I took a nasty spill a few days ago off my horse and my knee took the worst of it." She pulled up the hem of her gown to see that it was, once again, reddened and inflamed.

Charlie knelt. "Jesus, Emma! You shouldn't even be on this." He looked around and noticed a foot stool. Standing, he grabbed it, dragged it over, and positioned her leg to rest on it.

"Thank you, Charlie!"

"It looks like New York agrees with you," he said and pulled up another chair. "I honestly would not have recognized you if the Major had not mentioned your name."

"I can honestly say the same!"

Charlie had been an awkward boy, his arms and legs long and gangly as if they weren't made for his body, but the man before her was tall, muscular, well built—and extremely handsome. The only thing that remained the same was the crooked, boyish grin that now made him even more attractive by adding to his charm.

"I was sorry to learn of the passing of your parents," she said sympathetically.

"Thank you for that. I still find it strangely odd to think they are both gone now."

"That feeling never goes away," she said quietly.

He laid his hand over on hers and they sat in silence for a brief time, each having a personal moment of remembrance.

"How do you like living in New York?" he asked, breaking the awkwardness.

"I have had an extraordinary life here thanks to my Aunt Lucy. I don't know what I would have done without her."

"Is she here?"

Emma nodded. "Yes, and I am sure she would love to see you. I must say, I was surprised to hear you had joined the army."

"We all must do our duty to what we believe a just cause, no matter what others might think."

Emma thought that a rather odd answer and was just about to question him on it when the door opened.

"Here you are!" exclaimed Lucy. "I have been looking all over for you."

"Aunt Lucy! Come here! You remember little Charlie Taylor from Virginia."

"I do now!" She crossed the room.

Charlie stood to greet her. "Mistress Wolfe! It is an honor to meet you again."

"Welcome to New York, Charlie!" She turned to Emma. "Oh dear!" Lucy saw Emma's propped-up knee. "That looks much worse than it did before we came here."

Emma winced. "It's had an interesting night! Gratifying, but interesting!"

"Yes! It is time to get you home and back in bed." Lucy eyed Charlie up and down. "You are a strapping young man. Think you can manage to carry her?"

He smiled warmly at Emma. "I do believe I can."

After getting her settled comfortably in at home, Emma and Charlie stayed up half the night talking and laughing, catching up on the years they had missed together.

Late the following morning, Emma slowly crept down the stairs holding onto the rail for support to find Lucy at her desk writing out a note.

"Good morning, sweetheart! How are you feeling?"

Limping over, Emma took the chair opposite her on the other side of the desk. "I suppose I will live, but I won't be dancing the night away anytime soon."

"You should still be in bed," scolded Lucy. "You overdid it last night."

Emma shrugged. "I don't know. I think my swollen knee is a small price to pay for getting the chance to hit John André where it really hurt."

Lucy snorted. "I wish I had seen that when it happened. I am going to have to start following you around at these events."

"What are you doing?" asked Emma, noticing the quill in Lucy's hand.

Lucy looked down. "Oh, I may have accidentally

overheard some of the officers talking about some movements in town, so I am making a 'grocery list' for Washington."

"I will take it out."

Lucy shook her head. "Absolutely not! You can't ride in your condition."

Emma stood up and leaned against the desk. "The horse does all the work, and besides, I could use some fresh air. I have been stuck inside enough the past week."

John stopped to shake the cramp from his hand. He had spent the entire afternoon putting together reports and going over some intelligence information he had received. He had taken a quick dinner at his desk and had just glanced through the window to see the sun setting low in the sky. The work had been more tedious than usual, but it helped to keep his mind off Emma.

Shifting in his chair, he tried to get comfortable, still sore from the punishment she'd inflicted the previous evening. He shouldn't have caught her off guard with such an unexpected action, but he just wanted to stop her, and it was the first thing that popped into his mind. Smiling to himself, he rested his hand on his thigh and recalled the feel of her so close to him. The few seconds of unadulterated bliss he had felt with his body and lips pressed to hers was worth any amount of suffering he endured today. She wanted him, even though she would never admit it, and now that he knew, he would not rest until he tasted those lips once more.

A knock at the door interrupted his thoughts. He picked up his quill to appear busy and called out, "Come in." Looking up, he saw it was the man he had put on guard duty, keeping an eye on the drop spot in the park. "Well?"

The man crossed the room and sighed. "There isn't a time of day when someone is NOT at that tree. Everyone from families to lovers, to drunkards, to our own men—even the wealthiest heiress in town visits that tree. But, at the end of the day, I did find this concealed inside the trunk."

John took the piece of folded paper and read it. "It's a grocery list," he said and flipped it over. "Why did you bring me a grocery list?"

"Because of where it was," he replied. "It was deliberately placed inside the tree, not merely dropped inadvertently beside it."

John jotted down what it said, word for word, before handing it back. "Place it back where you found it to see if it is retrieved and if it is, see if you can determine by whom."

"Yes, sir!"

John nodded. "That will be all. Thank you."

The man tipped his hat and started out of the room as John stared at the list.

"Wait!" called out John as he reached the hall. "Which heiress?"

"Miss Eldridge."

The man had John's full attention. "What was she doing there? Was she meeting with someone?"

"No, sir. She just sat underneath it with a book and read for nearly an hour. I did hear some of the shopkeepers say it was good to see her back at her usual place reading after the accident. From what I could piece together, she goes there alone quite often."

"Is that right?" John stroked his chin. "Thank you. You may go."

Midge lit the candles in the library where Emma had planted herself on the sofa with a pillow beneath her knee to rest it and closed the doors behind her. She was nursing a glass of whisky after supper while Lucy sat at her desk going through a stack of invitations that had arrived earlier in the day.

"The Alberts are having a dinner party to celebrate the engagement of their daughter, Mary, on Wednesday. Are we attending or not?"

"Not!" snapped Emma. "Cheap wine and bad food make for a very long night."

"No, it is," muttered Lucy, scribbling down her response. Setting it aside to dry, she remarked, "So, Charlie's arrival was rather unexpected."

Emma smiled. "It was really good to see him. You know, I didn't realize how much I missed Charlie and Francis until they showed up here. My memories of growing up with them were some of the best of my life. I don't know how I would have ever gotten through without them. I mean, I made friends here in New York, but none ever quite like them."

"Sort of like your mother and I growing up," said Lucy wistfully. "She was my best friend and we had so many wonderful times together. Unfortunately, as we got older, we just found ourselves wanting different lives and we drifted apart. I wish more than anything we had not—it is one of the only regrets I have in this life." Lucy laid down her quill. "I am glad you had them, especially when you needed them the most. And I am so happy you have the chance to reconnect now—consider it a precious gift from the fates."

Midge opened the door slightly and slipped in. "Major André is here to see you, Miss Emma."

Emma's face darkened. "Tell Major André he can go fuck himself— and be sure to quote me word for word."

Midge looked to Lucy who shrugged and grinned. "Very well."

Emma was polishing off her glass when Midge returned. Clearing her throat and suppressing a grin, she announced, "Major André would like me to point out he believes it physically impossible for him to 'go fuck himself' because of the anatomical arrangement of the male body. However, if it pleases you, he promises to thoroughly research the subject in depth just to be certain and get back to you on it. In the meantime, he begs for a few moments of your precious time."

Lucy looked to Emma, concealing the smile on her face with her hand. "I am dying to hear your response to that, my dear niece."

Wrinkling her nose, Emma thought for a moment. "Tell Major André if his 'member' is as large as his ego, it should be more than long enough to easily reach around so he can position it to, in fact, shove it up his ass, and literally, go fuck himself."

Lucy snorted and laid her forehead on the desk, smacking the top as her entire body shook with silent laughter. Raising her head with tears in her eyes, she managed, "I am certainly glad to know I got my money's worth from that expensive finishing school I had you attend."

Emma chortled and waited for Midge to return. Coming inside and closing the door, she went to stand next to Lucy and relayed his final message of the night, doing her best to keep a straight face. "Major André offers his apologies for bothering you this evening. He had no idea you had taken notice of the size of his rather large member, but he appreciates the compliment just the same. He intends to return home to thoroughly research the aforementioned subject but provided he cannot find a way to carry out the intended action as you requested, he wishes you to know that he will move on to the next acceptable alternative by taking matters into his own hands, ultimately achieving the same result in the end. He also wants you to know he will do so while keeping the image of you, and you alone, first and foremost in his thoughts and mind, since it was in fact, your idea. He bids you 'goodnight' and 'sweet dreams', promising to return at a time when you are in a more gracious mood to receive him. He can only assume that your lack of decorum and use of such colorful language stems from the fact you aren't feeling quite yourself—perhaps because your knee is troubling you after being reinjured from making contact with something rather 'large and hard' last night—or maybe you are feeling disagreeable because you are in the throes of some womanly issue. Whatever the case, he wishes you to feel better, suggesting several glasses of whisky and a good night's sleep to improve your demeanor."

Midge and Lucy locked eyes and the two women could hold back no longer. They held onto each other and erupted into a boisterous bout of laughter that went on until they could hardly breathe.

Emma yanked the pillow from underneath her leg and flung it at them.

Lucy shook her finger at the door. "He may be a Redcoat, but God help me, I can't help but like that man."

Emma, Francis, Jack, and Charlie sat at a table in one of the local taverns having ale and reminiscing after an early supper.

144

"Do you remember when we caught that green snake and stuffed it in your mother's teapot when the priest came to visit?" asked Emma.

"Oh, I had completely forgotten about that," replied Francis. "Mother was mortified, and I thought she was going to collapse on the spot when that thing's head popped out of the end of the spout."

"And Father Wallace made us sit for an hour and a half to listen to a sermon about the evils of handling serpents!" added Charlie. "It started as a ten-minute lecture, but every time one of us would laugh, he added ten additional minutes to the time."

"It was impossible to keep a straight face," said Emma, now clutching her stomach from laughing so hard. "Because every time Francis or I would look at Charlie, he would stick out his tongue and flick it as the snake did with his head sticking out of the spout."

"The only reason I did that was because I knew Mother wouldn't spank us with the priest there and his story was a great deal less painful to bear."

The entire table erupted in laughter.

"Did you get in trouble with your parents over it?" Jack asked Emma.

"No, not at all. Papa and Mama were too busy laughing when I told them."

"Your mother and father were the kindest, sweetest souls God ever put on this Earth," said Charlie and laid his hand over on hers. "I daresay Francis and I missed them almost as much as we missed you."

John took notice of the placement of Charlie's hand when he came through the door and stopped to greet them. "Good evening all!"

"Major André," said Charlie and Jack, and both went to stand.

"Don't get up on my account," he looked to Francis, "Mrs. Donald," and lastly to Emma, "Miss Eldridge."

"Major!" Emma replied curtly.

"Would you like to join us?" offered Charlie. He flinched when he felt Emma's kick to the shin and reached down to rub it while shooting her a questioning look.

"No, but thank you for the offer," replied John. "I have some business to attend to. I just wanted to say 'hello'."

"'Hello' and 'goodbye'," muttered Emma dryly as he started away.

Upon hearing her words, John stopped, straightened his shoulders, and turned back around. "On second thought," he said and reached for an empty chair which he planted directly next to Emma's. "It seems the person I am meeting is not here yet, so I would be delighted to join you until then. Thank you for the kind invitation, Captain Taylor."

Emma scooched closer to Charlie, a look of disgust on her face.

"It seems these three had quite the adventures growing up," explained Jack as John sat down.

146

"Oh really!" John looked directly at Emma. "I love stories! Please, continue."

"Why don't you tell us one instead? I am dying to know all about your fiancé and how you met," snarked Emma.

"I am sure you are the only one interested in that and I will be happy to tell you all about it when it's just the two of us alone, so I don't bore the others."

"How is your research coming along?" she asked as soon as he took a sip of his ale.

Never missing a beat, he replied, "I am still looking for information, but I will be sure to keep you informed of my progress. How is your knee feeling?"

Emma smiled sweetly at him. "It's still a little sore, but some things are well worth the pain."

The rest of the table had gone awkwardly quiet as the two bantered back and forth.

"How do you find New York thus far, Captain Taylor?" John asked, smoothly shifting the topic.

"Very well, so far. I look forward to seeing everything it has to offer."

Emma reached over and rubbed his arm. "And I look forward to showing the city to you and Francis," she said sincerely. "I am so happy to have both of you back in my life."

Charlie put his arm around her shoulder and squeezed.

The action caused John's jaw to tighten. "Unfortunately, I am afraid Captain Taylor will be quite busy. I have a great deal of work for him to do and more piling up by the day."

"*You* seem to find plenty of time to socialize, Major," pointed out Emma. "I am sure Charlie can manage to carve out some time as well."

"Speaking of which, Captain Taylor," John shifted his gaze to Charlie, "I will need you to report to my home first thing in the morning for a new assignment. You will need a clear head for it, so you may want to go easy on that ale this evening."

Taken a bit off guard, Charlie pushed his tankard aside. "Of course, sir."

"In fact," added John, "you might want to get a good night's rest as well."

Charlie nodded. "In that case, I should be getting Emma home."

When he stood, John smiled. "I will escort Miss Eldridge home for you." It was more of an order than an offer.

Charlie looked down at Emma, the expression upon his face relaying the fact he was just put in an awkward position by his superior.

"I wouldn't dream of having your betrothed become upset with you for being seen with another woman," she said to John sarcastically. "Besides, I have my carriage." She looked to Francis and Jack. "May I offer you a ride?"

Francis shook her head and leaned against her husband. "It's a lovely night. I think we would rather walk."

Emma nodded and stood, as did everyone else. "We will

148

have to do this again soon. Good night!"

As she started out, John attempted to follow, but fortunately, the person he was there to meet came in and she was able to slip out without another word.

Emma sat outside on the bench across from John's house the next morning with a newspaper concealing her face. When Charlie came out, she lowered it just enough to peek over the top.

Grinning when he caught sight of her, he crossed the street and came over wagging his finger. "You are going to get me in a great deal of trouble with Major André. Given the number of assignments he just gave me, I get the distinct impression he does not want me to have a moment to spare for you."

Pulling her skirts aside, Emma reached between her feet to pull out a basket. "Well, a soldier has got to eat to keep up his strength—he can't fault you for that," she said with a smirk and moved over to make room for him.

"What's going on between the two of you anyway?" he asked as she unwrapped a napkin holding some bread and handed it to him.

"I don't know what you mean! The Major is engaged to another woman," she answered in a childishly mocking way.

Charlie laughed. "Emma, I have known you a very long time, and even though I have not seen you for a few years, some things never change—that tone of voice tells

149

me there is indeed 'something' between the two of you."

"Not really," she said in a more serious voice, not meeting his eyes.

"Well, I am happy to hear that," he said and took a bite of the bread, smiling at her as he chewed. "The Major seems to have some 'sort' of involvement with a great many women from what I understand."

"Yeah!" Emma mumbled staring ahead and bit into a piece of cheese.

"Are you going to share that?" he asked.

Emma laughed, broke off a piece, and handed it to him. "How busy are you going to be?"

"With all the assignments the Major just gave me, I might be able to go to bed a week from Tuesday," he replied with a chuckle.

"I'm sorry, Charlie."

He put his arm around her and pulled her to him. "It's not your fault. I signed up for this."

"Do you think it will be over with soon—the war, I mean?"

"I certainly hope so."

"What will you do when it is?" she asked.

Charlie shrugged. "I suppose I will go back to Virginia. Francis and Jack will surely settle somewhere else and that will leave the family estate to me, provided it is still standing by then. As far as what I will do, I honestly have no idea. I haven't thought that far ahead."

"I am surprised you haven't married," she said.

"Me? You are the one well on her way to becoming a spinster," he teased.

"Being a spinster is not as bad as one might think," she retorted. "Aunt Lucy is proof positive a woman does not need to be married to be happy. Do you remember when we were waiting for her arrival, how bad we thought she would be? Boy, we missed that one by a mile."

"Thank goodness!" he said. "She is quite a woman, isn't she?"

"Unlike anyone you will ever meet, and I love that woman more than anything in this world."

Charlie stuffed the rest of the bread in his mouth and stood up.

"Where are you going?"

"Major André is watching from the window. I had better go before he finds something else for me to do. Thank you for the food and the company."

Emma reached for his hand. "Anytime. Come by the house when you get a few minutes free."

He leaned down and kissed her cheek before hurrying off.

"I want what you have," demanded John angrily, watching Captain Taylor kiss Emma's cheek from the window.

"I have not secured a prospect yet," huffed Sarah and poured herself a glass of wine. "And you get nothing until I have something."

He turned with his hands clasped behind his back. "How about you just have a horrible, fatal accident and I take my chances with what I don't already have?"

Sarah rolled her eyes. "The problem is none of these gatherings we are attending have enough suitable men attending them. They are all either already married, or don't have enough money. I just need one good party with a bunch of rich, unmarried men to find someone."

John glanced out the window where Emma was putting things back in her basket.

"Maybe I can kill two birds with one stone," he muttered.

"What was that?"

"One party and a roomful of unmarried rich men—I will give you that in exchange for the information. This engagement is being called off in four days regardless, and it is the best offer you are going to get. I suggest you take it!"

He'd spat the words in a threatening voice that gave Sarah pause. Something about his tone made the hair on the back of her arms stand up—it was terrifying.

"Yes!" nodding her head vigorously, "I think I will take that offer."

"Good! Now get the hell out of my house and don't forget to bring my payment to that party, otherwise, you will regret it."

She set her glass down and wasted no time departing.

Emma decided to take a nap that afternoon and when she came downstairs, she was surprised to see John standing in the hall with his hat in his hand.

"Good afternoon, Miss Eldridge."

"Major? I thought I made it clear I did not want to see you."

"That you did!" He smiled. "And I am not here to see you."

"Then why are you here?"

Midge came out of the library. "Mistress Wolfe will see you now, Major André."

Emma eyed him peculiarly as he went in, gave her a wink, and closed the doors behind him.

"Midge, what is that all about?" she called in a hushed tone.

Midge came halfway up the stairs to meet her. "He arrived and asked to be alone with your aunt."

"Alone with Lucy? Why would he do that?"

"I have no idea."

Emma looked to the closed door and frowned. "I'm not sure leaving those two alone in a room together is such a good idea given Aunt Lucy's fascination with the man."

The two women sat down on the steps where they were and waited. Nearly thirty minutes later, John and Lucy emerged.

John tipped his hat, a pleased look on his face, as he went to the front door. "Ladies!" he smirked and let himself out.

"Why does he look so happy?" demanded Emma. "Did you and he—?"

Lucy scoffed. "I wish!"

"What the hell was that all about?" questioned Emma and descended the stairs.

"I am not entirely sure," replied a somewhat dumbfounded Lucy. "Come into the library and I will fill you in."

"He wants you to do what?"

Lucy folded her arms as she paced the floor. "He wants me to put together a party at his house and only invite wealthy, unmarried men who are actively looking for a wife."

"I don't understand!"

"I am not sure I do, either." Lucy scratched her head and sat down next to Emma. "He said it concerned army business and I would need to use the better part of discretion when sending the invitations."

"Did he specifically ask for those with loyalties to either army?"

"No! Just unmarried, wealthy men and no women allowed, including you and I, which is even odder because I have never thrown a party I wasn't there to enjoy."

"What did you say?"

"I couldn't exactly refuse him. When he brought you

back to me after the accident, I told him I was in his debt—he is now choosing to call in that favor."

Emma fiddled with her ear and scrunched up her face. "You don't suppose it's some sort of weird sex thing, do you?"

Lucy suddenly looked intrigued. "Well, you did tell him to go fuck himself. Perhaps he figured out a way to do it and is putting on a demonstration for the rest of the lonely men in town who have no women for that purpose, which would certainly be worth the price of admission."

"LUCY!" Emma clamped her hand over her mouth and laughed.

Lucy touched her on the thigh and chortled. "Like you wouldn't want to see that for yourself."

"I would be lying if I said I didn't!" Emma shook her head. "No, John André is up to something. We just need to figure out what."

"Well, you had better do it fast. He wants this to take place the day after tomorrow."

"So soon? That man is definitely up to something."

The next morning, Emma was walking past the dressmaker's shop when she happened to catch a glimpse of Sarah Tate through the window. Unable to resist, she ducked into the store and pretended to shop.

"Oh, Miss Tate!" she exclaimed. "I didn't see you over there."

It took a moment for the woman to recognize her. "Oh

155

yes, Miss Eldridge. We met at that party last week. How good to see you again."

"Are you here to see about your wedding gown?" inquired Emma.

"No! I was looking for something special for a private gathering tomorrow evening."

Emma tilted her head. "Is that right?"

Holding up two gowns, Sarah asked, "Tell me, Miss Eldridge, which one of these would you pick if you wanted to turn a high society man's head?"

"Neither!" she replied, now even more confused.

"Oh really?" Sarah looked them over. "Why not?"

"Because they aren't what a woman of standing would wear. The fabrics are of lesser quality to keep the price reasonable for the ladies of New York. Don't get me wrong, they are beautiful gowns and look lovely on any woman who chooses to wear them, but a wealthy man would notice the difference. These are also made and fitted afterward—not tailored to the woman specifically."

Sarah put them down. "You obviously have impeccable taste—would you mind helping me?"

"Of course, although I am a bit confused. Why would you need to impress Major André when you are already engaged?"

"Oh, this isn't for John." She leaned in and stated rather grimly, "To be perfectly honest, I don't think it's going to work out between us. That man has a temper, so I thought I might see who else New York has to offer in the way of husbands. Now, what would you suggest?"

"I would suggest having one made, but since you don't have a great deal of time, they do keep a few higher quality ones for unexpected occasions." Emma pointed to another part of the shop. "The gowns you are looking for are kept over there."

Sarah rubbed her hands together and headed in that direction with Emma slowly following behind.

"Where are you from, if you don't mind me asking?" asked Emma, trying to piece things together.

"I was born in Maryland, but I have lived in Philadelphia and most recently in New Jersey." She held up a purple gown. Emma shook her head. "And how did you and the Major meet?"

"Oh, just from being around. You know how it is! How about this one?"

"No, yellow is not your color."

Sarah nodded. "You are right."

"Your engagement seems rather sudden. How long have you and John known each other?"

"Not that long really."

Emma reached for one and handed it to her— a green silk gown. "This is the one you want."

"Oh, that is perfect," she cooed. "May I try this on?" she asked the dressmaker.

While Emma waited for her to come out, it occurred to her that something about all of this didn't add up and the thought unsettled her. Her concentration broke when

Sarah emerged, looking radiant.

"Well, what do you think?"

"I think you look stunning," she said with a smile.

"How much?" Sarah asked the shopkeeper. When she heard the cost, she looked deflated. "I can't afford it," she whispered and touched the fabric longingly.

"What if I buy it for you?" offered Emma.

"Why would you do something like that?"

Emma came over to her. "Any woman who looks that good in a gown deserves to own it and because I want to see you get exactly what you deserve out of life."

Sarah's face lit up. "I don't know what to say."

"It will be our little secret," Emma smiled, "and say you will come back to my house with me. I have the perfect earrings to go with that. You can try them on while we have a few drinks and figure out who the best man in town is for you."

"Aunt Lucy, we have a guest," announced Emma as they came inside the house.

"Oh?" called Lucy from upstairs.

"Yes, Miss Tate. Will you bring down those emerald earrings from my room? I want Sarah to try them on."

"Alright?" Lucy eyed her warily, but Emma nodded encouragingly.

"Come," Emma said and led Sarah into the library. "Let me get you a drink."

"Your house is magnificent," remarked Sarah, looking

around in amazement, stopping to pick up things and look at them closer, as if she were adding up their worth in her head. "Say, you don't have any unmarried men in your family, do you? The older, the better!"

"No, I am sorry, I don't," replied Emma, unsure of what to make of the woman.

"Here you go, dear," said Lucy to Sarah and handed her the earrings. "There is a mirror in the hall."

"Thank you," she replied, her eyes wide with delight as she bounced off.

"What is going on?" whispered Lucy.

Emma poured the strongest whisky they had. "Something is very off with her and John, and I intend to find out what it is."

"I hope you know what you are doing," warned Lucy.

"Oh, they look beautiful on you," declared Emma bringing over the whisky. "Here, let's drink to finding you a more suitable man."

Lucy sat back and watched Emma work her magic. After an hour of solid drinking and a little coaxing in the right direction, Sarah Tate had spilled her guts about the whole affair—how she had obtained the information from her lover, fled to New York, and blackmailed John and General Clinton into going along with her demands. The party the next day was her last chance to find a husband before John washed his hands of her completely."

"You know," mused Emma, "John André is a keen man.

I hope you have that information somewhere safe."

Sarah Tate was a lightweight when it came to drinking, which was surprising for a woman who made her living in a whorehouse. The whisky went straight to her head and as it turned out, she was a sloppy drunk. Sprawled out on the sofa, still wearing the earrings and on the verge of passing out, she slurred, "Oh, he—won't find—it. I put it—" her eyes started to close.

"Where did you put it?" asked Emma.

"I put it—" she turned on her side and snuggled in as something between a snore and a snort escaped her.

Emma plucked her ear. "Where the hell did you put it?"

Sarah swatted her hand away and mumbled, "Under the pulpit in the abandoned church near the checkpoint."

With her arms folded and her thoughts coming together, Emma walked over to join Lucy. "If tomorrow is the end of John's dealings with her, she will have to retrieve the information sometime before then, which means we need to get to it tonight."

"What are we going to do with her?" asked Lucy, walking over to the slumbering woman to remove the earrings from their guest. "She can't exactly stay here."

Emma drummed her fingers on the table. "Go get Jacob and give him some drinking money. I think he needs an evening at the tavern."

Around midnight, Emma wrapped herself in a black cloak as Lucy brought her a lantern and a loaded pistol.

160

"I am not sure about this idea," she fussed, extremely nervous about her niece's plan.

"Do you have a better one?" asked Emma and tucked the gun safely in her belt.

Lucy held out the lantern by the handle. "Just promise me you will be careful."

Emma took it and hugged her aunt. "Always!"

The abandoned church was one the British army had taken over for their own use to store supplies in. It was about a twenty-minute walk from Wolfe Manor and within sight of the checkpoint.

Emma stuck to the side alleys and darker corners to avoid being seen. Most of the town had turned in for the evening and the only ones left roaming were drunks, soldiers, and the women who got paid for their services after dark. Emma stopped as she rounded a building and saw two soldiers negotiating with a prostitute.

Backtracking, she altered her course, finally reaching her intended destination not long after. The church only had one way in and one way out, and that entrance faced the checkpoint. Using her cloak to conceal the light from the lantern, she flattened her body against the outside wall and inched her way closer to the door. Waiting for a chance when the guard's backs were turned, she made a run and slipped through the partially opened door. Once inside, she pushed back her hood and set the lantern on the floor.

All the pews had been removed and over half of the place was loosely packed with barrels and crates. The other half was being used to house hay.

Emma worked her way to the front of the church and located the pulpit.

"Now, where are you?" she asked aloud and moved the light closer. What she sought would not be out in the open but concealed somehow.

Kneeling, she ran her hand over the wood, looking for any clue. Her hand stopped when she felt a small gap on the inside near the top and a rough patch of wood that had been pried loose. Using her fingers to work and shift the space, she was able to pull the unattached board free.

After carefully setting it aside, she reached in and felt around, eventually pulling out a satchel. Smiling triumphantly, she made sure she had everything and put the panel back in place. Slipping it over her shoulder, she was just about to stand up when she heard the door push open and the voice of a giggling woman.

Emma quickly pulled the lamp closer to her body and covered it with her cloak once more. Peeking around, she saw one of the soldiers had come in with a woman and the couple had made their way over to where the hay was. He removed his coat and she started to untie the top of her gown. Emma cursed to herself when she realized this was where the men would come to bring women when they were on duty.

Praying it was a paid transaction that would be over

with soon, her hopes were dashed when she heard the man profess his love. Emma was trapped for the foreseeable future.

Settling with her back pressed to the inside of the pulpit, she did the only thing she could do—she waited.

Emma listened to the sounds, even peering around the corner every now and then, curiosity getting the better of her. She had never actually been with a man, but she knew how things worked—Aunt Lucy had gone into great detail when explaining to her about the birds and the bees, telling her everything including how to take precautions that would prevent her from ending up with a child from the union.

Seeing it, however, was something entirely different, and, judging by the sounds these two were making, it was more enjoyable than Lucy had let on. When the intensity and the vocals seemed to pick up, she looked once more, her gaze seemingly transfixed as she watched the two reach their grand finale. Feeling something stir deep inside, she wondered what sort of noise John André made when he reached that point.

Pushing the thought from her mind, she got up on her knees prepared to leave since the amorous couple's business seemed to now be concluded. She sat back down when she heard another man shout, "Hurry up, Sam. I need to get a few kegs of gunpowder out of there."

"Damn it!" she mouthed when she opened her cloak for

a small bit of light and looked closer to see she was surrounded—by gunpowder stacked to her left and bales of hay to her right.

If she was caught in there with that bag, she was done for. There would be no way to explain it away, and the army would have the information she couldn't afford for them to lay hands on.

With only one entrance and exit, she racked her brain to come up with a plan. Deciding the best course of action was a distraction, she looked down at the satchel in her hands. It was better to destroy it than to let them have it. Taking a few handfuls of straw and stuffing them in the bag with a wary eye to the gunpowder, she said a silent prayer she was doing the right thing.

Emma opened the door of the lantern and removed the candle, now nearly gone out. She took a few papers from the bag and lit them along with the pieces of straw. Once a flame had taken hold, she slung the bag into the hay as far away from her as she could, tossed the candle in after—and waited anxiously.

Once the fire caught, it erupted into a blaze. Covering her mouth with her cloak, she moved to the space between the barrels and inched her way towards the entrance.

When the soldiers noticed, they started to shout orders and flung open the doors, rushing to extinguish the flames. When they saw how near it was to the gunpowder, they instructed the men to move back.

Taking advantage of their diverted attention, Emma slipped out unnoticed. Once clear, she tossed her pistol aside and ran—but not fast enough.

The church exploded in a brilliant eruption of flames—blowing out windows and sending parts of the building flying through the air.

Emma felt the heat slam into her backside as she fell, covered by pieces of the church as it rained down upon her. She lay still, with no strength or desire to move. Her ears rang and her hearing was muffled to the point she could not make out the sounds around her. All she could do was close her eyes and ask God not to take her just yet.

John sat in front of the fireplace with a glass of whisky celebrating the fact it was his last day of having to deal with Miss Sarah Tate. The last straw was having one of his men, Charles Taylor of all people, inform him she had been found passed out drunk in a stable by one of the taverns this afternoon. No doubt, he would tell Emma about this even though he ordered him not to mention this to anyone else.

He sincerely hoped the information she had was worth it, otherwise, he very well might strangle her with his bare hands.

The sound of the explosion and the shaking of the house brought him to his feet. Heading for the door, he grabbed his coat and rushed into the street to see townspeople and soldiers headed towards the edge of town.

"What's happened?" he demanded of a man on horseback.

"The old church by the checkpoint exploded."

John pulled on his coat and hurried in that direction, arriving at the same time as General Clinton. Barking orders, he set the men to putting out the fire and went to locate one of the guards on duty.

"What's happened here?"

"Some hay being stored near the gunpowder caught on fire," the man replied, wiping soot from his face with his sleeve.

"Was someone in there?"

The man looked away and coughed. "Yes, sir," he said in a low voice.

"WHOM?"

"I was, sir. The lantern I was using must have turned over."

"Were you alone?" asked John, his tone suggesting he already knew the answer.

The man hung his head and didn't reply.

"Were you having carnal knowledge of a woman while on duty?" John grabbed him by the collar and punched him in the face before shoving him to the ground, the man refusing to fight back. "How many people died here tonight because you couldn't control your urges? The number of casualties?"

The guard wiped the blood from his nose. "None that I

know of, sir."

John looked down and spat, "You had better damn well hope there aren't any!"

Turning when he heard someone shout, "There is a woman over here under some of the debris. I think she is dead," John wiped his mouth with his hand and looked down at the guard. "I will deal with you later!"

John pushed through the men who had gathered around. He cursed when he rolled her over and looked upon her face.

"I'm sorry for your loss, Major André," said the man sincerely who found the body.

John nodded an acknowledgment and stood up, anger overtaking him as he stalked away.

Emma came to—her mouth and throat dry, burning. Coughing, she slowly shoved off the boards covering her back and forced herself up. Her eyes stung and tears rolled from them. Looking over her shoulder, she could see the flames and men trying to put them out. She knew she had to get away before she was found. Thankfully, she had run away from the street and was in a section that was more out of sight.

Staggering to the nearest building and using it for support, she managed to avoid running into anyone before making it home.

Lucy met her at the door and Emma fell into her arms.

"Oh, dear God!" Helping her to the sofa, she touched

her face and pushed back her hair, looking her over. "Are you alright?"

"I need water!"

Lucy rushed over to the buffet, returning with a poured glass which Emma drank down greedily.

"What happened? Was that explosion your doing?"

Emma rested her head on the back of the couch. "It was the only way, otherwise I would have been caught and they would have gotten the information. Now, no one will have it."

Lucy looked on worriedly. "Should I send for the doctor?"

Emma shook her head. "Just help me upstairs and let me sleep in tomorrow."

It was near two o'clock in the afternoon before Emma woke the next day. Moving slowly, sore in spots she didn't know she had, she made her way downstairs still in her nightgown.

"How are you feeling?" asked a concerned Lucy.

"Oh, I am 'feeling' everything."

"Can I get you anything?"

"Whisky," answered Emma, which Lucy obliged.

"Major André stopped by this morning to call off the party for this evening."

"I suppose he has his hands full," Emma groaned while curling up with her glass.

"He has no need of it. Miss Tate was killed in the

explosion last night."

Emma straightened up. "What?"

"My guess is she went to retrieve the information for tonight and was in the wrong place at the wrong time."

"It's my fault," muttered Emma.

"No, it is not!" Lucy touched her shoulder. "She was playing a dangerous game and she lost. That was not your fault."

"We play the same dangerous game," Emma pointed out.

"Yes, we do, and we know the risks. She did as well—she should have been a better player. Now, I will have a bath and something to eat sent up for you. In the meantime, write a note and offer the Major your sincerest condolences, so your own ass is covered." Lucy's face softened. "Are you sure you don't need to see a doctor?"

Emma shook her head and got up, whispering, "No, just send up more whisky."

Lucy nodded and stood to kiss her cheek. "I am so proud of you, even though you make me worry myself sick. I got down on my knees and thanked God you came home safely last night. In the future, please be more careful. I won't have the will to live if something happens to you. I love you."

"I love you, too."

John stopped by to see Emma the next day after she had spent a great deal of time with Sarah's death on her mind, weighing heavily on her conscience.

"I wanted to thank you for your kind note," he said.

"I am truly sorry for Miss Tate's death," she replied, shifting in her chair, still uncomfortably sore from the explosion and beside herself at the thought of being indirectly responsible for her death.

John took notice. "Are you alright? You don't seem like yourself today."

"I have just been feeling rather poorly the past few days, that's all."

"I am sorry to hear that. I won't keep you long." John studied her. "I wanted to finally take the chance to explain about the situation with Miss Tate and apologize for the undo amount of grief I have caused you."

"Oh?" She pretended she didn't already know the story.

He looked down. "The engagement was not real—it was part of my work. I can't go into details, but I want you to know there was never anything between us, not even a kiss. I was simply following orders."

"Did she know the engagement wasn't real?" asked Emma.

"She did indeed. It was her idea, as a matter of fact, and she insisted no one else know. I wanted to tell you all along, but it would have voided our deal."

"Did you get what you wanted from her before she died?"

"No," he said quietly. "At any rate, that matter is finished now, and I was hoping we could pick back up

170

where we left off."

"It's so effortless for you, isn't it?" She stared off into nothingness. "To just turn your feelings off and on so easily."

He appeared confused. "Not really? I never had any feelings for her or Miss Thompson."

"I am not sure you have feelings for me," Emma retorted matter-of-factly.

"Of course, I do!" The man looked stunned. "Why on Earth would you say something like that?"

Emma sighed. "Because if you had any true feelings for me, you would not have let me believe you were betrothed to another. Do you have any idea how much that hurt me? The emotions I have gone through since I heard the news? I thought—"

He cut her off. "Emma, I understand, and I am truly remorseful for the pain I have caused you. That was never my intention, but you know my work comes before all else."

"And that's the problem, John. I will never be a priority for you."

"That's not true," he argued.

"It is, and you know it! There will always be another woman with information who is worth more to you than my feelings, and I am not sure you can convince me otherwise."

"I can—I will. I want to spend time with you and see where this might go."

"I don't think it is going anywhere."

John rubbed his chin as he regarded her. "Well then, it seems I have my work cut out for me. You, my dear Emma, may be my biggest challenge yet."

"I am not sure you should waste your time— or mine."

He got up, leaned over, and kissed her on the top of the head. "You have never been a waste of my time, and I look forward to proving you wrong. Feel better, Emma. I will be seeing you soon."

She shook her head and watched him leave.

Tired of her moping, Lucy ordered Emma out of the house two days later.

"Go shopping, ride to the park to read, find some young man to drive wildly out of his mind—just get out of this house, sweetheart. You need some fresh air. It's not good for you to be cooped up in here with your thoughts."

"Maybe you are right," she conceded.

Emma grabbed a book and took her time riding to the park. Approaching the tree, she was surprised to see a familiar face already sitting in her normal spot.

"Ah, good morning, Emma!" said John cheerfully from where he sat.

"What are you doing here?"

"I discovered this wonderful place to sit and read," he held up his book. "What about you? What are you doing here on this fine day?"

Emma held up her own book.

172

"How about that? Great minds must think alike. Please, join me," he said and scooted over. "I have plenty of blanket to share."

"Don't you have some sort of army business that needs attending?" she asked, standing with her arms folded.

"Well, one must make time for the important things in life," he said with that devilish smile. He patted the spot next to him. "Please, I insist!"

Emma rolled her eyes and went to sit down.

Cautiously, John rested his arm on his bent knee and remarked, "You seem to be having some difficulty moving around recently. Have you not entirely recovered from your accident?"

"No," she lied. "It seems my bruises still have bruises. Some days are better than others, but you would know that if you had visited while I was recovering."

"I had no idea," he said, his voice full of concern. "Perhaps we should have the army surgeon look you over in case the town physician missed something." Removing his coat, he folded it and placed it behind her back as a cushion.

"Thank you and, no, I just need to move around a little more." She pointed to his book. "What are you reading?"

"I am rereading Shakespeare's, Romeo and Juliet. It is one of my favorites."

"There is a rather depressing love story for you," she remarked dryly.

"You don't like it?" He took her by the hand and

173

repeated the words from the play, "'My bounty is as boundless as the sea—my love as deep; the more I give to thee—the more I have, for both are infinite'."

Emma jerked her hand back and opened her book, pretending to concentrate.

"What are *you* reading?" he inquired with a grin and glanced over. "Ah! It seems I am not the only one who is a Shakespeare fan. Perhaps you are a romantic at heart, after all."

"'Love is merely a madness'," she read from the page it was opened to.

"'The lady doth protest too much, methinks'," he said, reciting a line from 'Hamlett'.

She countered with another from 'The Tempest', "'Hell is empty, and all the devils are here'."

"Do you believe me a devil, Emma?" John asked in a low sultry voice, moving close to lightly stroke her cheek with the back of his hand.

She leaned into his touch and sighed. "'The Devil hath power to assume a pleasing shape'."

John went in for a kiss, but she stopped him by pressing her finger to his lips. Deciding to change the narrative by changing the playwright, she quoted William Congreve by whispering, "'Heav'n has no rage, like love to hatred turn'd, nor Hell a fury, like a woman scorn'd'."

Emma patted his face, got up, and brushed off her gown. "Good day, Major. Enjoy your book," and she walked away, smiling to herself.

John laughed, rested his arm on his bent knee, and watched her go. "Well played, Miss Eldridge," he said with an impish grin. "And know this— the game is officially afoot!"

"How was the park?" asked Lucy when she came in.

"Full of Major John André," she replied and slammed the door. "He was sitting at the tree."

"Our tree?" Lucy set down the papers in her hand. "Should we be concerned?"

"He was either there because he knew I was going to show up there eventually—which would mean he has had someone watching me—or he has been keeping an eye on that tree for a different reason. I don't think we should use it anymore."

"Agreed! Did he seem suspicious when you showed up?"

"No!" she scoffed, "He seemed salacious."

Lucy giggled. "Well, I suppose given the choice, that is the better option for keeping us off the gallows." When Emma groaned, Lucy frowned. "Go upstairs and get some rest."

"Get out of the house, go to bed," mocked Emma as she climbed the stairs. "Make up your mind, woman."

"What's all this?" asked Emma when she came into the library after a long nap. On the desk was a small box with a single rose lying on top. "Don't tell me General Clinton has turned into a romantic."

"It's not for me," replied Lucy. "It was delivered for you while you were resting." Tapping the top, she added, "I believe there is a card attached."

Emma lifted the rose to her nose and inhaled the sweet fragrance before opening the card.

It bothered me to see you in such pain this morning, so I paid a visit to the apothecary. Adding this mixture to your bath water to soak in should help ease your soreness.

"The Prince of Darkness is a gentleman!"

"More Shakespeare! Oh, I will admit, you are good," she muttered and opened the box to find the most delightful smelling bath salts she had ever experienced. "Just not good enough."

Lucy took the card to see for herself and smiled. "Damn! If you don't want him, send him down to my room. I could use a man with balls that big in my life, especially if his cock is as large as his ego."

Feeling a great deal better after the bath soak, Emma decided the next day to go by the apothecary and get more to have on hand.

"May I help you, Miss Eldridge?" asked Mrs. Reade, who ran the shop while her husband tended patients.

"Yes! Someone brought me some bath salts for pain and

soreness. They worked such wonders, I wanted to get more."

"I have several. If you tell me who purchased it, I can get the exact one."

"It was Major André."

"Oh yes, he was here yesterday," Mrs. Reade reached for a jar, "and this is the one he bought. I remember him asking some questions, but I didn't realize it was for you. I am glad to hear they helped." She started scooping the salts out. "I have to say, he has been one of my best customers since he arrived."

Emma cocked her head. "Oh?"

Mrs. Reade cut her eyes over as if trying to warn her. "He is particularly fond of a rose water in a special bottle that can be added to the bath to fragrance the skin. He has purchased several as gifts, for a few young ladies in town, from what I understand. He seems to get around quite a bit."

"I have heard the same thing," grumbled Emma.

"Can I get you anything else?" asked Mrs. Reade as she boxed up her purchase.

"No, that will do. Thank you!"

As Emma was walking along the street, she felt a familiar energy fall in beside her.

"Hello, Emma!"

She didn't even have to look. "Hello, Charlie. Where have you been hiding?"

Emma accepted his proffered arm.

"The Major has me running ragged and that, along with the church fire investigation, has been keeping me plenty busy. I had been hoping to get by to see you, but I haven't had the chance."

"Investigation? Wasn't it caused by an unattended lantern?"

"That's the consensus, but we must conduct a formal inquiry, which means we have had to interview everyone in the area. It seems there was a pistol found in the woods that has raised some questions."

Emma winced and a few choice words crossed her mind. She had tossed it aside because she didn't want the gunpowder to accidentally ignite while it was on her person as she ran, but it hadn't even dawned on her it might survive the explosion.

"And then there is the question of why Major André's fiancé was there," he added. "Although, he seems more concerned about why she was there specifically, and less about the fact she is dead."

"I am sure he is grieving in his own way."

"Or maybe not!" muttered Charlie and stopped.

Emma noticed his gaze fixed on something and she followed it.

Major John André was sitting in the front window of one of the taverns with a woman whose face she didn't see because her eyes locked on the fact his hand was resting on hers.

At that very moment, John glanced out and caught sight of her and Charlie together.

John offered her a sincere look of contrition before going back to work.

Gripping Charlie's arm tighter, she said, "Will you escort me home please?"

Smiling, he kissed her hand. "Nothing would make me happier."

7
CHAPTER SEVEN

Emma and Francis stepped inside Rivington's
Coffeehouse and looked around for a table. Mid-morning
was the busiest time for the establishment and the place
was always crowded. Emma groaned inwardly when she
saw the only available table required them to walk past
John, who was sitting alone with his back to them,
seemingly absorbed in some correspondence. She was
hoping they would be able to slip by unnoticed, but
Francis stepped around her and headed straight for the
man to say 'hello'.

"Good morning, Major!"

"Ah, Mrs. Donald," he said, laying the letter aside and
standing to take her hand. "What a pleasure to see you.
What brings you out this fine day?"

"Emma and I thought we would venture out for some
much-needed time together."

John turned and bowed in her direction, simpering with
a twinkle in his eye.

Emma cursed under her breath but followed her friend.

"And Miss Eldridge! The sight of you always brightens
my otherwise dull day." He offered his hand and Emma

rolled her eyes.

"Major André," she managed to say, begrudgingly letting him take her hand.

Amused by her reaction, he intentionally took his time to plant a lingering kiss on it.

Emma looked away, but her gaze fell to the letter he had set aside. Though she only got a brief glimpse, the one thing she did manage to see was the signature—and it shook her to her very core, drowning out everything and everyone around her. For a moment, time stopped, and she was taken back thirteen years to the event that had changed her life forever. Rattled beyond belief, she felt her legs give way and was only brought around by John's hands firmly on her waist and the words he called out, "Emma? Emma? Are you alright?"

She shook her head and suddenly remembered where she was. "What?"

"I said, are you alright?" he repeated, concerned. "Your color has suddenly gone ashen, and you look as if you are about to faint."

Forcing a smile, she said, "I just—haven't eaten today. I will be fine."

Not entirely convinced, he escorted her to the empty table and waved Mr. Riverton for immediate service.

"Thank you," she mumbled.

"Are you sure that's all it is?" he whispered in her ear.

"I am perfectly fine, Major. Thank you for your concern," she said dismissively.

"Very well. Good day, ladies." He went back to his table, but his eyes remained cautiously on her.

"What happened?" asked Francis as she sat down.

"I just got a little light-headed," she lied. "Shall we order?"

Emma tried her best to focus on their conversation but was distracted to the point her mind and eyes would wander back to the letter on the table. She forced herself to sip her coffee every so often and acknowledge Francis.

"Oh, look at the time. As much as I am enjoying this, I must go meet Jack," Emma heard Francis say. As her friend stood, the young woman said, "Let's get together another day."

Emma stood and kissed her cheek. "Of course. I will pay you a visit soon."

She sat back down after Francis departed, her thoughts consumed by that letter. She would have it no matter what the cost. That's when she noticed John André had just tucked the information she needed into the pocket of his coat and was preparing to leave. There was no way she was letting him walk away with it. She got up from her chair and sat back down next to him at his table.

"You know, John," she purred and slid her left hand over on his, "you and I have not had nearly enough time alone to get to know each other and I think that is our problem." She started to sensually stroke his fingers. "I have decided I really would like to get to know you better."

He eyed her suspiciously. "Well, this is quite a change. Are you sure you are feeling yourself?"

"I give up, John. I have been trying to fight my feelings for you and I cannot do it anymore," she said sincerely. "Life is short and can be taken away at any moment. I don't want to waste any more time."

He sat unmoving as if trying to determine if she were being sincere.

Emma discreetly let her right hand drop underneath the table to rest on his upper thigh. "I have the entire afternoon free, and I would like to spend it alone with you." Slowly, she let her fingers wander.

John thought for a moment before he slid back his chair, stood, and offered his hand. "That is quite a coincidence. It seems my afternoon just freed up as well."

Accepting his proffered hand, Emma stood, doing her best to hide how nervous she truly was.

They made small talk as they strolled to the house he was quartering in. After escorting her inside and into the parlour, he called out to his servant, Nelly, to tell her he was not to be disturbed under any circumstances.

Emma watched him closely as he closed the doors to the room, removed his coat, and laid it across the back of a chair. He loosened his cravat and walked to the side buffet to pour two glasses of wine.

Sitting down on the small sofa, she smoothed her gown and surveyed the room, wondering exactly how she was going to get what she wanted. She smiled as he handed her the glass and sat down next to her.

Crossing his legs, John casually laid his arm across the back of the couch, settling in close.

"Emma, I must admit I am surprised. I had come to the conclusion you wanted nothing to do with me," he said and sipped the wine.

"You did?" she asked. "Well, as you are aware, a woman of my standing cannot come right out and say such things. It would not be proper."

"Yet, you just did in the coffeehouse," he pointed out, his gaze fixed on her.

Emma turned up the glass and drained it, trying to think of some witty response. When John leaned in for a kiss, she stopped him with the empty glass, pressing it into his chest. "It seems I need a refill."

John laughed softly at his inept timing. "So, you do." He got up and went over to bring the decanter. "You seem a bit tense," he noted as he poured. "Perhaps there something I can do to put you at ease?"

"Do I?" she asked. "Maybe I am a little."

John topped off his wine, placed the bottle on the table, and sat back down. "Forgive me, but I was under the distinct impression at Riverton's that you wanted to be here alone with me."

"I did—I do!" she responded quickly. "I just—"

He cocked his head. "You what? Come now, tell me the truth. Do you really want to be here are or are you playing at some sort of game? Perhaps trying to punish

184

me for some of my past deeds?"

Emma looked down into her wine and said nothing.

John sighed and set his glass down on the table beside the sofa. "I don't know what else to say or do to prove my feelings for you are sincere. I don't have the heart to play games with you and if you are playing them with me, perhaps you should just go."

He started to get up, but her hand shot out to stop him.

Emma's eyes cut over to his coat and nothing else mattered except getting what she wanted. "No games," she said and pressed her lips to his.

John was pleasantly surprised, greedily accepting and reciprocating the kiss. Pushing back a bit, he rested his forehead on hers. "Let's go upstairs to my bed where we will be more comfortable," he whispered hoarsely. "Let me prove to you how I truly feel about you."

"No!" she exclaimed and reached out to touch his chest, pulling up his shirt and over his head. "I want you here and now."

John gently leaned her back against the arm of the sofa and brushed her lips with his before moving to stroke the curve of her neck with the tip of his nose.

Emma's eyes locked on the ceiling and she tried to remind herself to not get lost in the surge of desire she was experiencing—and she was feeling a great deal of it. But as much as she wanted him, she wanted that letter even more.

John's attention moved to the top of her breasts and he

185

slid his hand over the curve of her hip while methodically gathering the fabric of her gown, the hem slowly coming up.

"Please let me take you upstairs," he moaned. "I have waited so long for this day and I want to touch and taste every inch of your beautiful skin."

Her face flushed and her breathing became ragged when she felt the firmness of his large manhood pressed against her. A feeling unlike anything she had ever experienced overcame her and nothing seemed more important than his touch. Deciding the letter could wait for just a little while longer—after all, what was one more afternoon after thirteen years, she was just about to give in to him completely—when Nelly, his servant knocked on the door. "Major André? There are some people here to see you," she called out nervously.

"GO AWAY!" he growled angrily over his shoulder. He lifted his head and smiled at Emma before tenderly kissing her lips.

"Do you think you should see who that is?" she whispered in his ear. "It may be important."

"No, my sweet. I will allow no one to interrupt our delightful afternoon," he replied with a lustful smirk on his face that said nothing would deter him from his ultimate goal.

Emma let her fingers drift downward and she was just about to unfasten his breeches, ready to give him everything—until she heard another woman shout—

"John André! Get out here NOW!"

"DAMN IT!" grumbled John and dropped his head. "I need to see to whatever this matter is."

"I understand," she said, panting and out of breath, and she sat up, shoving her skirts down.

He pointed to the room connected to the one they were in. "You can go through the dining room and exit through the side door so no one will see you. I am sure you do not want word to get back to your aunt." He stopped to kiss her. "We will continue this later. I give you my word." He snatched his shirt from the floor and stormed over to the door before flinging it open and shouting angrily, "WHAT?"

Emma rushed out of the room—but not before stopping to deftly retrieve the papers from his coat pocket. She shoved them down the front of her dress as she moved and paused when she made it into the doorway to adjust them. That's when she looked over her shoulder and caught sight of the source of their interruption—a dark-haired woman who seemed to be feeling quite unwell.

"Damn it!" Shaking her head, she chided herself for almost giving in to temptation. "He is shoving you out the back door while he has another one coming in the front. You are a fool for thinking he cares for you," she said to herself and got out of that house as fast as she could.

Emma could hardly contain herself as she hurried home.

187

Once inside, she went into the library, closed the doors, and fished the letter from the front of her dress. Taking a seat on the sofa, she unfolded it, then quickly read over the contents. The details were brief, to the point—and coded—simply giving what she could only assume was a current troop location and an intended movement date for an unnamed Continental camp, but the part she needed to see was the signature.

She had not misread it or been mistaken—it was, without a doubt, signed by one Lieutenant Sherman Finch.

It was the first she had seen or heard of the man's name in thirteen years and the thought of it made her stomach churn. Every detail from that day flashed before her eyes and she suddenly felt like she was going to vomit.

Instead, she sat there, staring blindly at the page. She wasn't sure how long she had been there when Midge tapped on the door and pulled it open, but when she looked up, she noticed the sun had started to go down. "Miss Emma, Major John André is here to see you and he does not seem pleased."

"Damn it!" she said under her breath and managed to shove the letter underneath a book on the nearby table just before John pushed past Midge into the room.

"Is there anything you need from me?" Midge asked Emma, her eyes cutting over to John.

"We will only be needing some privacy," John replied, his eyes fixated on her. "Please close the door on your way out." As soon as they were alone, John crossed the room and pulled her from her seat by the arm. "Where is it?" he demanded angrily.

"Where is what?" She tried to break free, but his grasp remained firm. "John, you are hurting me."

He loosened his grip and determinedly escorted her over to the sofa in front of the fireplace, forcing her to sit. "You know damn well what I mean. There was something in my coat pocket you took when you left and I want it back, along with an explanation."

Emma sat unmoving, staring down at the floor.

"For the love of God!" exclaimed John and shook his head. "You do realize we hang traitors, no matter who they are? Are you spying for the Continental army?"

"Is that what you think?" she asked, deflecting the question. While she had done plenty of spying for the opposing army, she found it rather ironic the one time she got caught had nothing to do with it.

"What am I to think?" he asked. "You wouldn't be the first woman to do it, and while it would personally distress me greatly to turn you in, I do have a duty."

She slowly got up, went to the table, and retrieved the letter. Handing it back to him, she muttered, "That is not why I took it."

He accepted it and waited for her to continue, wondering why the young lady who usually had so much fire within her suddenly looked more like a shell of a lost little girl.

"I saw the signature at Riverton's and that is why I took it. I have been searching for that man for thirteen years and that is the first mention of him I have come across in all this time. I could not let you walk away without seeing if there was any indication on that paper as to where he was."

"You were willing to go to great extremes for that name," he said, his anger somewhat tempered, now more curious than anything. He folded his arms and watched her intently. "Why? What about that man was worth giving up your virtue?"

A single tear dripped down her cheek. "He is the man I watched murder my parents."

John blew out a long breath and crushed the paper in his hand. "Dear God, Emma!" He sat down next to her and listened as she told him everything she had not already told him about that day—how one of the other soldiers told her his name and to remain quiet about it so she would not meet the same fate.

"Why didn't you ever tell anyone who he was? He could have been held accountable for his actions."

"It's more likely he would have lied. His own men were afraid of him and it would have been the word of a ten-year-old girl against his. Who do you think they would have believed? Even at ten, I knew he would have walked away and that would have been the end of it. Instead, I chose to keep it to myself and wait until the time was right to ensure he answered for their deaths."

"This man was worth—" He covered his mouth with his hand as a thought occurred to him. "Emma, have you ever even been with a man before— in that way?"

She looked down and shook her head.

"And you were willing to lay with me just to get this?" Her silence was his answer. "Why? Why would you trade your virginity for—" he demanded as a slow awareness came over him.

"You don't intend to—" he half-laughed until he saw the expression on her face.

Disbelief filled his voice. "You do! You mean to carry out justice yourself. Are you mad?"

She slowly turned to face him and a few more tears streaked her face. "What would you do? What if the same thing had happened to your parents and you were the one who was forced to experience everything all over again in your dreams each time you shut your eyes? Could you walk away and let it go so easily?"

John sighed. "No, I don't suppose I could." He reached over, gently brushed her tears away with the back of his fingers and gazed at her face. "Why didn't you just ask me about him?"

Emma shrugged. "Would you have told me? Will you tell me now? Who is he to you?"

He paused, searching her face as if debating if he could trust her. Looking down at the letter, he realized nothing had been truly compromised because to anyone else, this seemed like an innocent note.

"Just an acquaintance. I am sorry for what happened to you and under any other circumstances, I would kill him myself if it meant no tears ever fell from your eyes again, but there are things about this man you don't know. My dear, sweet Emma, Sherman Finch is a dangerous man and one extremely valuable to our cause. We cannot afford to lose him."

"So that's it! He just gets away with murder?" She pushed his hand away and stood. "I couldn't afford to lose my parents, but I didn't have any choice in the matter!"

"Emma," he said, his voice wheedling.

"No! NO!" she shouted hysterically before crumpling to the floor and breaking into a sob.

John went to her, put his arms around her, and pulled her against his chest trying his best to comfort her. "He will pay, I give you my word. It will just have to wait until this war business is finished. After that, I will see to it myself."

John remained with her much of the night, managing to get enough brandy into her to calm her down. When she finally fell asleep on the sofa against his chest, he gently laid her head on a pillow and covered her with a blanket before tenderly kissing her forehead and quietly departing the house.

The following morning, Emma woke with a horrible

192

headache as the previous night's events started to fill in.

"What happened to you?" Lucy was drawing out a map on a sheet of paper when she stumbled into the dining room.

"It's a long story." Emma poured herself a cup of tea and sat down. "Where did you get off to last night?"

"I was in the neighborhood and my carriage happened to bust a wheel just as we passed by General Clinton's house right after his morning meeting with some of his advisors on troop movements. Would you believe he still had his maps out?" she said, feigning shock.

Aunt Lucy was a woman of many talents and one of those was the ability to look at something once and remember every little detail. It was a trait that had become most helpful when stealing glances at important information.

"How long did you make poor Jacob sit out there and pretend to fix a broken wheel?"

Lucy shrugged. "No more than an hour and I gave him the rest of the day off with enough money to have a rather enjoyable afternoon at one of the brothels for his trouble."

"It's a good thing we have loyal people around here," remarked Emma, rolling her eyes.

"Indeed! What about you, dear niece?"

Emma explained about the letter, her trip to John's house, and his subsequent visit afterward.

"That horrible man is still alive? Dear Lord!"

193

Emma nodded.

"What was in the letter?" asked Lucy.

"Troop movements maybe?" Shaking her head, Emma searched her memory. "It was coded but not like they usually are. I guess Finch couldn't take the chance of being caught with a British code book, so I assume he has some sort of other system."

"Well, what exactly did it say?"

"Dear John—something about Finch stopping in to visit his Aunt Rose while he was traveling because he was missing her famous shepherd's pie. It went on to say she was doing well after being kicked by her favorite steed in the stable. Apparently, she is looking forward to a visit from John once she is healed. The physician, Doctor Eastwood, says she will be able to get around in a week's time. It doesn't make much sense, does it?"

"No, it doesn't!" Lucy got up, went to the library, and returned with a map she laid out on the table.

Emma cleared the dishes out of the way. "What's on your mind?"

Lucy smoothed out the page and circled her hand over New York. "There isn't enough information for troop movements, but maybe for something else—like a possible meeting?"

Emma came around to stand beside her aunt. "Maybe you are right." She picked up the quill, dipped it into the bottle of ink, and started to scribble on a piece of paper.

"What are you doing?" asked Lucy.

"Writing out the keywords so we can see if there is a connection," she replied with a grin. "Rose—traveling—shepherd's pie—favorite steed—stable—Doctor Eastwood—week's time." When she was done, she laid it next to the map so they could study it closer.

"Alright, obviously John would have to travel to meet Finch—" pondered Lucy.

"Eastwood is not a common name, is it?" muttered Emma.

"Not particularly."

Emma planted her finger on their location in New York. "Eastwood?" Looking to the right, she said, "What if?" Drawing an imaginary line to the right, she tapped a spot and cursed under her breath. "There is pretty much nothing except woods sprinkled with a few towns to the east of our current location."

"Steed!" exclaimed Lucy. "What if he didn't mean 'steed' but instead meant to imply 'stead'? Hampstead is in the woods just to the east and it is a place where loyalties tend to shift daily depending on which army is closest by at the time, And as I recall, there are a few taverns out that way which would make for a good meeting place."

"How in the world do we know which one?" questioned a frustrated Emma.

Lucy placed her hands on her hips and shook her head. "Shepherd's pie? Why in the world would he mention shepherd's pie of all things? Unless—there is a place that

195

specializes in an extremely tasty shepherd's pie?"

"Do you happen to know any of the names of the taverns out that way?" asked Emma.

"No, but I know someone who might." Lucy stepped to the doorway and called for Midge.

Emma folded her arms and looked at her questioningly.

"Did you need something?" asked the housekeeper.

"Midge, you have family out in Oyster Bay, don't you?"

"Oh, yes ma'am!"

"On your travels out that way, do you recall the names of any taverns out in Hempstead?"

Midge nodded. "Of course! There's 'Miller's Tavern', 'The Copper Pot', 'Johnson's Alehouse'—" she tapped her temple as she paused to think, "and that one that is off the beaten path called 'Roslyn's'."

Emma and Lucy exchanged glances.

Continuing, Midge added, "They are a good ways out, but from what I have heard, they have the best shepherd's pie you have ever tasted. Need anything else?"

"No, thank you, Midge. You have been most helpful!"

Once she was out of earshot, Emma turned to Lucy. "Do you think that message was as simple as that?"

"Why wouldn't it be?" whispered Lucy. "Anyone other than you or I, or John André, reading that note would not give it a second thought. You wouldn't have, for that matter, if you hadn't seen the signature."

Emma blew out a long breath. "A week's time, although there was no date and I do not know how long John has had the letter."

"What exactly are your intentions, my dear niece? It's not like you can waltz in there and murder the man in front of a British army officer. You will be swinging from a tree before the end of the night. Besides, Finch is a dangerous man, and you have no business trying to take him on alone. I simply will not allow it."

There was no point arguing with her aunt. Lucy loved her like she was her own daughter and would do anything to keep her safe. Whatever Emma did, she would have to do on her own and behind the woman's back.

"You are right, of course. For now, it will have to be enough to know he is alive and can be found," she lied. "Besides, John has assured me he will answer for what he did as soon as the army is no longer in need of his services."

"I am glad to hear that!" Lucy embraced her. "You have waited this long, a little longer won't make that much difference."

Emma smiled, but her mind was already formulating a plan.

"There is a Miss Eldridge here to see you, Major."

"Thank you, Nelly. Show her in."

Emma stepped inside the room with her head bowed in a contrite manner.

John looked up from the sofa where he sat with his legs crossed reading a report. He tossed it on the table and focused his attention on her.

"I wasn't sure if you would see me," she said and shifted on her feet nervously. "I wanted to apologize for what I did, and I wanted to thank you for staying with me last night."

John sucked in a deep breath but said nothing.

"Aren't you going to say anything?" she asked after an awkward silence.

"I don't know what to say to you, Emma. What this man did to you and your family angers me to no end. I am furious that I need him to win this war more than he needs to pay for causing you such pain," he paused, "I am beyond enraged he damaged a ten-year-old girl so badly, that as a young woman she felt the need to offer her body in exchange for a mere glimpse at his name because she is filled with such a need for revenge." John stood and went over to her. "It tears me apart inside to know you didn't trust me enough to come to me with any of this."

"I wasn't sure I could trust you."

John's brow furrowed. "I don't understand. Why would you not?"

Emma sat down on the edge of the sofa. "It's all the lies and the other women, John. You went to bed with Colette for information, you pretended to be engaged to another woman, and let me believe you had led me on, and even yesterday, you are pushing me out the back door while another woman waits at the front. How do I know you

198

are telling me the truth?"

He knelt on one knee before her. "You want the truth? Well, here it is—the woman from yesterday is an old friend. She is here with her husband visiting and they are expecting their first child. She rushed in because she was violently ill. I ended things with Colette because the information Sarah offered was more important and I only bothered with Sarah because I was ordered by General Clinton. I never once lay with Sarah and in fact, I have bedded no woman since the night of your accident. I have written up the paperwork to send Charles Taylor away from New York three times and burned them because every time I see him near you, jealousy unlike any I have ever experienced before overtakes me." He took her face in his hands. "Thoughts of you fill my mind day and night, to the point there is no room for anything or anyone else. I care for you a great deal and I will do anything to prove it to you."

"Anything?"

"Name it!"

Emma swallowed hard and looked him in the eye. "Give him to me. Tell me where he is."

Clearly taken off guard, John shook his head in disbelief and dropped his hands. "Ask anything of me except that."

"Please!" she begged and reached out for him.

John pulled away and stood. "Why in God's name would I?"

She got up. "That man took everything from me, and it

is my right to see justice served."

"Justice?" He half-laughed. "How would it be justice for you to go after him and he slaughters you the same way he did your parents? Where would be the justice in that? Emma, I will do anything for you, but I will not be responsible for your death and if I told you where he was, that is exactly what would happen. The answer is 'no'. I'm sorry. Ask anything else of me, but not that."

"Then we have nothing else to discuss," she said quietly.

"Emma, you have to let this go," he pleaded. "You have a good life here, but you are so consumed with rage and revenge it prevents you from thinking clearly."

"I suppose having your parents murdered in front of you as a child tends to make you a little angry," she said before turning and walking out of the room.

"EMMA!" he shouted, but she was already gone.

"Damn it!" He went over to the buffet and poured a whisky which he downed in one shot.

Cringing, Nelly stepped inside, "Major André? There is a Colonel Asheton here to see you. He says you are expecting him."

"Yes! Send him in and close the doors behind him. We need some privacy."

Emma bumped into a man going inside as she came out the front door.

"Pardon me," she muttered and glanced up.

"It's quite alright," he replied, tipping his hat and smiling.

She gave him a second look when she caught the faint smell of sandalwood coming off him, having the oddest feeling she had met him somewhere before. There was something oddly familiar about him, but she couldn't for the life of her figure out what it was. He seemed to regard her as well, before turning and going into John's house. Once out of sight, she stopped and went over to kick a nearby tree out of frustration.

"Well, that didn't go as planned!"

Her plan had been to cozy up to John, get him to spend some time with her so she could find out when his meeting was with Finch, but she had allowed her emotions to overwhelm her and revealed her hand too soon. Now he would be on guard and never let her know anything else about that bastard. She needed a new plan—and an idea came to her when she saw a man grooming his horse.

"Gabe! Come in and sit down!" said John. "May I offer you a drink?"

"It's a little early in the morning for the strong stuff, isn't it?" asked Gabe, eyeing his old friend warily.

John looked down into his glass. "Is it? It's been a long day already."

Gabe Asheton had been the finest intelligence officer the British army had ever seen and had taught John a great deal about the trade of espionage. He was a dear friend who had retired a couple of years prior, although the army was currently trying their best to draw him back in. Fortunately for John, he was visiting from out of town.

"I was rather surprised to get your note this morning asking me to pay you a visit and to not let anyone else know I was doing it." Gabe held up a folded piece of paper. "What's this all about?"

"Army business." John offered him a seat and sat down across from him. "I need some information I think only you can provide about an agent I inherited from you— one Sherman Finch."

"Is that bastard still alive?" Gabe scoffed. "I am surprised someone hasn't knifed him in the back."

"Believe me, I would like to," remarked John. "What can you tell me about him?"

"He was a soldier willing to do anything asked of him— a trait that helped him rise through the ranks quickly." Gabe held out his hands. "He is heartless, cunning, and seems to have no moral compass whatsoever. He was the perfect man for the position I placed him in. I assume he is still there?"

"Oh yes!" John's jaw tightened. "He provides a great deal of beneficial information."

"So, what's the issue?"

John got up and went to his desk. Returning, he handed some papers to Gabe. "If I am not mistaken, that is your signature at the bottom of this report."

Gabe unfolded the stack and read over it. Scratching his chin, he nodded. "It is indeed. Roger and Martha Eldridge—unfortunately, I remember this incident a little too well. It happened not long after I arrived in Virginia, some years ago in '67. I was asked to come out and investigate because no one was quite sure how to handle it otherwise at the time. It always bothered me we weren't able to find out who was responsible. As I recall, their young daughter witnessed the murder of her parents, but she couldn't give us much information—only that British soldiers were involved. I believe Emma was her name—the poor thing was traumatized beyond belief." Gabe refolded the report and handed it back. "Why are you asking about it now?"

"I recently learned that young girl lied." John sat back down. "She saw everything that happened that day, and she told me it was one man who killed both her parents. When one of the soldiers found her, he shielded her and instructed her to remain hidden underneath her bed, but not before telling her the name of the man responsible."

Gabe's face clouded over, and he suddenly became extremely interested in the answer. "Who was it?"

John took a long sip of the whisky before answering. "Sherman Finch."

Gabe exhaled sharply and paled a bit. "Dear God! I had no idea! How on Earth did you find out?"

"That young girl is now a wealthy heiress who lives

here in New York, and I have become rather fond of her. I want nothing more than to see this man pay for the despicable crimes he committed, but I desperately need the information he provides."

"Well, that is quite a quandary. I can see why you are drinking the hard stuff this early in the morning." Gabe stood and went to the side buffet. "As a matter of fact, I believe I will join you. Does she know?" He made himself a drink and then sat back down.

"That he works for me? Yes, though she doesn't know in what capacity—only that his work is important. She is hell-bent on revenge, not that I can blame her, and upset with me because I will not give him up. Her 'friendship' is not something I am willing to let go of so easily."

"What are you going to do?"

"What can I do, Gabe? As always, it comes down to a choice between a woman and the army, and we both know who wins out in that case." John polished off his drink.

Gabe looked down into his glass. "Can I offer a little advice as an old friend?"

"I am all ears."

Scooting to the edge of his seat, Gabe leaned closer. "Retire from the army, go back to England, and take this girl with you. If she is wealthy, you can live off her money while you paint, write, and entertain people with your war stories at parties. Leave this miserable place behind and go back to polite society where you can live a long, happy life and die in your bed at the age of a hundred after having made love to her the entire night before. Fuck this war business! It's not worth the price."

John looked up the see the expression on Gabe's face. He didn't seem to be suggesting—he was instead pleading. "I am a soldier, Gabe, and as enticing as that sounds, I will see this war through to the end, no matter what the cost."

"I don't say this lightly," Gabe downed his glass and sighed, "but, between you and I, old friend, your loyalty to the Crown very well may cost you everything!"

A cold chill ran down John's spine as if someone had walked over his grave.

Standing, Gabe placed his hand on John's shoulder comfortingly. "I think you just answered your own question. I wish you luck with the matter, and I hope Sherman Finch gets what's coming to him, sooner rather than later."

Emma located Jacob in the stables feeding the horses. Looking around to make sure they were alone, she said, "Jacob, I need your help."

"Sure, Miss Emma. Do you want me to saddle up Mac for you?" he asked and set down the bucket he was holding.

"No! I need some information."

He stopped what he was doing and gave her his full attention. "What kind of information?"

"Well, you go and drink with some of the other stablemen, right?"

He nodded.

"Major André will be taking a day trip out to Hampstead sometime in the next week, but I don't know which day. Do you think you can find out for me?"

"It should be easy enough after a few drinks," he replied with a shrug.

"And the drinks are on me!" She pressed several coins in his hand. "Thank you, Jacob! There is just one other thing. The information is for me, not Aunt Lucy. I don't want her to know anything about it."

Jacob scratched his head. "I don't know, Miss Emma. I work for Miss Lucy and it's starting to sound like she wouldn't like it too much."

Emma winced. "It's personal," she said. "Um—Major André and I have been getting close recently and I just want to make sure he is not getting 'close' with another woman behind my back," she lied. "I don't want to look like a fool if he is seeing someone else in addition to me."

Jacob studied her for a minute before finally giving in with the shake of his head. "Alright, Miss Emma, I will find out for you and it will be our little secret."

She kissed him on the cheek. "Thank you, Jacob!"

8
CHAPTER EIGHT

Five days later, Emma got up before dawn, dressed, and left her aunt a note stating she would be out with a friend, returning later in the evening. Jacob had come through for her and she knew John would be meeting Finch that day.

Having deciphered the destination from the note, she would already be there when Finch arrived.

While packing her saddlebag, she went to her wardrobe and opened a hidden compartment she had installed in the back several years prior, used as a place to store weapons. She removed two flintlock pistols and a powder horn; holding them in her hands, she considered the fact these would be the instruments used to finally bring her some peace. After shoving them in her bag and fastening the buckle, she quietly slipped out, saddled Mac herself, and rode off.

Emma arrived at the tavern mid-morning, before it got busy, and paid a great deal of money for a room close to the stables with a clear view of the road. Riding out with one of Lucy's maps, she surveyed the surrounding area, before returning and instructing the stable boy to feed and water her horse and to leave him saddled so she could ride on a moment's notice. After having a hot meal sent up, she loaded the powder and balls into the pistols, moved a chair to the window, and ate as she kept watch.

By noon, nearly a dozen people had come and gone, none of them the man she was looking for. Standing to stretch, a new arrival dressed in plain clothes dismounted his horse and caught her attention. Something about the tilt of his head and the way he moved seemed familiar.

He turned and went inside just as she moved nearer the window for a better look. Adrenaline and anger surged throughout her body with such intensity, she felt her shepherd's pie threatening to come back up.

Sherman Finch had not changed much in thirteen years, the only difference being his hair was now grayer and his belly a little softer, but it was most certainly him.

Gripping the gun tightly, she stopped herself from going downstairs when she noticed John had arrived from the other direction. She almost missed him for the fact he was wearing breeches and a thin shirt, not his usual uniform. If he knew she was there, he would never let her get anywhere near Sherman Finch, much less close enough to fire a shot.

She watched John lead his horse into the stables and emerge a few moments later.

No matter—she would just stick to her plan: when

Finch departed, she would follow him until they reached a stretch of heavily-wooded road about three miles out from the direction he came, a spot she had determined remote enough to go unnoticed. She just needed to make sure it was clear of any other people at the time—and she would have her revenge.

In the meantime, she needed to get ready. Putting on her cloak and pulling up the hood, she descended the back staircase and slipped into the stable unnoticed. There was a cluster of dense trees not far up the road from where Finch came, and she would wait on horseback there.

Emma had just begun to wonder if he might have departed with John in the other direction when she heard the approach of a horse. Peeking around the tree, her heart raced and all she heard was the rush of blood in her ears. Ducking as he passed by, she waited until he was about fifty feet ahead before falling in behind him. Keeping her head down and nodding to a few travelers going the opposite way, she kept her pace so he would not become suspicious, slowly closing the gap to about twenty feet as they came up at the beginning of the stretch. There was one rider coming from the other direction, and as soon as he moved along, she would make her move.

Emma turned her head to the side as he went by and glanced over her shoulder to make sure he was far enough away before spurring her horse to run so she could overtake Finch. As soon as she passed, she pulled

Mac to an abrupt halt, blocking the road.

Finch stopped his horse, confused and taken off guard. "What the hell are you doing?" he demanded.

She pulled one of the pistols from the bag resting at her hip and pointed it in his direction. "Doling out a little justice," she replied and leaned forward in the saddle. "You and I are going to move off the road into the woods so we can have some privacy," she said and pointed with the gun. "Don't even think about fleeing. I am a pretty damn good shot."

Seemingly more curious than anything, he nodded and flippantly followed her instructions. Once they were out of sight of the road, she ordered him off his horse and dismounted herself. "Keep your hands up where I can see them!"

"Well, this is a twist," he goaded, his hands up, but in a relaxed manner indicating he was not afraid. "Usually, men are dragging women into the woods against their will, not the other way around," pausing to leer, "Although, if you want to have your way with me, a pretty little thing like you won't find me putting up much of a fight."

"You are a vile and disgusting human being, but I know that better than anyone," she sneered, a repugnant look on her face.

Finch tilted his head, intrigued. "Have we met? No! I would remember someone who looked like you."

"We haven't officially, but I know exactly who you are.

You are the bastard who murdered my parents, and the time has finally come for you to pay for your crime."

"I have killed many people," he shrugged, unfazed. "I am afraid you are going to have to be a little more specific."

"Thirteen years ago, when you and your men stopped at a house in Virginia. You were a lieutenant then and when my mother fought back against your advances, you shoved her to the ground, causing her to hit her head and die. When my father rushed to her side and accused you of murder, you stabbed him in the back. I know because I watched it all happen from my bedroom window."

He leaned against a nearby tree. "Ah yes, the teacher and his divine wife." He smiled wickedly. "You know, I don't even remember their names, but I do remember how lovely your mother was and how disappointed I was I didn't get the chance to fuck her, especially given the fight she was putting up. You look a great deal like her— the same full lips, the same firm tits, and, now that I think about it, you seem to have a little bit of the same fire she had as well. Why don't you and I have some fun together? I am sure I can make you forget all about your mommy and daddy issues."

"Oh, I am going to have plenty of fun all by myself just watching you die," she spat, her rage coming forth. "And their names were Martha and Roger Eldridge. I want you to know exactly what sins you are paying for when you arrive in Hell."

"Oh, I will be in Hell soon enough," he said with a smirk, "but it won't be by your hand and not today."

Her finger rested firmly against the trigger and Finch took a step towards her. Just as she was about to squeeze, she heard the unmistakable sound of the hammer of a gun being cocked directly behind her.

"Put the gun down, Emma!" she heard John say.

She turned her head to the side, the muzzle still aimed at Finch's heart, to see the weapon pointed at her back.

"John?"

"Please! For the love of God, PUT IT DOWN EMMA!" he pleaded.

She shook her head vigorously. "NO!" she screamed and tightened her grip. "He has to pay for what he did."

"And I have told you before how much I need him to win this war. Give me the gun!"

Her eyes cut to over her shoulder. "Are you going to shoot me, John? Is his life more important than mine?"

A desperate expression filled his face. "Don't put me in this position, Emma. I need you to set your feelings aside and walk away."

Her hand started to violently shake, and the barrel of the gun tipped down just a bit.

John took advantage of the hesitation to step closer and removed it from her hand.

"Told you!" gloated Finch, and he moved towards her. "Emma Eldridge!" he crowed, relishing his triumph. "A fine name for such a lovely girl."

John raised his gun and aimed it at Finch's head. "You will forget this ever happened and if you ever go near her, I will kill you myself," he threatened. "Get your arse back to that rebel camp and get me the information I need. Right now, it is the only thing keeping you alive. Get out of my sight!"

"Yes, Major André," smarted Finch with a dramatic tip of his hat, his eyes full of lust as he looked over at Emma.

"This isn't the last you have seen of me," she said to him as he walked past her. "This is far from over."

He climbed onto his horse and smirked at her. "I look forward to it," he said and galloped out of sight.

John made sure the man was back on the main road before letting out the breath he had been holding and wiping his mouth with his sleeve. "Emma! What the hell did you think you were doing?"

"Why did you stop me?" she demanded, so infuriated she had to consciously force herself to breathe. "He deserves to die for what he did!"

"Don't you get it?" John got directly in her face, equally incensed, tossing her gun to the ground and shoving his own into his belt. "He was seconds from taking that gun from you and once he had it, he would have raped and killed you if I hadn't come along. I have told you how dangerous that man is, yet you continue to ignore my warnings, having no regard for your own personal safety."

213

"Would you have pulled that trigger and shot me to save him?" She started toward her horse.

He moved to block her. "Emma, I would never intentionally hurt you, but I have told you, I need him to finish this war and I will see this business finished if it is the last thing I do."

She went to step around him, but he firmly grasped her by the arm. "Where do you think you are going?"

"Where do you think I am going? I am not going to let him just ride away!"

"Oh no, you don't!" He grabbed her around the waist and hoisted her over his shoulder.

"What are you doing?" she screamed angrily and slapped at him.

"Saving you from your own, destructive self while giving him enough time to get far enough away so you can't reach him. Since you seemed determined to continue to disobey me, you are forcing me to take drastic measures, even if it means I have to tie you up!"

"You wouldn't dare!" she hissed.

"You would be astonished to learn some of the things I have dared to do," he retorted and stalked back towards his horse.

"PUT—ME—DOWN!" she snarled and clawed at his back with her nails. When that didn't work, she leaned forward and bit him on the back of his shoulder.

"You want down!" he bellowed and reached for something in his saddlebag. "FINE!" and dropped her on

214

her back to the ground, directly into a patch of fresh mud. Before she could react, he fell upon her and pinned her down with his knees.

"What are you doing?" she demanded and tried to push him away as he straddled her.

"You want to act like an animal, then I shall treat you like one!" He caught her by the wrists and used the two pieces of rope he had taken from his horse to bind her hands and feet.

Eyes wide and nostrils flaring, she growled, "How dare you do this to me?"

"I know you cannot see it now, but I am only trying to protect you." When he was done, he relaxed a hair and reached around to rub the spot she bit, drawing back blood. Removing a handkerchief from his pocket, he pressed it to the wound. "Damn it, Emma! What the hell is wrong with you?"

"You fucking bastard!" she roared. "I will kill you for this!"

John shook his head and 'tsked'. "Such foul language for a refined young lady!" He looked at the handkerchief in his hand and shoved it in her mouth. "That's better!"

Emma screeched and banged her feet against the ground as John got up and brought her horse over to his. He picked her up and slung her, face down, over his animal before climbing in the saddle and taking Mac by the reins. He spurred his mare in the side, and they were off.

An enraged and humiliated Emma seethed as John

hummed a lively tune while they rode. Fighting back at this point was a waste of energy, so Emma decided to conserve her strength. Grunting whenever John picked up the pace, she didn't know how long they rode until John pulled his horse to a stop.

He dismounted and pulled her down before slinging her back over his shoulder again and handing the horse off to someone else. When he turned to have the stable boy place his saddlebag over his shoulder, she saw they were back at the tavern.

John carried her inside and located the tavern keep. "We will be needing a room."

The confused little man looked up at John and then at Emma questioningly. "We were just married," explained John with a smile. "Her father arranged it and she wasn't very happy with his choice."

Emma squealed and used her tied hands to slam into the spot where she bit him. He tensed and grimaced at the fresh round of burning pain—she laughed—and he smacked her sharply on the fanny, causing her to release a string of muffled obscenities. "Her father said she was a wild cat," he whispered to the man with a wink. "I can't wait to find out for myself. It should be an interesting night, to say the least."

The old man stroked his chin amused, looked her over, and chuckled. "Lucky you!"

John pulled a generous amount of coin from his pocket and laid it in front of him.

The keep eyed the money and smiled. "What will you be needing, sir?"

Looking around, John sighed. "Two hot meals, an enormous amount of drink, a room with a key lock that works on the inside—and a great deal of privacy."

'Would you like a hot bath brought up, as well?"

"Yes," he replied and looked down at the dirt on his hands, "I would actually."

The keep handed him a key. "The last room at the end of the hall. I will have everything brought up right away, so you won't be disturbed after that."

"Thank you!" replied John and turned towards the staircase.

"Congratulations, ma'am," said the man with a little wave of the hand as they started away.

Emma glared back at him with a murderous look on her face.

Once in the room, John dumped her unceremoniously into a nearby chair. "Not the worst place I have stayed," he said as he looked around. He went over to the water basin and washed his hands and face.

Emma mumbled something.

"What was that?" he asked, drying off with a towel.

She repeated the incoherent words once more.

He came over and looked down at her. "I will remove the gag, only if you promise not to scream. If you do, I will put it back, where it will remain until I deliver you to your aunt. Do you understand?"

Emma just stared at him.

John folded his arms. "Well? Those are my terms, take them or leave them."

Looking away, Emma grunted and gave one simple nod.

John grinned and reached for her mouth, but hesitated. "Do I have your word?" he asked dubiously.

She wrinkled her nose and nodded again.

"Alright," he said and pulled the gag free.

Emma closed her eyes and gulped in the fresh air.

"You were saying?" He tossed the bawled-up handkerchief aside.

Licking her dry, parched lips, she asked, "How long are you going to keep me here?"

"Until I have talked some sense into you regarding Finch and this ridiculous lack of concern you have for your own well-being when it comes to him."

"Well, you had better get comfortable," she retorted dryly, "because Hell will freeze over before that happens."

"That's what I am afraid of," he complained and got up to answer a knock at the door. The tavern keeper delivered their requests before John stepped into the hall to have a few words with him—she was unable to make them out. When he returned, John secured the lock, shook the key for her to watch, and bent down to slide it through the gap underneath the bottom of the door, into the hall.

"What did you do that for?" she questioned.

John straightened up. "Well, I can't have you rifling through my pockets while I'm sleeping—or worse, while I am unconscious because you hit me over the head with something before foolheartedly riding off into the night. This will ensure you won't do any of those and will allow me to unbind your hands and feet unless you would prefer to remain tied up the rest of the night. It would be extremely uncomfortable for you, but it would make my evening less taxing."

"My aunt is expecting me back for supper," she argued through clenched teeth.

Crossing the room, he jeered, "I am sure it is not the first time her errant niece has been late getting home. In fact, she probably expects it by now."

"You're intolerable!" she berated as he knelt and loosened her binds.

"So, I have been told," he replied with a wink and a mischievous grin.

Emma threw the rope aside and rubbed her now numb wrists to get the circulation going again.

John sighed and regarded her. "You're a muddy mess. Why don't you take advantage of that tub over there and get cleaned up?"

"I wouldn't need cleaning up if you hadn't dropped me into a puddle!" she sassed back.

"I swear, I didn't know it was there," he lied, trying to keep a straight face. "Go on, while the water is still warm."

She looked at the tub and back at him. "You expect me to bathe in front of you—naked?"

"That is how it is typically done," he countered.

"Dream on!" Emma got up, went to the door, and started to bang on it with her hands. "HELLO! Can someone open the door? The key is in the hall!"

"No one is coming to open that door until morning." He stood and poured himself a tankard of ale. "I made certain of it. You are wasting your time, so you might as well get comfortable for the evening."

Emma smacked the door, rested her forehead against it, and huffed. There was no possible way she could catch up with Finch now, even if she were able to get out of this room. It would be dark soon and she was, indeed, stuck there for the night. She slowly turned to glower at him.

He had taken a seat and was watching her intently.

"Bath!" he commanded. "You are filthy, and to be perfectly honest, my horse smells better than you do at the moment."

"I don't have any clean clothes," she said and went over and poured herself some of the ale, "and if you think for one minute I am parading around here without anything on for you, think again."

"As enticing as that sounds," he laughed, "I have an extra clean shirt in my saddlebag you are welcome to and, I am even willing to turn my back while you bathe, although I can assure you, I am familiar with the womanly form. I have even seen a few without clothes on."

"Too many!" she grumbled and tasted the ale. It didn't warm her like whisky and the truth was, she was freezing. That puddle still had plenty of water in it and she had gotten soaked.

"Fine!" she conceded and slammed the tankard down. "Turn your chair around!"

"As you wish!" John moved his seat just as she asked and sat back down, careful to conceal he had done so in front of a small mirror hanging on the wall.

Emma quickly undressed and stepped into the blissfully hot water, sinking to her chin. "Damn it!" she cursed when she realized the soap was on the table.

"Something wrong?" he called over his shoulder.

"I forgot to get the soap." She started to get up, but he stood.

"I will get it for you. Stay put."

John picked it up and walked it over to her.

"Close your eyes!" she demanded.

"I most certainly will not!" He handed it over and sat down on the foot of the bed. "Now that I have you trapped, you are going to listen to what I have to say whether you like it or not."

Emma made a wry face and rubbed the soap together in her hands.

"I know you want revenge, Emma," he said gently, "and

221

I promise you, your parents will be avenged if I have to pull the trigger myself. It just cannot be right now. I need you to be patient."

"Why? Tell me why his life is so important?"

John rubbed his chin with his palm. "Sherman Finch has been entrenched in one of Washington's camps as one of them since the beginning of the war under an assumed name. That is why you have not been able to find him by his actual name all this time. He has brought valuable information to me which has saved a great many casualties on our part, more than you can imagine," he paused, "Because of him, I have been able to ensure many ten-year-old girls will actually have their fathers return home to them—rather than having to grow up without one like you did."

Emma shifted to face him and swallowed hard. "I don't care," she said half-heartedly and turned her face to hide the tears forming in her eyes.

John got up and walked over to her. "Yes, you do! I know in your heart you would give anything to not have another child grow up without a parent the way you did." He kissed the top of her head and went to get something clean from his bag for her to wear.

John stared out the window as she dried off and slipped on his shirt.

"I often wonder what my life would be like now if they had lived," she said, out of the blue. "I love my Aunt

Lucy with all my heart, and I thank God every day for her. She has given me an extraordinary life, but not a day goes by I don't think about them. Are your parents still alive?"

"My mother, yes, but my father passed some years ago."

"Do you have siblings?" she asked.

John nodded. "Several."

Emma pulled a quilt from the bed, wrapped it around her, and sat down. "My father was a teacher and always impressed upon me the importance of education. I wonder what books we would have read and had lengthy, animated discussions about."

John rested his head against the windowsill and watched her as she continued to speak, her voice soft and wistful.

"My mother loved to cook—people raved about the sweets she made for miles. She would have taught me all those little tricks and secrets that made them so good and how to place them perfectly on a plate to make them more appetizing. If given time, I may have had a brother or a sister, perhaps several, who I could have complained about following me around and pulling my hair." She wiped her nose on the blanket and pulled it tighter around her. "My father will never give me away when I get married. My mother will never hold her grandchild for the first time and tell me how to settle my baby when he cries for no apparent reason. I will never have a sister to have tea with and talk about our broken hearts or a brother to defend my honor if I am insulted by some rogue. That man didn't just kill my parents—he stole part of my life—and I need you to understand why I cannot let it go."

John could not stay away from her another moment. He went over to her and took her face in his hands.

They gazed into each other's eyes as their faces slowly moved closer together. Surrendering to the feelings they had been fighting for so long, John took her in his arms, and they kissed, slowly at first until their passion ignited and each knew, neither would allow anything to come between them that night. They took their time exploring each other's bodies before John took over and showed her the true pleasures of lovemaking.

When the time came to breach her virtuous barrier, he held back. Stroking her face, he asked, "Are you certain you want me to do this? Once I take your innocence, there is no getting it back and I want to know, without a doubt, it is what you genuinely want."

"It is! I want you more than I have ever wanted anyone—and I want you to be the one to do it."

John was gentle, understanding, and whispered sweet nothings in her ear as he guided her through the pain she barely noticed because of his caring effort. Pushing her to her peak by building the rhythm, he ensured they reached their orgasmic explosion together.

He covered her in kisses and brushed the hair back from her face as he lay with her wrapped in his arms. "How do you feel?"

"I don't know how to describe it," she said and snuggled against him, "but I know I don't want it to ever end." She fell asleep in his arms, curled against his chest as he lightly stroked her back with his fingers.

Emma woke him sometime in the middle of the night and he made love to her again, and once more before dawn.

After an early breakfast, they slowly dressed and prepared to leave for home.

"Are you up for riding?" he asked, planting kisses on the back of her neck. "I understand the first time can be 'uncomfortable' the next day."

"I'm fine," she assured, "unless you want to stay another day."

"Nothing would please me more, but your aunt would probably send out a search party and this might be difficult to explain," he groaned and rested his chin on her shoulder.

As he gathered his things, he asked the one question that had been nagging at the back of his mind. "How did you know?"

"Know what?"

"I was coming to meet Finch?"

Emma froze. Thankfully, her back was to him, and he couldn't see the reaction on her face.

"I need to know," he said. It was not the tone of 'John',

the man who made tender love to her a few short hours ago, but the one of 'Major André, the Head of British Intelligence' demanding an answer."

"I followed you," she replied.

"That's one lie!" he stated aloofly and came around to stand in front of her. "Your horse was already here when I arrived—I saw him when I stabled mine. That's how I knew to follow Finch. I ask again," he took her firmly by the arm, a stern expression on his face. "How did you know?"

"You're right, it was a lie." Panic threatened to overtake her. "Frankly, I am embarrassed to admit the truth," she said, hoping he would somehow believe whatever story she was about to come up with.

"Go on."

She drew in a deep breath and exhaled sharply. "The letter I took from you. It said your Aunt Rose was expecting a visit from you in a week's time. I was hoping she would know where Finch was and that I could get the location out of her after you led me to her. I paid my stableman to get yours drunk—to find out when you were planning to be gone for the day and where you were headed to. He told my man you were going to Hampstead."

"How did you know about the tavern specifically?"

"I didn't!" She laughed nervously. "It occurred to me, a little too late, my plan was greatly flawed in the fact I was indeed ahead of you and not behind you, which, of course, would have made more sense. I had become so anxious at the prospect of finding the man, I got ahead of myself because I wasn't thinking entirely clearly. I became frustrated with my stupid mistake and stopped off here to have a meal and try to come up with a plan that might actually work. No one was more astounded than I when Finch walked right into this very tavern. I was so taken aback, I hid and watched from afar as you joined him. I found my rage growing by the moment and by the time he left, I could think of nothing but killing him," she half-smiled, "I'm completely mortified by my lack of reasoning skills. I know it was a foolish thing to do, but it was the only word I had of him since that day, and I could not just let it go. I suppose given my thought process, I wouldn't make a particularly good spy."

She watched for his reaction, having no idea if he believed her or not. Realizing, the odds were against it, she braced herself and prepared for the worst.

His face remained stoic for what seemed like an eternity before it softened, and he kissed her. "No, I don't suppose you would make a very good spy. But, Emma, no more going off half-cocked. Not only is Finch dangerous, but so are the areas outside of New York. You could have been kidnapped or worse. Promise me, no more coming out alone and that includes your little riding excursions like the last one. I need to know you are safe."

She nodded and leaned into him. "Whatever you say,"

she lied.

When they arrived back at Wolfe Manor, Lucy was beside herself with worry.

"Oh, thank God!" She rushed to Emma and embraced her. "Where have you been?"

Dreading having to explain, she opened her mouth only to have John interject. "I am afraid it is my fault, Mistress Wolfe, and I must offer my sincerest apologies. You see, I spirited Emma away for a picnic out in the country and we were having such a lovely time, the day got away from us. We started back and my horse threw a shoe. By the time we located a blacksmith, it was getting late, so we stopped at a tavern and stayed the night—in separate rooms, of course."

Lucy eyed him suspiciously, then Emma. "Uh-huh!" she said with a dubious look on her face.

"I take full responsibility," he added. "Please don't be angry with Emma."

Lucy turned to her niece. "Are you alright?"

"I am," she replied sincerely.

"Right now, my only concern is Emma's welfare." Lucy narrowed her eyes at John, and he lowered his gaze, attempting to appear contrite. "You and I will discuss the matter later. You may go now, Major."

He bowed. "Good day, ladies!"

Lucy slammed the door behind him and pulled Emma into the library. "Now tell me what's going on."

"I went after Finch," she replied and sat down.

"You did what? Emma! What were you thinking?"

"I was thinking I wanted him dead."

"What happened?" Lucy poured a drink and brought it to Emma.

Emma took a long sip and rested the glass on her leg. "John stopped me. I had that bastard dead to rights and all I had to do was pull the trigger, but John prevented me."

"Why would he do that?"

"Because Sherman Finch is entrenched as a spy in one of Washington's camps and John needs him."

"You are certain?"

"I am." Emma nodded. "I may have missed my chance to kill him, but I know where to look for him now. With any luck, when they discover he is an agent, maybe they will let me be his executioner."

The revelation washed over Lucy. "We need to warn Washington as soon as possible."

"This will require a trip," said Emma.

"Why do you think that?"

"Because I am the only one who knows his face and can identify him."

Lucy shook her head. "It's too dangerous."

"So is having that man sending information back to the British. From what little John did tell me, he is worth a great deal."

"But you don't even know which camp he is in."

"It should be easy to determine if we use the tavern as a starting point. He arrived about noon and would have to be back before nightfall, so it must be within a defined area that's no more than four hours ride from there. I watched him approach from the west. That should narrow it down some."

"Washington's main army is in Middlebrook right now, so he can't be with them." Lucy frowned. "He has to be with one of the smaller regiments that moves around, so it will be difficult to pinpoint."

"Getting away for the rendezvous may be difficult as well," pondered Emma. "John has warned me about leaving town and I am afraid he may be keeping a closer eye on me now."

"Any ideas?"

"When I met with Washington's man, Tallmadge, he told me a way to signal in case of an emergency and we needed assistance. I think this qualifies. I will take care of it first thing in the morning."

Taking Emma by the hand, Lucy said, "Alright, now, tell me the rest of it."

Emma winced and raised the glass to her lips. "I don't know what you mean."

"You became his lover," Lucy simply stated. "I can smell his scent all over you."

"I did," she confessed.

"Well? I want to know the truth—how was he?"

"Lucy!" Emma feigned shock, but it morphed into more

230

of a grin. "That's a rather inappropriate question."

"That good, huh?"

"We should not be discussing something so personal."

"Nonsense!" exclaimed Lucy. "I have created a unique situation for you—you have no need to marry, which means no man will ever have the authority or the audacity to tell you what to do. You are free to be your own woman and, if you find a man who can put a smile on your face like that after one night in his bed, my dear, have at it. You will hear no judgment on my part. Life is entirely too short to spend with boring men who have no idea how to please a woman with the tool God gave them. But," she wagged a finger, "I will offer one word of warning—John André is not like most men, so be sure while you are enjoying the pleasures of his flesh you are not doing something foolish like falling in love with him. That would be most unfortunate for all concerned."

Emma sat at her vanity after having brushed out her now clean, shiny hair. It had a bit of natural curl to it, making it more wavy than straight, and it hung almost to her waist. She had taken her time having a relaxing, hot bath and dressed in a simple white nightgown. The smell of mint soap lingered in the air, but she found herself having some regret John's scent had been erased from her skin.

Staring into the mirror, memories from the previous night filled her mind and she smiled. The sound of something hitting her window repeatedly interrupted her thoughts. Laying her brush aside, she went over and pulled back the curtains. Seeing the cause of the noise, she opened the window. With one hand resting flat on the sill, and the other flat against her cheek being held by her propped elbow, she called down, "Good evening, Major!"

John's face lit up. "'See how she leans her cheek upon her hand. O, that I were a glove upon that hand, that I might touch that cheek'!"

"What are you doing down there, Romeo?"

"Hoping to get a glimpse of my fair Juliet," he replied. "That, and the fact your aunt might meet me at the front door with a pistol if I did otherwise."

"Well, lucky for you, Aunt Lucy is out playing cards with some of the ladies, so I believe you are safe for the time being. Meet me at the door."

Grabbing a robe, she rushed downstairs and let him in.

John closed the door behind him as his eyes swept over her. Taking her in his arms, he greeted her with a long, greedy kiss. "Dear God, you look like an angel sent straight from above," he stopped to cup her face, "I could not close my eyes tonight without seeing you. I hope you were not in too much trouble with your aunt."

Emma bobbed her head back and forth. "She had a few words to say about the matter, but otherwise, everything is fine."

He took her by the hand and started towards the library,

but Emma stopped, instead pulling him towards the staircase.

"Emma, your aunt will have my hide," he protested.

"You let me worry about her," and she put her arms around his neck.

John hesitated. "I do not want to besmirch your reputation."

"You didn't seem to mind back at the tavern," she retorted. "Are you saying you don't want to take me upstairs right this minute and ravage me in my bed?"

"I never said that," and a slow grin spread across his face.

She pressed her lips to his. "Every minute you spend down here protecting my honor is one moment you could be doing something else much more worthwhile and far more pleasurable."

His eyelids became heavy, laden with desire. "Well, when you put it like that!" John scooped her up and carried her up to her room.

Emma woke sometime in the middle of the night when she heard Lucy come in. Reaching for John, she was disappointed to find the spot where he had been empty. A smile came to her face when she caught a whiff of a scent. Closing her eyes, she went back to sleep and dreamed of his touch.

After making the note drop, Emma was riding back

towards home when she noticed a grim-looking Charlie
speaking with some of the other men in front of the
mercantile. She pulled to a stop when he waved and
started over.

"Good morning, Emma," he said rather solemnly.

"Good morning, Charlie! What's this all about?" she
asked and nodded in that direction.

"Army business. Major André has ordered security
within the city to be tightened. Someone in town is
passing information to the other side by way of a tree in
the park, using it as a drop. We rounded up a list of
suspects this morning, who the Major will be
interrogating."

Emma felt her body go numb, a sense of fear overtaking
her, and black spots filled her sight—the next thing she
knew, she was off her horse and Charlie's arms were
firmly around her, holding her up as he escorted her
inside the nearby coffeehouse.

"Secure her horse!" he shouted to one of the other men
who was holding the door.

Charlie helped her into a chair, wrapped his coat around
her, and knelt before her, his palm on her forehead
looking greatly unsettled. "You don't feel feverish," he
stated, "I will send for the physician."

"What?" She started to come around. "Why would you
do that?"

His face clouded over. "Emma, you practically fell out
of your saddle and you have turned a ghastly shade of

234

gray."

"I'm fine," she said and touched his shoulder. "I—skipped breakfast this morning—that's all. I get like that sometimes when I do."

Charlie turned and called out to Robert Townsend, who was serving coffee that day to bring over something. "Are you certain you aren't ill?"

Emma shook her head. Before she could answer, the front door flung open, and John came inside on a determined path directly towards them. "What is happening here, Captain?" he snapped, his eyes fixed on the coat draped around her.

The young man climbed to his feet. "Emma—Miss Eldridge isn't feeling well, and I brought her inside, Major."

John's concern immediately shifted. "Emma?"

"I'm fine, John. I forgot to eat this morning."

He turned to Charlie. "I will see Miss Eldridge safely home. You are dismissed. I am certain the assignment I have given you is enough to keep you busy for the rest of the day."

Charlie hesitated and looked to Emma for guidance.

She reached over and touched his arm. "I am well in hand with the Major. Thank you for your help, Charlie."

"I will check on you later," he said. "Major!" he acknowledged and turned to go.

"Captain Taylor," he called out, "aren't you forgetting something?" He removed the coat from around Emma

235

and shoved it into his chest. "You are to be in full uniform at all times. No exceptions!"

"Yes, sir," he replied and departed.

John took a seat as Townsend brought over coffee and a plate of freshly baked bread with preserves.

"You don't have to be so rough on him," she scolded. "He was just trying to help me."

"He has work to do." John rested his arms on the table and leaned in. "What happened?"

"Nothing! Really!"

"Tell me the truth, Emma!"

"I didn't eat this morning," she lied.

"Skipping meals seems to have become a habit with you—one that needs to be rectified immediately." He slid the plate over in front of her while keeping a watchful eye. "Eat something, please!"

Emma took a bite of the bread and slowly chewed but her stomach churned as the weight of Charlie's words slammed into her.

"Do you have a busy day ahead?" she inquired, hoping to garner more information.

"I do have quite a bit of tedious business today, but I will make time to see you safely home."

"What kind of shit work did you stick Charlie with?"

"Why do you ask?" John scrubbed his chin and suppressed a grin. "Has he been complaining to you?"

"No, not at all, but I am afraid he may be suffering indirectly because of our relationship. You haven't exactly made a secret of your disdain for our friendship."

John sighed. "You do know he doesn't see you merely as a friend."

Emma was taken aback. "What is that supposed to mean?"

"You really can't see it?" A look of bewilderment crossed the Major's face. "Emma, he is in love with you. I daresay, he probably has been since you were children."

"That's ridiculous!" Emma waved him off. "Our relationship isn't like that."

"It's not to say he doesn't want it to be." He laid his hand over on hers. "I have seen how he looks at you— take it from someone whose job it is to notice little details such as that."

She put her bread down and took a sip of the coffee, obviously bothered by the thought. "Well, I don't have the same feelings for him."

"That's good to know," said John with a smile. "Come on, let me take you home."

He escorted her back to Wolfe Manor and before she opened the door, he caught her by the hand. "I may not be able to see you for a couple of days. I have some pressing business that needs attending, and it may take a considerable amount of time."

"I understand," she said, obviously disappointed.

John stepped closer and touched her face. "It is not because I don't want to see you, I want you to know that." He leaned down and kissed her before opening the door and watching her go inside.

Emma closed the door and rushed into the other room. "Midge! Where is Aunt Lucy?"

"I'm right here," called Lucy from the top of the staircase. "What's the matter?"

"John knows about the drop spot in the park. He has rounded up several people for interrogation."

"Damn it!" exclaimed Lucy, and she descended the steps. "Who?"

"I don't know, but we cannot let someone else pay the price for what we have done."

"Of course not!" She put her arm around Emma. "Did you leave the note at the bakery?"

Emma nodded.

"Don't worry, we will figure something out."

By the end of the day, the word was out. The army had taken six men into custody for questioning and their family members were being told nothing. The entire town was on edge and it had neighbor eyeing neighbor with a deep degree of suspicion.

9
CHAPTER NINE

Two days later, Emma and Lucy were having drinks in the library, each with their own book in hand. Emma had not seen nor heard from John and she had begun to wonder if he had learned something about her that kept him away.

The two women both heard a slight creak of the floor coming from the dining room and they exchanged looks.

Lucy reached for a book on the table beside her and pulled it into her lap. She opened the cover to reveal a loaded pistol she discreetly slid beside her and covered with her skirts.

Emma lifted the top of an ornate box on the table in front of her and removed the insert to pull out a second gun.

They nodded to each other and at the same time, turned to aim at the doorway.

When the man stepped inside and was greeted with the unexpected welcome, he held up his hands. "Wait, Emma! It's me! It's Ben Tallmadge."

Emma let out the breath she was holding and lowered her gun.

Lucy, on the other hand, didn't flinch.

"It's alright, Aunt Lucy!" she assured, "Washington sent him."

"How can you be so sure?" she demanded dubiously.

"He is the one I met with before. You can put the gun down."

Lucy eyed him up and down before reluctantly laying the weapon on the table.

"You must be Mistress Wolfe," said Tallmadge with a grin. "The General said you would be hard to miss."

"Well, George should know," she said with a wink, and without elaborating.

Tallmadge and Emma both turned to give her a peculiar look.

"May I offer you a drink?" asked Lucy, rising from her seat.

"Are we safe meeting here?" he questioned and glanced through the window before moving to close the curtain.

"As safe as anywhere right now." Lucy handed him a filled glass and offered him a seat.

"Thank you. I got your message there was an emergency. What's going on?"

"You have a man reporting to Major André in one of your camps," explained Emma.

"What makes you so sure?"

"The Major confirmed it to me when he stopped me from killing the bastard."

Tallmadge regarded her. "I think you had better tell me

the whole story."

Before she could reply, a knock at the door startled them all.

"I will get rid of whoever that is," said Lucy.

Emma set her glass on the table. "You had better let me go instead." She closed the doors to conceal their guest and looked around. Upon answering, she was more than a little surprised to see Charlie standing there with his hat in his hand.

"Charlie! What are you doing here so late?"

"I wanted to check in on you," he replied and looked around.

"I am not feeling very well," she said and slumped a bit. "Why don't you come back tomorrow?"

"But I was asked to come," he whispered.

"Asked? By whom?"

"That would be me," called out Tallmadge from the door he had cracked open. Waving them over, he said, "Hello Charlie!"

Charlie went over and shook hands with the Major. "It's good to see you, sir."

"And I am very glad to see you!"

Emma closed the door and stared at the two in disbelief. "What the hell is going on?" she demanded.

Tallmadge smiled. "Charlie is with us."

"When you say, 'with us'?" questioned Lucy.

"I have been working for Washington since the beginning of the war," explained Charlie. "I am one of a handful of men loyal to him who were asked to join up with the other side and send information back."

Emma pressed her palm to her forehead. "Oh my God! I am getting a headache. So, you are an agent for Washington in the British army and Finch is an agent for Major André in the Continental."

Lucy put her hands on her hips. "How on Earth do you keep this stuff straight?"

"Ask the women who are living in New York and passing information to Washington?" countered Charlie.

"It all balances out, I suppose," offered Tallmadge with a chuckle.

"How long have you known about me and Lucy?" demanded Emma.

Charlie cringed as Tallmadge answered for him.

"We pulled a few strings and had him sent here after a woman found her way into our camp and made off with some crucial information, including the location of the drop point you were using. We have been trying to get it back ever since, even though I understand this woman is no longer alive."

"Sarah Tate!" muttered Emma, a tinge of guilt in her voice. "You don't have to worry about that information anymore. It was incinerated in a church fire recently."

Charlie folded his arms and narrowed his eyes at her. "Don't tell me you had something to do with that?"

Emma scratched her nose. "I found out about the satchel and its location and was in the process of retrieving it when things went horribly wrong. I am afraid it boiled down to destroying it or letting the British have it. I had to make a quick decision."

Tallmadge looked surprised, but exceptionally pleased. "You did the right thing, and it is a relief to know it is not floating around out there anymore." He went back to explaining about Charlie's presence. "Washington became concerned, not only about that, but when he learned of your accident after our last meeting. He wanted someone to help keep an extra eye on you and to be here if you found yourself in some difficulty."

"How did he—never mind—I don't want to know."

"When he learned we grew up together, he knew it would give me a reason to stay close to you," added Charlie.

"Does Francis know?"

"No, and it must stay that way. Despite the fact he is a Redcoat, Jack is a good man, and they truly love each other. He will take her back to England and give her a good life when this is over. I would not have allowed the marriage to happen if I did not genuinely believe that."

"Yes," agreed Emma, "she deserves some happiness, and the less she knows, the better."

"Wait, who is Finch?" asked Charlie suddenly.

"Sherman Finch is a British agent in Washington's camp and the man who murdered my parents."

Charlie and Tallmadge both seemed stunned by the revelation.

243

"What?" they asked in unison.

Emma pointed toward the library. "Come on! You both might as well hear this at the same time.

When she was done explaining everything, except the part about sleeping with John, she sat back and sighed.

"Dear God, Emma, why did you never tell anyone the man's name?" fussed Charlie, now angry. "He could have paid for what he did to them—to you!"

"Oh, make no mistake, he is going to pay—and I will be the one to make it happen," she promised, no doubt in her words. She slowly took a sip of her drink as if lost in the thought of planning his death.

"First things first," said Tallmadge, "we need to get him out of the position he has wormed his way into. Do you happen to know which camp he is in?"

Lucy got up and went to her desk, returning with a map. "No, but we may have narrowed it down a bit. Perhaps you can fill in the rest." She spread it out on the table before them as Emma laid out the parameters she had established.

Tallmadge and Charlie poured over the map. "There are no major camps out that way, but there are two smaller mobile regiments that fit that bill." Tallmadge looked up. "Do you have the name of his alias, a description, or does he have any identifying marks?"

Emma shook her head. "I am afraid I am the only one who knows what he looks like. It is an image I have carried for thirteen years. You are going to have to take

244

me there so I can point him out and then I want to be the one to kill him."

"Absolutely not, Emma! You will be putting yourself in too much danger and that will not happen on my watch!" Charlie was visibly upset.

"How else are you going to find him, Charlie? Waltz into Major André's office and ask for his name? If he wouldn't tell me, he sure as hell isn't going to tell you. You are not exactly his favorite person."

"Is there something I should know?" questioned a curious Tallmadge.

"The Major has developed a fondness for Emma," grumbled Charlie, "And he doesn't care for her having friends."

"That would be friends of the male persuasion," corrected Lucy.

Tallmadge averted his eyes and drummed his fingers on the desk, the tension in the room rising with the awkward silence.

"There is no other way," Emma finally said.

Lucy chimed in. "I agree with Charlie. I don't like it. How would you even do it? You forget, he knows who you are now—and you did try to kill him."

Tallmadge stroked his chin. "Maybe if we could conceal you somehow, where you could see the men, but they couldn't see you."

"You cannot be serious!" Charlie pushed back. "Washington will have your hide if anything happens to

Emma."

"And the British may win this war if Finch gets a hold of the wrong information. I think it's a risk worth taking, but only if Emma agrees."

"I'm in!"

"NO!" shouted Charlie.

"You have no say in the matter," she said calmly, "It's my decision, and killing that man is worth any risk to me."

Charlie turned to Lucy. "Talk some sense into her!"

Lucy half-smiled. "There is no talking her out of anything when she makes up her mind. Believe me, I learned that a long time ago. Instead, I learned my efforts were better put to use making sure she was as safe as possible when she does make a decision."

"I am going with you!" demanded Charlie.

"You can't!" countered Emma. "You need to stay here and try to protect the people who are being interrogated for what Lucy and I did."

"What's this all about?" inquired an even more concerned Tallmadge.

"Major André has hauled in several citizens for questioning because of the information he received about the drop we were using," explained Emma. "Innocent people."

Charlie shook his head. "There isn't much I can do anyway. Major André is—determined—to root out the guilty party and he is taking a great deal of pleasure in his work."

A shiver went down Emma's spine at his words—John was so gentle and kind with her, but how would he be if he only knew the truth about all she had done?

"You can give him a traitor," suggested Tallmadge.

"And who do you propose we sacrifice?" scoffed Charlie. "That's not how we operate."

"That's not what I meant." Tallmadge gripped his shoulder. "You don't have to produce an actual person—just the premise of one—and lay a trail leading to somewhere they will never follow."

"Oh!" Lucy's face lit up. "That is an excellent thought and one I like the idea of a great deal. Imagine how foolish they will look pursuing a person who doesn't exist. Let me take care of putting that puzzle together."

"Charlie, Emma is right. We need her. I will not let her out of my sight—I give you my word. I will give my life to protect hers if need be." Tallmadge turned to Emma. "Can you come up with a reason to be gone a few days?"

"The Major won't let you out of his sight that long," derided Charlie.

She thought for a moment. "Well, I wasn't feeling well at the coffeehouse, so perhaps my illness just became an extended one that will last a few days."

"He will see right through that!"

"Not if the physician, and her aunt, insists she has no visitors," mused Lucy aloud, "The Major will not dare press the issue with me if I put my foot down especially after—"

"After what?" asked Charlie.

Emma shot Lucy a look of warning.

"Nothing! Nothing!" the older woman said innocently, "I just meant, he will not dare go against the wishes of someone so close to General Clinton."

Charlie turned to look at Emma, his eyes narrowed, but said nothing.

"You are close to General Clinton?" asked Tallmadge.

Lucy patted him on the back. "Oh, you are very young and naive, aren't you?" she sighed. "How else do you think you get the kind of information you get?"

Tallmadge blinked and it dawned on him what she meant. His cheeks flushed red, and he looked down, clearly uncomfortable.

"When shall we go?" Emma asked Tallmadge to change the subject.

"As soon as you are ready."

Lucy held up her hand. "We need to lay a bit of groundwork first. Charlie, run out to Dr. Reade's house and tell him Emma has become extremely ill and we need him to come right away."

"She doesn't look very ill," he pointed out.

"You let me worry about that. Emma, run up and change into a nightgown," she said and looked around the room, "Major Tallmadge and I will be right up."

A few minutes later, Emma stood in her nightgown as

Lucy and Tallmadge came in with a bucket of water.

"What are you going to do with that?"

"Sit down," ordered Lucy, "and put your feet and hands in it."

Emma obeyed and yelped. "This water is freezing."

"And now, so are your feet and hands," explained Tallmadge. "It will make it more believable when you say you have chills."

Lucy reached down and splashed some of the water on the front of her gown. "And the sweats."

"I will have them both at the rate you two are going," Emma fussed and shook herself.

Tallmadge looked her over. "She still looks too healthy." He went over to the fireplace and ran his hand in the cool ash before coming over and rubbing a bit underneath each eye to make darkened circles.

"Excellent idea!" Lucy touched him on the back. "You are a smart man and I like smart men." She went over to Emma's vanity and brought back a bit of powder, using it to make her face appear pale.

"Much better!" said the Major with a smile.

Lucy turned and eyed him up and down. "Say, are you married? Or do you have a sweetheart?"

"No?"

"How do you feel about mature women with a great deal of experience in the boudoir?"

"LUCY!" Emma scolded as Tallmadge's face turned bright red.

249

But her aunt only winked at her and grinned. "Now, you are going to have to sell it. When Dr. Reade gets here, pretend you are on your deathbed." She held back the covers for Emma as she unbound her hair and shook it loose. "Bring me that candlestick."

Tallmadge handed it over and Lucy waved the flame in front of Emma's forehead until they heard the front door open. "Major, hide in the wardrobe."

She set the candlestick aside and Emma laid back, moaning as if in pain.

"Thank goodness you are here, Dr. Reade," said Lucy as the older man and Charlie came inside. "Emma just collapsed, and I am extremely worried."

He immediately went to her bedside, pulled back the covers, and started to examine her. Emma writhed back and forth, making odd noises as if in a delirium.

"She is running a fever," he said, feeling her forehead.

Charlie looked to Lucy questioningly and she simply shrugged in response.

"Her color is terrible, and it appears she has also been sweating quite a bit. Any chills?" He felt her hands and feet.

"Oh yes," answered Lucy, feigning an enormous amount of concern.

"Nausea? Vomiting?"

"She did have a bit of a stomachache?" added Lucy, wondering why she didn't think of that.

"Emma, can you tell me where it hurts?" the doctor

asked.

Emma rolled her head back and forth in response and began to make sounds along the lines of a painful whine as she pulled her knees up to her chest.

"What do you think it is?" asked Lucy.

"It could be any number of things. It doesn't appear to be smallpox. There is no rash, which is a good thing because there have been some small outbreaks nearby. It could be something as simple as something she ate that had gone bad to some other contagious illness that is going around—or it could be something far more serious. I will give you some herbs to brew for a tea for the fever and some laudanum for her discomfort. I think we should give it a couple of days and see if she is any better. If not, we can explore other options. Keep her in bed and I would advise you against allowing any visitors in here in case she is contagious."

"Whatever you say, Doctor!" Lucy escorted him out.

Once he was gone, Tallmadge stepped from his hiding place and Emma got out of bed.

"You have your few days," said Lucy when she returned. "I know there's no point in trying to talk you out of it, so please be careful and make sure you come back in one piece."

Emma embraced Lucy tightly.

Lucy glanced back at Charlie, and said, "I am going to pack a few things for you while you get dressed. Major Tallmadge, would you be so kind as to join me?"

He looked back and forth between Charlie and Emma. "Yes, ma'am!"

Once they were alone, Charlie went over and took her by the arms.

"For the love of God, Emma," he pleaded, "don't do this. We can find another way."

"There is no other way!"

"You are playing with fire, Emma. Major André is not a stupid man, and he will not look the other way if you are found out. If it comes down to you or the army, he will choose the army every time."

"You let me worry about him."

Charlie looked down. "You have not seen the side of him I have. I am sure he is kind, sweet, and doting to you, but that same man ordered Colette Thompson's father beaten to within an inch of his life today in front of her for information she did not possess."

"What?" asked Emma, greatly disturbed by this new piece of information.

"John André is good at his job because he will do whatever it takes to get what he wants. He doesn't love you—not the way I do."

A dumbfounded Emma stared back at him. "You what?"

Charlie took her face in his hands and planted a slow, loving kiss upon her lips. "I have thought about you every day since you left Virginia. I begged Washington to send me here when I learned you might be in danger and would not take 'no' for an answer. Emma, I—"

"Stop!" she whispered. "I can't do this right now. I have one goal and nothing else matters. Now, please leave so I can dress."

A dejected Charlie nodded and left the room, closing the door behind him, leaving Emma to process his words.

10

CHAPTER TEN

Emma and Tallmadge waited until just before dawn
before they made their way out of town on a secret path
to an old game trail that wasn't used much anymore.

"How did Charlie end up on this side of the war
anyway?" she asked that afternoon as they slowly rode
through a denser part of the woods. "His father is
probably rolling in his grave as we speak."

"From the pieces I have put together in the past few
hours, I would say we have you to thank for that," he
revealed.

"Me? Why would you say that? I haven't seen him
since we were children."

Tallmadge stopped to hold back a wayward branch for
her to pass before he answered. "When Charlie joined up,
he said it was because he had seen the damage the British

army had inflicted upon someone he loved, and he wanted to ensure it never happened again." He looked over at her when the path widened, and they were able to ride side by side again. "I take it you and Major André are 'involved'?"

Emma let out a deep sigh, her silence speaking volumes.

"I see," he remarked compassionately. "Forgive me, but I feel the need to ask, even though I am almost afraid to hear the answer—is that relationship because you are using him to your advantage for our cause, or is it because you have fallen in love with him?"

When she didn't respond for a second time, he cleared his throat. "A relationship like that can complicate things a great deal."

"Our relationship changes nothing," she said when she finally spoke. "My loyalty, first and foremost, is always to Washington and the Patriot cause. I want more than anything to see that army driven out of this country and back to England where they belong, with their tails between their legs."

"But the heart wants what it wants," he proclaimed. "I understand more than you know."

"My heart doesn't matter as long as my head is in the game. I am well aware of the risks involved when it comes to Major André and my personal feelings are not part of the equation."

"Which I suppose answers my question," he muttered.

"Careful there, Major. If I didn't know any better, I

255

would say you had some experience in the area," she noted.

He laughed. "I do indeed, although the choice between a woman and my country was made for me and without my consent. Well, you can see where I ended up."

"Do you regret it?"

"Every damn day!" He spurred his horse on ahead. "The camp is on the other side of these trees. Pull up the hood on your cloak and stay here out of sight."

Emma watched Tallmadge ride into the encampment and speak with the Captain in charge.

When he returned, he explained the plan—the Captain would call in each man individually to his quarters. Emma and Tallmadge would be concealed nearby, in a smaller tent, with a clear view of the comings and goings.

"You think this is going to work?"

"It's not an ideal plan," he admitted, "but it's the best I could come up with on short notice. It also ensures I am by your side at all times."

Emma agreed and a little while later, they were settling into a tent that was only big enough to hold a cot.

"I'm sorry for the tight accommodations," apologized Tallmadge, securing the tent flap, leaving just enough of an opening where they could see through to the commander's tent.

"It's fine," she replied and sat down. "It's a small price to pay to catch this guy."

For three hours, they watched to no avail. After the last

man left his tent, Captain Lewis came to join them.

"Is that all of them?" asked Tallmadge.

"Yes! That is every man I have."

"He must be in the other camp. We will ride out in the morning if you can spare this tent for the night."

"Of course! You are welcome to it." Lewis glanced at Emma. "I can round up another if you would like some privacy."

"This is fine," she assured. "Thank you."

John stretched his arms above his head and cracked his neck. The past two days had been long and arduous—and he was no closer to finding the informant who had been sending information to the enemies. He was, however, convinced it was not anyone he had taken into custody given the interrogation techniques he had used on them. He would have to start a new list of suspects, but today, he needed a break. After jotting down a note, he called Nelly into the room.

"Take this to Miss Eldridge at Wolfe Manor and wait for a response," he said as he handed it to her.

"Yes, sir!"

He leaned back in his chair and closed his eyes, dozing off for a bit as his thoughts drifted to Emma. A quiet, private supper alone and a trip up to his bedroom with her was exactly the distraction he needed. He was so relaxed he didn't hear Captain Taylor come in.

"Pardon me, sir," he said after clearing his throat.

257

John rested his arms on his desk and rubbed his eyes. "Yes, Captain, what is it?"

"I may have some useful information for you about the informant."

John got up, his focus back on his work. "What do you have?"

"After speaking with one of the street vendors, I found out there is one man who frequents the park with a keen interest in that tree we do not have on our list of suspects."

"Who is it?"

Charlie brought over a folded piece of paper. "His name is James Saunders. He came to town a few months ago and after asking around, he told some of the townspeople he resided in a home on Baker Street, but when I went there, the house was empty, and the neighbors said it had been for months being as it belonged to a family of known Patriots."

John snatched the page from his hand. "What does he look like?"

"A dark-haired man, clean-shaven, who is somewhere between the age of twenty and thirty."

"That describes half the men in this town," scoffed John angrily.

"I understand, sir, but another man recalled seeing someone by that description meeting with a known sympathizer on an old game trail that leads away from town three days ago."

"Where is he now?" demanded John.

"I have been unable to locate him but given the false address and the company he is keeping. I would venture a guess he might just be our man."

"I want him found and brought directly to me. Put as many men on this as you need."

"Yes, sir!"

Nelly waited at the doorway to be acknowledged.

"You have a response for me?" he asked.

She crossed the room and handed it to him.

"Do whatever it takes, Captain Taylor," he said and read the reply. "What the—"

"Is something wrong, sir?" asked Charlie.

John looked up. "Captain Taylor, do you know anything about Miss Eldridge being ill?"

"Yes, sir. Her aunt sent me to fetch the physician last evening."

"What's wrong with her?" he questioned, greatly concerned.

"A fever, sweats, chills, and some stomach pain. The doctor isn't sure what is causing it."

"That will be all," mumbled John, lost in his thoughts. "Show yourself out, Captain!"

"Yes, sir!"

As soon as Charlie was gone, John went to the hall, grabbed his hat, and rushed out the door.

Charlie watched nervously from outside as the Major headed in the direction of Wolfe Manor.

"Major André," greeted Lucy when she answered the door, "what can I do for you?"

"Mistress Wolfe, I just received your note and I have come to see Emma."

"I am afraid that is not possible, Major."

"If she is ill," he protested, "I wish to be by her side."

"Yes, Major, but my niece is finally asleep after an extremely long night, and I will not disturb her for you or anyone else." He tried to push past her, but she stopped him with a firm hand to the chest. "Furthermore, there is a chance she is contagious, and I will not risk anyone else getting sick. I am sure she will let you know when she is feeling better."

"I understand you are upset with me for keeping Emma out the other night, but if you are using this as a reason to keep us apart—"

Lucy put her finger in his face and cut him off. "Are you insinuating I am making this up?"

"The timing is rather suspect, don't you think?"

"Perhaps it was your little excursion that got her ill to begin with," she fired back. "I saw the state of her clothing the next day and it looked like she had been rolling around in the mud. I am assuming she didn't do it alone."

"I can explain, Mistress Wolfe," he said in an apologetic voice with his eyes downcast.

"There is no need for that!" Lucy stepped closer. "My

260

niece is a grown woman, and she can see whomever she likes whenever it suits her. I would not dream of trying to tell her what to do. If she chooses not to see you, have no doubt, it is only because it is precisely what she wants—and if you think I am lying about her illness, feel free to consult with Dr. Reade." She closed the door in his face and called out, "Good day, Major André!"

John placed his hat on his head and stormed off.

Tallmadge slept on his bedroll on the ground while Emma took the cot. She was uncomfortable and couldn't seem to settle in, so she lay awake listening to the sounds of the camp. She leaned over to see Tallmadge fast asleep and wondered if all soldiers slept that soundly on the ground.

Her thoughts drifted to Charlie and she turned on her side. She had no idea he had feelings for her, especially ones that ran so deep and for so long. Charlie had been one of her best friends as a child and, even after being apart for so long, they had easily picked right back up where they had left off. Spending time with him made her happy.

It occurred to her his appearance had put a small piece back in her soul, one that had been taken away when she left Virginia—and then there was the matter of John.

She had feelings for him—maybe even loved him—but what kind of future could they possibly have together? She could never be completely honest with him and if she were, he would see it as a betrayal—not that she could ever trust him completely either.

John used sex with women as a tool and there wasn't anything he could do to completely convince her his feelings for her were real—if they even were. He was skilled at playing parts, and he very well could be doing exactly that to meet his own physical needs. Living a life filled with constant doubts didn't exactly make for a happy one.

Emma pulled the blanket over her head and closed her eyes. She was trying to go to sleep when she heard it—a conversation just outside their tent between the Captain and a voice she recognized.

"What took you so long?" asked Captain Lewis.

"The other regiment moved, and it took a while to find them. What did I miss?"

"Major Tallmadge is here with a young woman looking for a traitor who has entrenched himself in one of the camps and has been sending secrets back to the British. They didn't find him, so they will be moving on to the next encampment in the morning."

"A young woman, you say?"

"Yes, and she is quite easy on the eyes," noted the officer in charge.

"Is the Major sweet on her?"

The Captain laughed. "Well, they are sharing a tent right now."

"Really? Who is she?"

"Her name is 'Emma', and that is all I know."

"Well, good for him," the man said with a chuckle, "I am going to look for some supper. Good night!"

"Good night, George. See you in the morning!"

Emma reached over and shook Tallmadge awake.

"What is it?" he asked sleepily.

"He's here," she whispered.

"Who?"

"Sherman Finch!" she growled. "I just heard him outside. The Captain called him 'George'."

Tallmadge sat straight up and reached for his pistol. On his feet, he went outside and returned with the Captain.

"Who is George?" he demanded.

"He is my second in command. He just returned from running some errands. Why?"

"It's him," said Emma, putting on her shoes and reaching for her gun.

"That's not possible," he argued. "George Fields has been part of our army since the beginning."

"He has been a planted spy since the war began," she said and got up. "Where is his tent?"

Stunned beyond words, Captain Lewis led them to one in the middle of the camp.

Tallmadge rushed in with his pistol cocked only to find it empty. "He is not here!"

"Find George Fields and bring him to me!" shouted the Captain, and all the men scrambled to attention. A thorough search revealed him and his horse both gone.

"Get after him!" ordered Lewis.

Tallmadge kicked at the dirt. "You are wasting your time. He is long gone, and you will never find him in the dark."

Tallmadge escorted her back to the tent and she slammed her gun down on the cot.

"NO!" screamed Emma. "Damn it! This cannot be happening again!"

"I'm sorry, Emma," offered Tallmadge sincerely.

"Where will he go?"

"Probably back to the British army after he lays low for a while. I will send the word out in case he tries to join up with another regiment and we will offer a reward for his capture."

She sat down and dropped her face in her hands. "I am tired of waiting!"

"I understand," he said and sat down next to her. Taking a flask from his coat, he took off the top and handed it to her. "If it makes you feel any better, we learned a hard lesson here today—the enemy is always closer than we think, and sometimes right under our own noses."

"Mistress Wolfe, I must insist upon seeing Emma and having the army surgeon see to her," said John, pushing the front door open wide and barging in with another man following close behind the next afternoon.

"MAJOR ANDRÉ! This is outrageous! What do you

264

think you are doing?" Lucy attempted to block him. "Dr. Reade has already seen to her."

"Forgive me if I want a second opinion," he snapped. "I wouldn't let that man treat a dog. I just need to see she is receiving proper treatment," he said as he climbed the stairs.

"You most certainly will not!" she shouted and chased after them. "You will leave my household to me!" She was three steps away when he reached for the doorknob. "Major André, DO NOT open that door or General Clinton will hear of it!" she threatened.

"So be it," he replied and threw it open.

The next day, they made the long journey back to the city and Tallmadge managed to get her to the back entrance of the house unnoticed. "Thank you for all your help, Emma, and I am sorry it didn't go as well as we would have liked, but I hope you will take some comfort in knowing he is no longer able to help the enemy. I give you my word, we will not rest until we find him." He planted a kiss on her hand. "We are, as always, in your debt, and don't hesitate to send for us if you need us."

"Thank you, Major Tallmadge!"

He offered her a smile as she watched him slip away.

Lucy stepped inside just as John yanked back the covers. Lucy tried to think of a reasonable explanation for why Emma wasn't in that bed when she heard the greatest sound to ever grace her ears — "John?"

"Emma," he said softly and touched her face. "I have been worried to death about you."

Lucy looked towards the ceiling and silently thanked God she was there.

"Are you *quite* satisfied?" asked Lucy angrily, crossing her arms and tapping her foot impatiently.

"I want Dr. Phillips to look her over," John replied firmly.

"I am feeling much better, really," assured Emma. "I am just still extremely tired."

Dr. Phillips came around, felt her forehead, and asked her a few questions as John hovered by with Lucy shooting daggers in his direction.

"I think Miss Eldridge is going to be just fine," agreed the doctor.

"Thank you," said John.

Lucy wiped an imaginary bead of sweat from her forehead for only Emma to see. "I will show you out, Dr. Phillips, while Major André has exactly five minutes to visit with my niece before I throw him out on his derriere," she announced loudly with determination.

"You shouldn't upset her like that," said Emma when Lucy and the doctor had gone.

"I will offer her my sincerest apologies," he promised and took her hand. "I was concerned about you and I could wait no longer."

"I just need—" she paused.

"What do you need, my sweet?" he asked and lightly stroked her face. "If it is within my power, you shall have it."

Emma curled on her side and burrowed into her pillow. "Just some rest, that's all."

John searched her face, certain there was something else bothering her, but he didn't press the matter. He kissed her forehead and brushed back her hair. "Then rest, my darling, and I will see you tomorrow—if your aunt doesn't gut me with a knife on my way out."

"Better keep your back to the stair rail!" she suggested and smiled despite herself.

He kissed her again and slowly closed the door behind him on his way out.

Emma met Lucy downstairs after John left.

"That was a little too close," said Lucy and collapsed in one of the chairs. "Well?" she asked anxiously.

"We found him, but he got away," she replied, void of emotion and drained of energy.

"Oh, sweetheart, I'm so sorry."

"Me, too. Twice now, I have missed my chance."

"Well, the third time is a charm," said Lucy with a smile. "I am just glad you are home safe."

Emma kissed her aunt on the cheek. "I'm tired and I am going to bed. I will see you in the morning."

"Good night, sweetheart!" As she started up the stairs,

Lucy called out, "I don't suppose that handsome Major Tallmadge is hiding upstairs somewhere, perhaps in the wardrobe in my room if there be a God?"

Shaking her head, Emma laughed. "No, he is gone."

"Damn!"

11
CHAPTER ELEVEN

One week later, Emma joined John for a late supper at his house. Still upset Finch had slipped through their fingers, she picked at her food, moving it around on her plate.

John wiped his mouth with his napkin. "Is the food not to your liking?"

"No, it's fine. I suppose my appetite isn't completely back yet."

Topping off her wine glass, he studied her. "Your illness was very odd. It came on suddenly and went just as quickly. Any idea what caused it?"

"It could have been anything I suppose."

"You seem very downhearted, and it is so unlike you," he pointed out. "Is there anything I can do to lighten your mood?"

Emma laid her fork aside. "I believe there actually is something you can do."

He moved his plate out of the way and rested his

forearms on the table, giving her his full attention. "Name it!"

She reached for his hand. "Take me upstairs and make me forget about everything wrong in this world for the rest of the night."

A slow smile spread across his face. Sliding his chair back, he stood and held out his hand. "Happily!"

True to his word, he spent the night making love to her and saw her home early the next morning.

"Your aunt is never going to forgive me now," he whispered in her ear.

"Probably not," she laughed, in a much better mood. "I had better go in alone from here."

"Alright!" He kissed her and started down the steps.

Emma turned and noticed the front door slightly ajar, which was most unusual, and a faint metallic smell wafting through the air. Lucy was a fanatic about keeping that door closed and secured. A strange, unsettling feeling suddenly washed over her.

"John?" she called over her shoulder.

He was near the street but stopped. "Forget something?"

"Can you come back here please?"

Something about the tone of her voice caused him to hurry. "What is it?"

"The door is unlocked, and it shouldn't be." She pushed it wide open and gasped when she noticed spots of a red, sticky liquid on the floor. She went to take a step inside, but John grabbed her by the arm, preventing her.

"Don't! Stay on the porch!" he ordered and went down to the street to call for some men.

Emma ignored him and went inside anyway. The house was unusually quiet, even for that time of the morning. Midge should have been rattling around in the dining room while she and Aunt Lucy were catching up on the latest scuttlebutt from town. Jacob should have also been in right about now asking if any of the horses would be needed for the day. Something was not right.

Following the trail into the library, she saw more of the red color on the floor, only here it was near flowing as if a bucket had spilled paint. There were a few chairs knocked over and something was in front of the fireplace that should not have been there. What was it?

Emma stepped around, careful not to put her foot in whatever those red puddles were, knowing her Aunt Lucy was going to have a fit when she learned someone had tracked up her expensive carpets. Making her way over to investigate, she stopped when her mind registered what her eyes now saw. She fell to her knees and screamed when she realized what lay before her—was her beloved Aunt Lucy in a bloody, mangled heap on the floor, eerily still, her eyes fixed open with a terrified expression locked on her face.

"Aunt Lucy?" she whispered and crawled over to the woman, gently pulling her head onto her lap. Stroking her now cold, blue-tinged face, she repeated, "Aunt

271

Lucy?" When she received no response, the dam holding back the tears burst and she unleashed a miserable howl that echoed throughout the hallways of Wolfe Manor.

John entered but stopped short at the sight of the horrific scene before him. Blood covered much of the room, including the wall and the furniture. He could see a knife laying on the nearby table, seemingly placed on display to be found. Lucy was on the floor in front of the fireplace, laid open from just beneath her breasts down. Emma was desperately holding onto the only part of her still intact.

Lucile Wolfe's life had been ended by a brutal attack, her insides having been dragged across the floor.

A few soldiers followed him in, averting their eyes from the monstrous deed that had been carried out, most unable to hold down their breakfast.

John ordered them to search the house before going over to Emma.

Kneeling beside her, he tried to get her to come out of the room with him and away from the carnage. "Emma, we need to go outside until we have secured the house," he said gently. "You do not need to see anymore."

She didn't hear him, only shook her head back and forth, muttering, "No! No! No! Not you, too! Please Aunt Lucy, just tell me you are fine. I need you. I can't do this alone. Your eyes are open, so you must only be hurt. We will send for Dr. Reade and he will come and fix you right up."

John tried to take her by the arms, but she shoved him off.

"NO!" she shouted angrily. "I won't leave her here like this alone. She hates being alone and can't you see she is cold and afraid? Tell Midge to bring her a whisky. That will warm her up—and get her some clean clothes. You know how she is about her appearance and this stain on her gown will simply not do. She will be mortified if General Clinton sees her like this."

John took a step back, and for the first time in his life, was at a complete loss on how to comfort a woman who needed him now more than ever.

Emma was in shock and her mind was on the verge of shattering.

Charlie suddenly appeared at the doorway. "Dear God!" he exclaimed as he looked around.

"Major André," said one of the soldiers who had returned.

John went over to him and he whispered something in his ear.

"Keep searching," he said to the man, who wasted no time getting out of the room.

"Emma, please come with me," begged John as he went back over to her. "You shouldn't be inside the house right now."

She ignored him.

Charlie walked over to her and placed his hands on her shoulders. "Emma?" Something about his voice brought her around.

"Charlie?" She leaned back into his touch, and something in her demeanor shifted. "Charlie, it's happened again," she cried. "Why does this keep happening? Why do the people I love keep ending up like this?"

"I don't know, but I am here for you now just like I was before—like I will always be."

She turned to face him, and he wrapped his arms around her comfortingly as she sobbed against his chest. "Come on, sweetheart," he said and helped her to her feet, "We need to get you out of here." Charlie was able to guide her outside.

John watched them go, stung by the fact another man was able to get through to Emma when he couldn't. Deciding to help her another way, he surveyed the butchery in the room, looking for some clue as to who was responsible for it. He took a handkerchief from his coat and went over to pick up the knife when his eyes came to rest on something on the floor at the foot of the table. Words had been scribbled in blood and he moved closer for a better look.

I will be seeing you soon, Emma Eldridge!

Those same words echoed in his mind because he had heard them before.

John felt the bile rise in the back of his throat and he

intuitively knew who had done this—Sherman Finch. He had come for Emma and when he didn't find her, he had left a distinct message instead. "I will kill you myself!" he vowed vehemently.

He went out onto the porch where Charlie had taken Emma to sit on a bench. The young man's arms were still around her and her face was buried against his chest as she wept. Some of the men had come back outside.

"Can someone go fetch my sister, Francis—Jack Donald's wife—please?"

"I'll go," offered a young man who looked as if he were trying to keep down the contents of his stomach, grateful for any excuse to get away.

Another man came through the door. "We have two more bodies, much the same as the first," he said in a low voice to John. "A woman in the kitchen and a man in the stable."

Emma's head snapped up, her eyes red and swollen. "Midge and Jacob too? Why would someone have done this? Who is despicable enough to do something as horrible as this to them?"

John wiped his mouth with his hand and closed his eyes. "Captain Simmons, I want this town sealed off and every available soldier searching for a man by the name of Sherman Finch. He may also be using the alias 'George Fields'. Have someone go to my house and bring my art supplies so I can sketch out a likeness. I want him found and brought to me. No one rests until he is caught."

"Yes, sir!" The Captain rushed off and started barking orders.

Emma pushed away from Charlie. "Finch? What makes you think he did this?"

John swallowed hard and blew out a deep breath. "He left a message inside."

"What message?" Emma stood up and rushed through the door into the library before John could stop her. "EMMA!" he shouted.

By the time John and Charlie reached her, she was on her knees in front of the words. "This is your fault," the words barely audible.

John reached for her. "Emma, please!"

She turned to glare at him, her face full of disbelief and rage. "If you had let me kill him when I had the chance, this never would have happened."

"Dear God, Emma!" he retorted, obviously stunned by her declaration. "Do you think for one minute I would have stopped you if I thought something like this would happen?"

"But you did!"

She slowly got to her feet and stormed past John and Charlie to the front porch.

Francis met her there and took her into her arms. "Oh, Emma! I am so sorry!"

Emma collapsed against her. "He did it again, Francis. The same man who took my parents took Aunt Lucy away from me as well."

276

Tears sprang to both their eyes. "You are coming home with me," said Francis, "and Charlie will stay with us as well. We will all be together again."

"She should stay with me," insisted John firmly. "I can keep her safe."

Emma looked to John, all emotion gone from her face. "I want to go with them," and she walked towards the street, Charlie close on her heels.

"Don't take it personally, Major," said Francis. "She just needs to be with us because we are familiar. We have been through this with her before and we will get her through it again. Perhaps your time is best spent finding the one responsible. That man has taken entirely too much from her already."

"You are correct, Mrs. Donald. Sherman Finch has forfeited his life. The only question now is how he will meet his fate. I will have men watching your home around the clock until he is found."

Francis nodded and started away.

"Mrs. Donald, take care of her, and if she asks for me—"

"I will send for you right away, Major."

"Thank you," he said as he stared after Emma.

Charlie remained by her side, holding her hand the rest of the day as Francis turned away person after person who came to offer their condolences. Emma was simply too upset to accept visitors, refusing to see even John.

That night, when darkness fell and the real pain set in,

Francis and Charlie laid in bed with her and held her as her grief was unleashed in a torrent. The sound was so unnerving, Jack went outside to escape the pitiful mewl, only to find he could hear it out there, as well. Even the men outside on guard duty seemed shaken, some wiping a few tears of their own for the poor woman's grievous loss.

By the time the funeral rolled around, Emma had no more tears to shed, and her grief had been replaced with something more tangible—a pure, unadulterated hatred with a need for vengeance— and nothing would stop her this time.

Emma stood alone by the three coffins soon to be lowered into the ground—the funerals had been scheduled as soon as possible due to the gruesome nature of the deaths. Everyone else had gone nearly an hour ago, except Charlie, who hovered nearby and, John, who approached.

"Emma," he said softly, when he reached her side, "I have not had the chance to offer my sincerest condolences. I came to the Donald's home several times but was turned away."

"I'm sorry, John. I wasn't really in the mood to see anyone."

"That's completely understandable and I know I am probably the last person you wanted to see anyway. I want you to know, if I had any inclination this would have happened, I would have put a bullet in his heart myself that day without a second thought. It weighs heavily on my conscience, and I hope someday you can forgive me."

"I don't need to forgive you because I don't blame you, John," she said softly, "And I am sorry I said those words to you that day. If I am being perfectly honest, I blame only myself."

"The only one to blame is Sherman Finch," spat John.

"Any sign of him?" she asked, staring down at the overturned soil.

"No," he replied, "but General Clinton wanted me to assure you we will not rest until he is found. He has assigned men specifically to the task of finding that bastard."

"Tell him not to bother," she leaned down and lightly touched the carved mahogany casket with a rose design holding her beloved Lucy, "I will take care of Finch myself."

"Emma! You cannot be serious. You have had a terrible shock, and you are not thinking clearly," he warned.

"Oh, John, my head has never been clearer," she assured. "You see, I have nothing left to lose, and a woman who finds herself in that position is an extremely dangerous creature to tangle with."

"Where are you going?" he asked when she stood and started away.

"Home! Where else would I go?"

He reached for her hand. "Stay with me tonight or let me come stay with you. Please! I want to be here for you."

Emma reached up and touched his face lovingly. "I need some time, John. Too much has happened, and I have a great many feelings to work through."

John planted a sweet kiss on her lips. "I understand," he said—and he did. He understood she would never look at him the same way again. A part of her would always blame him for what happened to her aunt whether she admitted it or not, and it was a hard thing for his heart to accept.

Emma sucked in a deep breath and opened the front door. She had not been back to the house since that day. Stepping into the library, a deep disappointment and sadness filled her when Lucy didn't step around the corner with a drink in hand to make some witty remark. Moving to the front of the fireplace, she knelt and touched the spot where Lucy had passed. There was no sign anything had ever happened—every drop of blood was gone, as it was from the rest of the room like nothing had ever happened. Emma jumped, startled, when she heard footsteps in the hall.

"I thought you might not want to be alone," she heard Charlie say, "but I can go if you like."

"You can stay," she said as she stood up and looked

around. "Aunt Lucy had so many things and a story for each one." She picked up a book of poetry from the table. "Some gentleman gave her this when he fancied her. She said it was the most boring thing she had ever tried to read, much like the man who gifted it." Setting it back down, she turned. "You know it has just now occurred to me I have no idea what happened to my parent's personal items that were in the house that day. I never went back after their deaths."

Charlie crossed the room. "I can answer that. When your Aunt Lucy came to bring you to New York, she had all their things packed up and sent to one of the family homes—near Fredericksburg, I believe. I suppose she thought you might want to have them one day."

"I do!"

"You are not going to stay here alone tonight, are you?" he asked, his eyes sweeping the room.

"I am. It is my home." The truth was, she didn't want to stay there, but she knew if Finch found out she was alone, he would come after her, and she would be ready for him.

"I can stay with you," he offered.

"Oh, Charlie," she reached out and touched his face.

Closing his eyes, he buried his cheek in her palm and delighted in her touch.

"My sweet Charlie who has been there for me in my darkest days."

"I want to be here for *all* your days," he whispered and

slowly moved to press his lips to hers.

She did not resist but instead accepted and encouraged his action.

Still absorbed in his kiss, Emma pushed the coat from his shoulders before pulling his face closer to hers. He pulled back and gazed into her eyes, a question in the air. She responded by untying the front of her gown and pushing it down. Taking his hand, she pressed it to her breast and used her other hand to pull his face to her chest.

Covering her with kisses, he picked her up and carried her upstairs to her bedroom where she spent the next few hours lost in him—mind, body, and soul.

Just before sunset, she got up and wrapped her robe around her before going to the window and looking out. "You should go," she said.

"Go? You want me to leave?" he asked and sat up.

"Yes."

"Emma, I am sorry," he apologized, confused and visibly upset. "I thought this was what you wanted."

She came back over and touched his face, smiling. "It was! I just want to be alone with my memories tonight, that's all."

He relaxed a bit. "Are you sure that is a good idea?"

"I know what I am doing. Now, go on before you get in trouble for lazing on the job."

He reached for his breeches. "I suppose I will officially be on Major André's shit list now," he said with a chuckle. "Although I have to admit, it's worth it."

"Well then, it's a good thing you work for the other side," she pointed out, as she watched him dress.

"Promise you will send for me if you become afraid, need anything, or just want some company."

Emma kissed him. "I promise."

Once she was alone, Emma went to her wardrobe and opened the false back. Pulling out her pistols, she packed them with powder and slid them under the covers on her bed. Going over to the window, she leaned against the sill and announced, "I am here! Come and get me, you bastard."

12
CHAPTER TWELVE

It had been three days since the funeral, and no one had seen hide nor hair of Sherman Finch.

Emma sat at her aunt's desk staring blankly into nothingness and barely listening to the words the attorney was saying. "I will just get you to sign the paperwork if that is all agreeable," said Mr. Barlow. "Miss Eldridge?"

"I am sorry, could you repeat that?"

He pushed a document over in front of her. "Of course! I just need you to sign here, so all the Wolfe family assets can be transferred to you. I have a complete accounting of everything put together in a report for you."

Emma picked up her quill, dipped it in the ink, and signed.

"Very good!" he said and shook the pounce over the ink. "It all belongs to you now."

"Thank you," she said and stood to show him out.

As the attorney walked away, a soldier approached. "I have a message for you, Miss Eldridge." He handed it to her and was off.

"Thank you."

She recognized the seal as John's and tore it open as she

went back inside. Her heart rate quickened when she read the words.

My Dearest Emma,
I need to see you. I have information to share with you about Sherman Finch. Come to my home as soon as you can.

John

It was near five o'clock when she knocked on the door. When no one responded, she tried again, more urgently. Finally, Nelly answered. "Yes ma'am?"

"I am here to see Major André."

Nelly sighed and glanced towards the parlour. "He is not to be disturbed," she stated as if she had grown weary of repeating the same phrase over and over.

Emma held up the note. "He sent for me."

"This evening?" She seemed confused.

Emma nodded and noticed the closed pocket doors. "Is he in there?"

"He is not alone, Miss Eldridge," she whispered.

"I don't care!" Emma threw the doors open wide.

John was absorbed in a young woman reclining on the sofa. The lady made a startled sound and quickly smoothed her gown when she saw they had company.

John recoiled and dropped his head in shame. "Emma, I can explain!"

"Don't bother. I'm sure it's only business," she snarked, not even a little upset. Looking to the woman, she demanded, "Do you know anything about a man named Sherman Finch or George Fields?" The woman shook her head. "Then, get out!"

When the woman looked to John for some guidance, Emma grabbed her by the arm and pulled her to her feet. "The back exit is that way!" she pointed and shoved her in that direction.

"Do you need anything?" asked Nelly cautiously from the doorway after watching the exchange.

"No, you can go for the evening," replied John. "Emma, what are you doing?" He went over and poured himself a drink. "Did you come here because you wanted to see me or just to look for information?"

"You're the one who sent for me, so tell me what you know!" She paced the floor, not even taking the time to remove her cloak.

John gave her a peculiar look and sipped from the glass. "What do you mean? I didn't send for you!"

Emma stalked over and held up the note.

After setting the glass aside, he unfolded it and read it. "Emma, I didn't write this!"

"It had your seal on it!" she said, and they exchanged worried looks.

John went over to his desk and opened the drawer to find his stamp was not in its usual place. He closed it and opened another, reaching for a gun he kept there. "We need to get out of here now!"

"Oh, don't rush off so soon," Finch spoke from the door, pointing a pistol at them. "We have so much to discuss." He had come in the way the woman had exited and caught them off guard.

John took Emma by the hand when he saw her body tense, ready to rip the man apart with her bare hands, gun or not.

"The only thing we have to discuss is the matter of your death!" spat Emma, "As far as I am concerned, the more pain involved, the better."

"Awe, are you a little upset about your auntie? I thought I was doing you a favor. You are an extremely wealthy woman thanks to me. The least you could do is show me some gratitude."

John felt her about to lunge and stepped directly between her and Finch to prevent it.

"What is all this?" demanded John. "Why did you leave your post to come here and do this?"

"I was forced to! Did your lady friend forget to tell you what she did?" he taunted, "I expect there is a whole lot she hasn't told you."

John turned to look at Emma. "What's he talking about?"

Emma's eyes narrowed on Finch. Her hatred was so completely focused on him that John wasn't entirely sure she even heard him ask.

"I will tell you what she did. After you forced her to let

me go, she went to your counterpart, Major Tallmadge, and told him there was a traitor among them. She even went so far as to accompany him to my regiment to point me out. Fortunately, I was away from camp at the time and caught word of it as I arrived back giving me time to get away."

All the pieces suddenly fell into place and John realized the New York 'leak' he had been searching for had been right under his nose, and in his bed, the entire time. "What have you done, Emma?" he asked in disbelief.

Her eyes shifted to him. "I'm sorry John, but I told you I would do whatever I had to do to make this man pay and I meant it. You wouldn't give him to me, but I knew they would, so I did what I had to do."

"What else have you told my counterpart?" he questioned.

Finch rolled his eyes and motioned them to sit with the gun.

When Emma didn't budge, John forced her to move.

"What is your endgame here, Finch?" demanded John. "What do you want?"

"There is only one witness to the murders I committed thirteen years ago and the two of you are the only ones on the British side who can identify me. Let's just say, I am bettering my odds for starting a new life under a new name."

"You think you will get very far after killing us?"

"Indeed, I do," said Finch and leaned against the arm of

288

a chair. "You see, I have had a great deal of time to think this through. I take it that piece of paper in your hand is the note Miss Eldridge received?"

John studied him as he snatched it from his grasp, and he continued to speak.

"You see, you invited her over this evening—this note being the proof—and the two of you will have a little lover's spat, after all, you did just have another woman here in your parlour. Everyone knows John André has not met a woman he could not, and would not, seduce. In a fit of jealous rage, she will accidentally kill you. Miss Eldridge, upon realizing what she has done and still out of her mind with grief over the death of her aunt, will find herself unable to live with the guilt, whereupon she will place this pistol, which is standard issue to the British army," he held it up, "to her head and pull the trigger. Of course, there will be a note explaining everything written in her hand. By the time an inquest is performed, and anyone suspects anything any different, I will be on a boat bound for England with a different name to start a new life."

"You have no proof we are lovers and anyone doing this investigation will see right through that," derided Emma.

"You are absolutely correct, Miss Eldridge, so when the two of you are found in bed together, they will have irrefutable evidence," he grinned sadistically, "and don't worry, I will make sure you have the 'just fucked' look before I kill you. Now, if the two of you will join me upstairs."

Emma looked to John with a surprising calmness on her face.

"Come on," he said and waved the gun. "Or I can blow your brains out now and just carry you up later. I have no issue getting blood on my hands, but I guess you already know that by the message I left you," he provoked.

"Let her go and just take me. I will get you whatever you need to get you out of the country, and you can kill me when I'm done," offered John.

"And I suppose she will just keep her mouth shut?"

Emma sneered. "There isn't one chance in Hell of that, and I will NEVER stop coming after you until you are dead. That is a promise I intend to keep!"

"Emma, shut your mouth!" warned John. "Let me deal with him."

"Like you dealt with him before?" she stood and faced John, her back to Finch as if he weren't there. "The problem is you thought you could control him, but you were dead wrong." She locked eyes with John and when he looked back, she cut her eyes to the fireplace where a poker was leaned against it, about a foot from her reach. Taking her meaning, he decided to ramp up the argument.

"Me? What about you running off to the enemy? What else did you tell them? Did you offer your body to get what you wanted?"

Emma growled and sidestepped a couple of inches,

glancing to see where she needed to be to strike a blow. "So what if I did? It's my body and I can do what I want with it. It's not like you haven't been with other women."

"That's different!"

Finch watched the two go back and forth, seemingly amused by the turn the argument had taken.

"Why is there always a different set of rules for women?" She wandered closer and managed to wrap her fingers around the handle. "When men bed a lot of women, they are heroes to other men, but let a woman bed any man she wants, and she becomes a whore!"

Leaning back to give her some room, he said, "Whores get paid, but I guess you got paid with information," he pressed to give her a reason to move closer to Finch.

"You fucking bastard!" she shouted and pretended to start towards John, but instead pivoted and swung the poker, hitting Finch directly in the nose with it causing an audible 'crack'.

When she reared back to do it again, he caught the iron, wrenched it from her hand, and threw it aside.

John attempted to rush him, but Finch was quick on his feet—he raised the gun and pressed it to his temple just as John reached him.

"Move and he dies, now rather than later!" Finch spat blood from his mouth and used his sleeve to wipe the steady stream from his nose before using his free hand to strike Emma hard across the face, knocking her to her knees. "Get her up and take her upstairs now!"

John reached for her arm while keeping an eye on Finch. "Emma," he said softly.

She rested on her knees for a bit, before letting him help her up. Dizzy, she could feel her face starting to swell as the taste of blood filled her mouth.

John wrapped his arm around her waist and slowly guided her towards the staircase as Finch followed. "Did it feel good to do it?" he whispered.

"Not good enough. Hold me tighter, John," she said and leaned against him. As he tightened his grip, a slow smile spread across his face. Once they reached John's bedroom, Finch slammed the door and sat down in one of the chairs. John stood protectively in front of Emma.

"Undress! Both of you!" he ordered.

"Fuck you!" she shouted over John's shoulder.

"Actually, I am going to fuck *you*, but we need to do a few things first. Major André, do you prefer to be strangled or bashed over the head?"

"Neither would be my first choice, but I suppose strangulation would be the cleaner of the two."

"Bashed over the head it is," sneered Finch and leaned back to try and stop the gush of blood from his nose.

"At least allow me the opportunity to say a proper 'goodbye' to Emma so I may taste the lips of a woman one last time before I leave this world," he proposed.

Finch regarded the two for a moment. "Fine! Get on with it!"

John turned to face Emma and smiled. Placing his hands

on her hips underneath her cloak, he said, "Emma, I hope you know you aren't just another woman to me. I care for you a great deal and I will always have feelings for you."

"I know John, and I feel the same way about you." She rested her forehead on his chest, and he wound his arms around her waist. "I hope you understand why I have done the things I have done. It was never to spite or hurt you—I was doing what I had to do to accomplish the only thing I have ever wanted more than anything in this life, now more than ever."

John took her into a long, passionate kiss, carefully tugging free the concealed pistol that was hooked in the belt at the small of her back, hidden by the gathers in her cloak. He discretely pulled it around until it was between them and used the words, "I understand completely," to cover the sound of him pulling back the hammer and cocking the gun. He brushed the hair back from her forehead, kissed the top of her head, and nodded. Emma took the pistol from his hand, smiled, and raised it just as he stepped to the side and out of the way.

Without hesitation, she squeezed the trigger.

The smell of gunpowder, the sound of the gun going off, and a cloud of thick smoke filled the room, taking a moment to clear. She watched and waited to see the results with bated breath as everything moved in slow motion. The shot was straight and true to its path—a direct hit to the center of the chest.

Finch looked down and began to tremble as a red

blossom bloomed across his breast and his gun slipped from his hand to the floor. He lifted his gaze and stared directly into her eyes as he slumped forward. His body convulsed and it was over—he lay dead, a stunned expression on his face—an unexpected ending he never saw coming.

"Give my regards to the Devil, you bastard!" Emma spat out the words, standing over his lifeless body. She dropped the pistol to the floor and began to shake. Collapsing to her knees in a heap, she blew out the breath she had been holding. She looked to John as the tears streamed down her cheeks.

He knelt and wrapped his arms around her, and she leaned into him.

"It's over! It's finally over!" she half-sobbed, half-laughed.

"Yes, it is!" John kissed the top of her head and held her until he heard men rushing through the front door. He helped her up and led her into the hall, shouting to the men who had made their way upstairs, brought by the sound of the gunshot.

"Sherman Finch is dead. Remove that filthy bastard from my house and dump his body in a gully somewhere for the vultures to pick clean. It is far more than he deserves."

An hour later, Emma sat on the sofa downstairs drinking a glass of whisky while John tended to the business at hand. She looked up to see Charlie standing over her.

He pointed to the bruising on her face. "That looks like it hurts."

"It hurts a lot less with whisky," she retorted with a grin and reached up to touch it, wincing slightly.

"I suppose it would." He sat down next to her. "How does it feel to know it's finally over?"

"Charlie, you have no idea the weight that has been lifted off my shoulders."

He took her by the hand, and she squeezed back.

They sat like that in silence until John came over and cleared his throat. "Emma and I have some things to discuss in private."

"Yes, sir!" Charlie answered sourly. "I will check in with you later."

John closed the doors so they would have complete privacy and went to stand in front of her, arms crossed. Major André, the 'Head of Intelligence' version was back. "Is there anything you want to confess to me? Like your dealings with the enemy?"

She sipped her drink and answered with a question of her own. "Is there anything you want to confess to *me*? Like the details of your dealings with the women in this town? The sheer number of them perhaps?"

John cleared his throat and looked away. "Perhaps not," he said quietly, "but that is comparing apples to oranges, sweetheart. Spying for the other side is punishable by death."

Emma sighed and looked down into her glass. "Don't you think the British army owes me a few lives?"

He sat down on the table in front of her and clasped his hands together in front of him, knowing full well she was right.

"John, every day you do what you have to do to get what you need, and this time I did what I had to do to get what I needed. I don't think either one of us wants to start spilling details, so maybe it is best we just let sleeping dogs lie."

"Perhaps you are right." Taking her hand, he gazed into her eyes and said, "I think I already know the answer to this question, but I will ask it anyway—where does this leave us?"

Emma intertwined her fingers with his. "You will always have a special place in my heart, but I cannot have a relationship with you when I am left to wonder whose bed you are in— or have just left."

"And I will always care a great deal for you, but I cannot have a relationship with you questioning if you are lending aid to those I am sworn to fight against." He kissed her hand. "Maybe we can try this again when this war is over, provided Captain Taylor hasn't convinced you to marry him."

"I have no need or desire to marry, and I don't see that changing anytime soon," she said and stood up. "I will be looking forward to your visit after the war." She leaned down and kissed him. "Thank you for everything!"

He watched as she walked out of his house for the last time.

Later that night, Charlie came to Wolfe Manor, where he stayed in her arms until morning.

"I am going to leave New York," she said out of the blue.

Charlie sat up. "Leave? Why?"

"I have nothing holding me here and truthfully, I need some time away."

"I'm here," he said.

"You mean until the British army sends you away or Washington calls you back. The life of a spy is a little uncertain."

"Emma, I don't want you to go."

"And I can't stay. Not in this house, not while everything is still so raw."

He kissed the side of her head. "Marry me!"

She turned and kissed his lips. "No! I care for you a great deal, but I don't want to get married. I watch all the time as women lose a huge part of themselves when they take a husband and I understand why Aunt Lucy was adamant I have the same choices she did. It was a great gift she gave me, and I will not give it up so easily."

Charlie looked stunned and hurt. "Emma, I—"

"Don't say it!" she pressed her finger to his lips. "What's wrong with just enjoying each other without saying the words?"

He sighed when he realized this was not a battle he was going to have any success with—he would have to bide his time if he wanted to win *that* war. Flipping her over on her back, he grinned.

"Well, I guess I am just going to have to keep wearing you down until you give in and agree to become my wife."

"I wouldn't get my hopes up—that is going to take a great deal of convincing," she said playfully.

He pinned her against the bed and rubbed his body against hers. "Oh, I think I am up for the job. I can be very persistent when I have made up my mind there is something I want."

"Well, I suppose we will see," she goaded. He tickled her until she erupted into laughter.

One week later, she sat at the desk in the library reading a letter containing condolences from General Washington while polishing off the last of the apple cake he sent along with it. She folded the letter and stuffed it in her reticule. Looking around, she smiled, remembering all the good times she and Lucy had there.

"Am I disturbing you?" she heard John say from the doorway, "I let myself in."

"No, not at all. Come in!"

Holding up a letter, he said, "I got your note," seemingly taken aback when he saw the furniture had been covered. "So, you truly are leaving?"

"Yes! I am closing Wolfe Manor for a while. I think I need some time away from here until I adjust to this strange, new life I find myself in."

"That may be for the best given some of your activities outside the home. I can only look the other direction for so long." He flashed that devilish smile she had come to love so much.

"And I appreciate your discretion more than you will ever know. I also need you to understand it was never about going against you personally."

"I know," he said, in a soft, comforting tone. Changing the subject, he asked, "Where will you go?"

"Where won't I go?" She laughed. "Did you know the Wolfe family has houses all over the place? There are at least three in the Colonies, two in England, one in Scotland, and a few other places I have never even heard of. The report of holdings from the attorney was nearly four inches thick."

"I had no idea!"

"Neither did I, and I am not even sure Aunt Lucy did."

John sat on the edge of the desk. "Perhaps I should try to get you to reconsider your decision to not marry and convince you to make me a kept man," he teased.

She stood up and pinched his cheek. "John André would be an absolute bore if he were tied down to one woman. I think you should stay exactly as you are for the sake of women everywhere."

Taking her hand, he remarked, "It's good to see you smile, Emma!"

"It feels good to smile, John."

"Where will be your first stop?"

She came around and hopped up on the desk beside him. "Virginia! Aunt Lucy had all my parent's personal items stored there. I think I would like to go through them."

"Virginia?" John rolled his eyes, "Of course!" he scoffed.

"Why do you say it like that?" she asked, confused.

John brushed his hat against the side of his coat. "I just signed paperwork less than an hour ago to have Captain Charles Taylor relocated to Virginia."

Emma pressed her lips together to conceal a smile, but a snort managed to escape. "Oh, John! I truly had no idea!"

They both laughed.

"Well, I suppose you will need these. You should know, I am reluctant to give them to you, because I don't want to see you leave," he reached into his coat pocket and produced a small, leather binder, "General Clinton asked me to personally deliver this. These passage papers should make your journey a little easier. He also asked me to send his regards and wish you well in your travels."

Emma accepted the bundle and looked down at it. "Thank you, and please let him know how much I appreciate this."

He stood and stepped in front of her before taking her face in his hands. "I am going to miss you, Emma."

"I am going to miss you too, John."

They shared a long, sweet kiss before she patted his cheeks. "If you ever make it to Virginia, come see me. I will always have a hot meal and a warm bed waiting for you."

"Will you be joining me in that warm bed?" he inquired impishly.

"Most certainly," she replied with a wink.

"In that case, I shall make it a priority."

He cupped her face and took his time kissing her tenderly before resting his forehead against hers and offering her a warm smile. They slowly meandered to the door, each gripping the other's hand tightly before saying their final 'goodbye'. She watched from the doorway until he was completely out of sight, a slight ache tugging at her heart.

Emma took one final walk around before closing the door and going outside to the coach waiting for her. Francis had stopped by earlier and they had promised to do a better job of staying in touch this time. Charlie had been detained and had sent his regards. All her things were already loaded on the ship, and it would be departing soon.

She said 'goodbye' to Mac before making a stop at the cemetery to have a long chat with Aunt Lucy and to leave flowers on the three graves.

As she approached, she noticed a man standing in front of her aunt's final resting place, his head bent, hat in hand.

"How did you know her?" she asked quietly as she went to stand beside him.

"I never had the pleasure of meeting her," he replied, glancing up as she approached, "but I wanted to pay my respects just the same."

Emma caught a whiff of sandalwood coming from him and realized he was the same man she had seen coming out of John's house.

Why was he so familiar?

"Have we met?"

The man smiled. "We have, Miss Eldridge, but it was a very long time ago and not under the best of circumstances. I am Colonel Gabe Asheton. I was the officer who interviewed you after the death of your parents all those years ago."

"Dear God!" exclaimed Emma and laid her hand on his arm. "Of course! I remember you now."

"I wanted nothing more than to get justice for that sweet little girl who had her parents ripped away so cruelly. Allow me to offer my sincerest condolences, and my deepest apologies, for my part in the death of the three people before us here today. I am partially responsible for what happened to them."

"How do you mean?"

"You see, I was the one who placed Sherman Finch in Washington's army as an intelligence plant. I knew what a horrible man he was, and frankly, I was tired of dealing with him. The world would have been better off if I had just rid it of him. Instead, I placed him in an assignment that managed to get him out of my hair as well as benefiting our cause as a whole, killing two birds with one stone so to speak. If I had any idea of what he would go on to do, I would have ended him a long time ago. I now have a daughter of my own, and I would give my soul to the Devil himself to never see her in as much pain as you were in that day."

Emma looked to Lucy's grave. "Well, if we are being perfectly honest, I have as much accountability as you."

Gabe turned to face her and waited for her to continue. "You see, if I had given you his name that day, perhaps he would have swung from a rope long before he had a chance to do all this."

"You were a frightened child, Miss Eldridge, who had just witnessed a horrific crime. You cannot blame yourself for not confiding in me after watching a British soldier murder them. It is no wonder you would not trust another wearing the same red coat."

"And, by the same token, you had no idea what a monster he was," she countered. "I don't see how you can fault yourself for that either. How about we both agree to lay the blame exactly where it should be— squarely at the feet of the man who committed the deeds?

And since he is dead, I think we should not spare him another thought other than wishing him an extra special place in Hell."

"You are a wise young lady, Miss Eldridge. I will agree to those terms if you will."

"Done!" She smiled warmly at him.

"Would you like to visit the coffeehouse with me?" he asked. "I would appreciate the chance to get to know you better."

"I am afraid I am on my way out of town."

"Oh?"

"Yes, I am headed to Virginia. I think it's time I put the past to rest once and for all."

"Interesting! You see, I retired, and my home is now in Virginia. If you find your way to Williamsburg, please look me up. The offer for coffee still stands."

"I would like that," she replied.

The Colonel placed his hat on his head and bowed. "I wish you well putting that past to rest, Miss Eldridge."

As he started away, Emma turned. "Colonel Asheton?" he stopped, "Thank you for your concern and for being so kind to me that day. Be sure to take care of that little girl of yours."

"It was my pleasure, and I most certainly will!" he smiled and walked away.

Emma carefully placed the flowers and arranged them before saying her final farewells.

When she returned to the carriage, she wasn't the least

bit surprised to find Charlie waiting for her.

"I was hoping to catch you before you departed," he said.

"I am glad you did," she replied and stepped into his arms.

Smoothing back the hair from her face, he sighed. "I am going to miss you."

She kissed his lips. "I have a feeling I will be seeing you sooner than you think."

Offering her a puzzled look, he helped her to get settled into the coach. "Take care, Charlie."

"You too, Emma!"

He smacked the side to let the driver know she was ready and waved as it pulled away.

Emma watched from the window as they rolled down the street. She would miss New York, but she also knew she wouldn't stay away for too long—it was her home. After boarding the ship, she watched the shoreline fade into the distance and found herself looking forward to seeing what adventure life had in store for her next.

The End

.... Or is it just the beginning?

About the Author

Tempie W. Wade is the award-winning author of The Timely Revolution Book Series, a Revolutionary War time-travel adventure.

Her first book, A Timely Revolution, was awarded best historical fantasy in the 2019 American Book Fest American Fiction Awards.

The writer is a lifelong resident of Virginia and currently resides in Williamsburg.

For more information, please visit
www.TempieWade.com

The Timely Revolution Book Series in Order:

Book One-A Timely Revolution

Book Two-More

Book Three-The Complicated Life of Maggie MacGregor

Book Four-Timely Revelations

Book Five-The Steep Cost of Fate

Book Six-Secrets and Lies

Book Seven-TBA

Book Eight-TBA

Book Nine-TBA

The Timely Revolution Book Series is a work of historical fiction/fantasy based during the Revolutionary War with the added element of Celtic Fae lore. The first book, A Timely Revolution, won Best Historical Fantasy in the American Book Fest American Fiction Awards for 2019. Books are available on Amazon.

www.ingramcontent.com/pod-product-compliance
Lightning Source LLC
Chambersburg PA
CBHW050552260626
47157CB00002B/537